≋ THE ≋
Island of Mad
Scientists

↘ THE ↙
Island of Mad Scientists

Being an Excursion to the
Wilds of Scotland, Involving Many Marvels of
Experimental Invention, Pirates, a Heroic Cat,
a Mechanical Man and a Monkey

By Howard Whitehouse
With illustrations by Bill Slavin

To the memory of my dear friend Vicki McGinnis, who was just as
determinedly caring as I have shown her, but not quite as German. Also to
her husband, Bill McGinnis, who is as smart and crafty as his fictional Scottish
counterpart but not nearly as tight with money — H.W.

The Island of Mad Scientists by Howard Whitehouse
Illustrated by Bill Slavin
This edition published in 2022

Xander Books is an imprint of
Winged Hussar Publishing, LLC
1525 Hulse Rd, Unit 1
Point Pleasant, NJ 08742

Copyright © Xander Books
ISBN 978-1-950423-28-6
LCN 2022937080

Bibliographical References and Index
1. Fantasy. 2. Adventure.

Winged Hussar Publishing, LLC All rights reserved
For more information
visit us at www.wingedhussarpublishing.com

Twitter: WingHusPubLLC
Facebook: Winged Hussar Publishing LLC

CONTENTS

DRAMATIS PERSONAE

Emmaline Cayley

A Pioneer of Aviation

Rubberbones

A Bouncing Boy

Aunt Lucy

The Best Sort of Aunt

Lal Singh

A Mysterious and Heroic Butler

Professor Bellbuckle

A Mad Scientist

Princess Purnah

A Royal Personage from a Distant Land

The Collector

Insane, Obsessive yet Organized

Samuel Soap

A Master of Disguise

Hercules & Titch

Little Thug, Big Thug

Harry & Maisie

A Holy Man and a Very Fine Cat

Angus

A Scottish Automaton

Mr. & Mrs. McGinnis

The Laird and His Lady

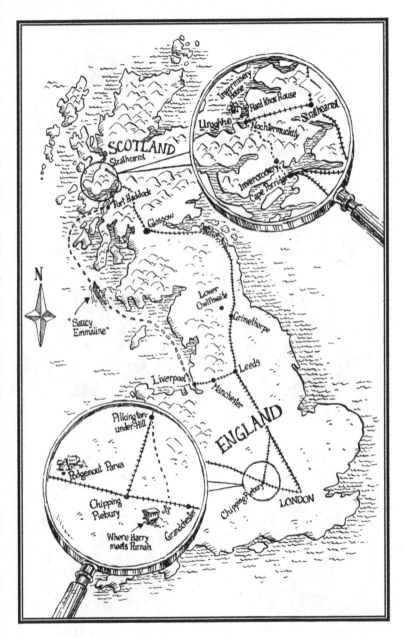

⚔ PROLOGUE ⚔

Some people collect coins or stamps. Others purchase books of old maps or Latin poetry. Rich enthusiasts may buy the works of long-dead painters or fashionable new artists. It's what they call a hobby, a harmless way of passing the time.

The strange old man was fascinated by science. In his long lifetime he had seen the invention of the railway, the telegraph and telephone, the steamship and the flushing toilet. He'd been intrigued when engineers in Germany had made a carriage run on exploding oil fumes. And he was an avid follower of the remarkable Mr. Edison, who was making a fortune with electrical devices. So, as a collector, the old man's tastes ran to all things scientific.

He collected scientists. When he was a youngster his father had told him that he ought to stop wasting time reading about science and begin collecting something (his father owned 70,000 porcelain thimbles), so the obedient son began kidnapping actual inventors. As the young man grew up he became rich and mad — and rich, mad people can generally do whatever they want.

He often came and looked at the scientists, always in strict alphabetical order. He kept them in a dungeon that he'd had installed in the deep old caverns beneath his home, an ancient towered mansion on the western shore of Scotland. The place was damp, freezing and thoroughly unwelcoming.

It was called Invermisery House, and it had been built in sixteen-something by a dour old man who believed that God disapproved of anything enjoyable. The Collector had snapped it up when it came on the market. What he liked about Invermisery House was that it looked out across the water to an island, no more than a half-mile away. This island, named Urgghh (which means "cold and nasty" in the Scots Gaelic tongue), was the home of the Royal Society of Experimental Science and Invention. On an isolated isle, with nobody to hurt but themselves (and hard- ly anything to damage), mad scientists from all over the world could experiment to their hearts' delight.

Those who knew the Collector thought that the dark caverns suited him. He was scrawny-chested with long arms and legs that twined beneath him when he sat. His eyes were black and goggled shortsightedly. His teeth were fang- like. There was a repulsive, spiderlike quality to him that was impossible to explain.

Since the Collector had a special interest in scientists, he liked to watch their activities through a high-powered tele- scope set up at his study window. Most of them were hope- less lunatics, but occasionally he'd spot one that might be worth adding to the Collection. Then he'd find a way of capturing that scientist, sometimes on his way back from the island, sometimes at the scientist's home or laboratory. He was careful to ensure that none of the mad scientists on the island noticed him watching them. He did not seize his victims on Urgghh or in the nearby village of Nochtermuckity. That would have been too obvious.

The Collector kept tabs on the amazing skills of his prisoners by setting up laboratories in the dungeons where they could experiment. He did nothing at all with the results of his captives' studies except file them, alphabetically, by thickness and by date. He had a very complete file room.

Right now, he was reading a selection of clippings pre- pared by his secretary. The gaunt, pale assistant, who was almost inhuman in his efficiency, announced, "I have researched the British and American periodicals for you, sir, and I am translating items from the foreign press."

"Thank you, Foglamp," replied the Collector as his fingers flicked through the cuttings. "That will be all for the moment." The neatly cut papers were gummed into file folders, each labeled with a typed name. The old man looked over two folders that were thin on announcements or celebrations of a successful career. The subjects of these were young and — he thought this ideal for his purposes — closely connected alphabetically. Unless he came across someone called Byrne or Cavendish, these two would go together. He'd collect both of them as a matching pair. They seemed to work as a team, as far as he could tell from the sparse items of news available. The newspapers hadn't properly followed up on the reports of "Local Vicar Criticized in Bell-Tower Kite Incident" (from a very small Yorkshire weekly), or "School Fire Mystery — Who Was the 'Flying Girl'?" Even the most recent, "Belgian Birdman Denies Substitution by Young Female Acrobat," was stronger on those angry denials than on solid information.

Yet the names were consistent. Robert Burns, aged twelve. Emmaline Cayley, aged fourteen. The Collector stood up, stretched his spindly body and scratched their names in chalk on a board on the study wall. He underlined them with a grating noise that Foglamp, standing alert outside the room, could feel in his teeth.

The Collector knew of a man who could help him lay his spidery hands on the two children, a clever (although regrettably criminal) fellow who made his living impersonating others. For a price, he'd make inquiries about the Cayley and Burns youngsters and — for a bonus — reel them in. The

Collector's withered lips stretched into a thin smile as his arachnoid fingers ran through a file of names and addresses. Sibley, Siddons, Soap. Yes, Soap — that was the name they'd agreed on.

⇙ CHAPTER 1 ⇘

In Which We Catch Up with Ourselves

Emmaline Cayley was packing for the trip. Comb, brush, toothpowder, sensible thick stockings, a hat that wouldn't blow away. She was not a froufrou sort of girl. She was a pioneer of aviation. Her mother's attempts to make her ladylike had been a complete failure. So everything went into one bag. She'd returned from London the day before, which made getting ready easy. What was much more difficult was deciding which of her scientific materials to bring along. Not just the notebooks and reference volumes but the tools and plans and all the waxed fabric, wooden struts, leather straps and metal thingumajigs (all of which she knew the names of) that were the raw materials for a flying machine.

Froufrou girls did not build aeronautical devices.

Emmaline sighed. It was ridiculous to take the makings of a gliding contraption with her. The trip was a winter holiday to a place as yet unknown, taken at short notice. It was more important to have mittens than her notes about a Russian inventor who might have flown for fourteen seconds in 1872.

Still, she tucked the copy of Professor Octave Chanute's *Progress in Flying Machines*, borrowed from Mr. Sherlock Holmes, inside her valise. She'd need some light reading on the train.

So, she was packed to leave. It had taken her fifteen minutes to get ready.

In the next room Princess Purnah was jamming her own choice of travel necessities into a suitcase. Emmaline could see that Purnah had no gift for packing. One might think that a princess would have relied on servants to pack for her, but Emmaline suspected that in Purnah's strange and ferocious homeland, nestled beneath the high Frizzibuttok Mountains, members of royal families traveled at the head of marauding bands of raiders or were trussed up as captives. Suitcases didn't come into it.

"Eeek!" said Purnah. "Cannot closings without squishy! Oople!"

Purnah was thirteen, as far as anyone could work out, and had learned English simply by overhearing it spoken while pretending that she didn't understand a word. The result was that she used it in a wildly ungrammatical way with lots of curses and threats in her own language. She spoke in Chiligriti, a tongue unknown to almost everyone anywhere but very well provided with curses and threats.

It was the middle of November, and they were running away from home. That had been Mr. Holmes's idea. A series of events had taken place in which agents of what the newspapers would call "a Foreign Power" had tried to kidnap Princess Purnah. This had involved a considerable amount of hurtling about the country in trains, cabs, balloons and steam devices. A man with no face and his masked minions had attempted abduction and murder. There was a Belgian birdman, the aforementioned famous detective and a lot of running and hiding. Buckets of rats, too, and a flying monster.

Rab had said it was "champion." Purnah had said it was a "hooty-hoot"!

Emmaline thought it was a good thing that it was all over.

Except that it wasn't over at all. Emmaline opened the case to rearrange the contents. Purnah's suitcase was completely filled with a mixture of cheap costume jewelry, kitchen knives and smooshed cream cakes from the village bakery.

"I think you will have to wash everything, Your Majesty," said Emmaline.

"I will licks the cream off!" declared the royal princess.

Emmaline shook her head in despair and went back to her own room.

She had plenty of time to wait, as Professor Bellbuckle was busy putting out the barn. She assumed he hadn't meant to set it on fire.

———————

Robert Burns (known as Rubberbones for his "indestruckable" physique) walked up the hill to Mad Mrs. Butterworth's house. He had spent the night at his gran's cottage, scratched the cat on the head and sorted out his belongings. He owned far less than Emmaline. An old sack contained socks and underwear, one shirt, a photograph of his mother, brother and three sisters, and seven paperbound novels with titles like Comanche Jim Rides Through and Dead Pirate's Gold! His grandmother had hugged the boy with a furious affection he hadn't expected and pushed him out of the house before she could burst into tears.

"I'll be back in a bit, Gran!" he called through the letter-box in the door.

"A bit" might mean an hour or a month when Rubberbones said it. In this case, he thought it might be a longish sort of "bit."

"Goodbye, Rab," she replied. She always called him by that name. "Yes, see you in a bit."

As he reached the Butterworth house he smelled something burning and rushed through the yard to find Professor Ozymandias Bellbuckle outside the kitchen door, drenched in water. Lal Singh was emptying a bucket into the open doorway to the barn, and Rab saw blackened wood around the frame. Mrs. Butterworth, Emmaline's Aunt Lucy, appeared from inside the barn with a bucket of her own. She greeted the boy cheerfully. "Hello, Robert! All ready? We are a little behind schedule, I'm afraid." She pinched his cheek affectionately and then turned to smack the professor with the bucket.

"Ouch! What in tarnation was that for?" demanded the professor. He was from Savannah, Georgia, and most people considered him quite mad.

"Ozymandias, dear, when I say 'Pack up the things you'll need for a few weeks away,' I do not mean 'Please start a fire in your workshop and risk burning my entire house to the ground!' You see the difference, don't you?" She struck him again, although not as hard. He groaned nevertheless. "I'm sorry, Lucy. I was making fireworks for our journey." "Most people find it possible to travel without homemade fireworks, Ozymandias. I've spent many a happy holiday without any sort of explosive devices in my luggage."

Rubberbones noticed that Lal Singh was trying to hide a smile. The Indian butler was always dignified, but sometimes he couldn't help himself.

Princess Purnah was the daughter of the late Mir of Chiligrit. Anyone with an atlas could find the tiny mountain kingdom at that point where India, Tibet, Bulgaria and the Russian Empire come together in a long knot of mountains, but they'd have to look hard. Chiligrit consisted of two moun- tains, a lot of wild people who liked to knife their own rel- atives and a ravine to throw the dead bodies into. Princess Purnah missed it very much. But her father had been killed — "foully slewed! Porok!" as Purnah described it — by his brother and cousins, and most of the family had disappeared into the mountains or perhaps off the mountains into the ravine. It was hard to know. Princess Purnah had been taken to safety by someone called the British Resident. Which might have been good, if the "safety" hadn't been the most unpleasant boarding school in the whole world, St. Grimelda's School for Young Ladies (established 1552). It was there that she had met Emmaline and, between them, they had escaped.

That was the problem. The British government — or at least that part of it called the India Office — considered Princess Purnah to be "an official responsibility." Purnah had no idea what this meant. Emmaline thought it meant that the government was a sort of nanny, although a rather vague and neglectful one. The India Office had placed Purnah at "St. Grim's," and demanded that she go back there. There were letters inside file folders. Fees had been paid. Documents had been signed. It was all settled.

"Pish that!" said Princess Purnah. "Tikkir the lots of 'em! I no go backs. I stayings with my friends Emmaline Cay-Lee and Errand Boy."

That was fine with Emmaline and Rab ("Errand Boy") and, more importantly, with Aunt Lucy, who had a house in the Yorkshire village of Lower Owlthwaite. Aunt Lucy seemed to think that you could take in stray princesses like lost kittens. But it was not acceptable to Mr. Botts of the India Office or to his superiors. Mr. Botts expected the princess to return to the school. So did the headmistress, the ferocious Mrs. Wackett, who didn't like it at all when "gels" tried to escape. St. Grimelda's had a reputation to uphold. No prison in Great Britain had a record like St. Grim's; Mrs. Wackett wasn't about to let "that chit of a foreign gel" go free. So Mr. Sherlock Holmes (a friend of the family) suggested that it might be a good idea if Aunt Lucy took the princess — indeed, the entire household — away for a while until things quieted down.

But where to go? Winter was coming. Aunt Lucy said she had money hidden in a pillowcase for this sort of emergency. Emmaline wondered whether she had money marked for different kinds of emergencies, like "the bag of cash in case I have to run off with a foreign princess." Maybe she did.

"Everyone come up with places we should visit," Aunt Lucy had ordered on the train back from London. They all wrote down three suggestions and put them in Rab's battered top hat. Princess Purnah scribbled "Chiligrit" on each of her papers. Rab's choices were "Africa," "Antarctica" and "Birmingham." The others kept theirs secret. Emmaline saw that Professor Bellbuckle had put down his hometown; she didn't say anything, although she knew that his family sent him money not to come back there.

Lal Singh, the ex-soldier from India who acted as butler and occasional bodyguard, had said that he would go wherever the Memsahib, Mrs. Butterworth, went; it was he that drew the "winning" suggestion from the hat. But he hadn't said what it was.

The sun had gone down over London. Two men waited in an alley that reeked of horse droppings and stale urine. They were physically as different as could be: one was a giant; the other was miniature in stature and build.

The little man spoke softly. "Cor! Stinks a bit 'ere, dunnit? He'll be along any time now. It's his regular short-cut 'ome. Fat man with skinny legs, it says 'ere. Wears an overcoat and a cricket cap. Squeaks for no reason, like a mouse. Twitches a bit when he walks, talks to himself. Got the chloroform pad ready?"

The giant nodded in affirmation.

A minute later a person matching this description stepped into the alley, mumbling under his breath.

The small fellow stepped in front of him. "Good evening!" he said. "Am I addressing the famous Professor Cavor? The inventor of the anti-gravity alloy known as Cavorite?"

"Ah, um, yes, I am he," stuttered the man in the cricket cap. "Can I help you?"

"You can accompany me!" replied the little man.

As Professor Cavor peered at him in confusion, squeaking faintly, the giant emerged from the shadows with surprising agility and stepped behind the scientist. With a swift motion he seized Cavor and pressed a pad over his mouth and nose. The noxious smell of chloroform mixed with the alley's stench. Within seconds the inventor of Cavorite fell unconscious. Then he was laid out in a traveling trunk and lifted onto a wagon.

"Off to Scotland, Professor," sneered the little man. "Good work, Titch!"

The giant sniffed at this nickname, which meant "tiny" in the slang of the streets. "All right, Hercules," he replied in a voice as soft as a choirboy.

⚒ CHAPTER 2 ⚒

The Horseless Carriage

The following day, with her belongings in a bag and the dogcart packed for the station, Emmaline still had no idea where they were all going. Aunt Lucy made her announcement as everyone gathered outside the house.

"We are going to Italy! We'll see the Colosseum and the canals of Venice and eat ice cream every day. There'll be donkey rides, and I shall wear a straw hat that looks ridiculous."

Emmaline thought about what she knew of Italy. It was shaped like a boot, it was warm — at least warmer than England, even in winter — and people ate food that looked like dead worms in tomato sauce. What else? Well, the Romans, of course, and the Pope, and opera, and the Renaissance and ice cream, if Aunt Lucy said so. Emmaline's interests were scientific, so she tried to think of Italian inventors. None came to mind.

"I shall kill snakes! I shall fight pirates! Glekk!" announced Princess Purnah. Clearly, she knew even less about Italy than Emmaline.

"I will pay homage to the great Leonardo da Vinci," said Professor Bellbuckle. "He drew up plans for a flying machine four hundred years ago."

Of course, thought Emmaline. I've got pictures of those in one of my books. Terribly impractical, but centuries ahead of his time.

Rab was thinking about Italy. Most of what he knew of the outside world came from cheap novels known as "penny dreadfuls." He couldn't recall any adventure tales that took place in Italy. Then he remembered something.

"I might see about being a gladiator. Just to find out if I like it."

Emmaline was wondering whether she should mention that there were no gladiators any more, but Aunt Lucy said, "Excellent plan, Robert," and strode toward the cart. Lal Singh had already put Ernest, the old horse, between the shafts. They were ready for sunny climes, and there was a train to catch in less than an hour. It was time to be off.

It would have been better if they'd been off ten minutes before, because a strange machine came puffing up the lane at considerable speed. Rab, who could tell these things, thought it might be doing twelve miles per hour. There were two men in goggles, perched on a tiny seat, bouncing as they came up the driveway.

"Good golly gumdrops!" called one of the men. "I'm glad I got here in time!"

He unwound himself from the conveyance, which was smoking and clanking loudly. Rab eyed it eagerly. The professor peered over his glasses at it. It wasn't a steam engine. It didn't seem to be clockwork.

"I think it's one of them motor cars," whispered Rab. "I saw a picture of one."

The other man climbed down from the device. "Quite right, young man. It's one of only a handful in England, although everyone will have one in a year or two, I'm sure. An 'automobile' as some say. Runs on petroleum oil. When cousin Winthrop asked if I'd run him up here in it, I was happy to do so. Four horsepower — imagine that!"

Professor Bellbuckle was busy imagining that. He had a history of inventing horseless carriages, powered by steam or rockets, but all of them had ended up broken or had blown up. He sniffed as if discontented.

"Cousin Winthrop" spoke to Aunt Lucy. She recalled him, more formally, as Mr. Botts of the India Office. There were people she'd have been less happy to see today, but not many. He'd pulled off his goggles to reveal a second pair beneath; Emmaline realized they were his glasses. He must be incredibly shortsighted. And he was ridiculously tall and thin.

"Ready for Princess Purnah to go back to St. Grimelda's, then?" he burbled. "All arrangements made. Back where she belongs."

Emmaline saw Aunt Lucy's hand tightening on the handle of her umbrella. She was quite likely to assault Mr. Botts with it. Stanley started to growl. Emmaline remembered that at their first meeting Mr. Botts had assumed that she herself was the princess. She stepped forward.

"Yes, quite ready. As you'll see, these nice people have got all my things prepared for the journey. I am so looking forward to returning to school. It was a terrible mix-up when I left there. There was a fire, and I became nervous and ran. Then I, um, got lost, and Mrs. Butterworth took me in. Her niece and I" — she indicated Princess Purnah — "whose name is Emmaline Cayley, have become great friends."

Emmaline wanted to gently nudge her aunt and the princess into agreement with her, but she couldn't. She hoped they'd pick up the idea.

Aunt Lucy did. "Yes, yes. We've packed up all the princess's belongings to take her back to the school. We'll miss her, of course, but she has to get her education."

Mr. Botts smiled — a toothy grin that managed to be oily and vacant at the same time. "Jolly good! I knew you'd see sense. Princess Purnah will be well taught at St. Grimelda's!" Now Emmaline wished she had nudged Purnah or possibly gagged her with a stocking. It was too late. The princess — the real princess — stepped forward and looked Mr. Botts straight in the eye. Actually, since he was two feet taller than she was, she looked him in the chest.

"I is Princess Purnah, and is no goings backs to school. Glekk! I is escapings to Italy, to kill snakes and fightings gladiators. You mine enemy! I shall have you slained and head put on spear in garden. Porok!"

This was exactly the wrong thing to say. Mr. Botts did not like to be defied. He didn't like to be fooled, either, and now he remembered how he'd mistaken Emmaline for Purnah. He lunged forward to grab the princess. Purnah ducked low and kicked him in the shin. Stanley barked and launched himself forward to embed his teeth in Mr. Botts's trouser leg. Aunt Lucy pulled herself up to her full five feet and a quarter inch.

"Unhand the princess, Mr. Botts!" Mr. Botts had not actually handed Princess Purnah at all; she was too quick for him. Still, he looked as if he might hand her if he had the chance, so Aunt Lucy thwacked him across the knees with her umbrella.

Emmaline was aware that she was the only one within hitting distance not doing any hitting.

"I say! Stop all that!" shouted the owner of the motor car. He stepped forward, chin out, remonstrating. "Ladies! Cease beating cousin Winthrop! It's most unseemly!" Emmaline thought he was quite impressive until Aunt Lucy caught him with a backhander and he went down like a rag doll.

Where was Lal Singh?

"Please be mounting the cart immediately, Miss Emmaline," came the butler's voice. "I may be compelled to assist the Memsahib." He'd swung the dogcart around and with a deft motion forced Ernest in between Mr. Botts and the angry females (and dog), who were inflicting grievous damage on the hapless bureaucrat. Emmaline climbed in, and in a moment the cart was wheeling down the driveway with Aunt Lucy, Purnah and Stanley aboard. Mr. Botts and his cousin floundered in the mud, waving fists and shouting. Rubberbones had been too interested in the horseless carriage to notice the dispute until it turned to actual blows. "Flippin' 'eck!" he muttered. There was a fight — a proper punch-up — right here in front of him. Princess Purnah wouldn't appreciate him pitching in; she'd say she could defend herself. And Miss Aunt Lucy didn't need help, what with that brolly flailing about. He didn't know what to do. It was a bit of a pickle —

A horn sounded, a great parp-parp, and Professor Bellbuckle yelled out, "Jump in, Robert! We'll take a field test in this contrivance." Rab leapt onto the motor car's bench seat and hung on. The professor jammed through the gears with much grinding, and the machine shot forward down the driveway.

"What do you think this handle does?" asked the professor.

He wrenched it, and the car spun in the dirt.

"Er, I think that's what steers it," replied Rab. "Straighten it up! Now left a bit!"

"What about this lever?" Professor Bellbuckle hauled hard.

The vehicle spun again. "The brake! Let it off!"

They were on the road down into the village. "Yee-haw!" trilled the professor. Rab wrapped both arms around what might be a luggage rack and hung on tightly. "Like grim death," as some would say. Grim death was what he was hoping to avoid.

"This really is most impressive," said the professor as he swerved down the lane. A duck leapt out of the way. "People should take more care with their fowl." He had a brisk way with the pedals, accelerating wildly, then braking sharply and clashing through the gears in a lively, clutch-burning way.

"Professor!" yelled Rab. "We've just stolen that bloke's car. We're a pair o' thieves!"

"Oh, no, Robert. That would be wrong. Morally. And legally. No, we are testing it for experimental purposes."

"We'll take it back, then?" Rab wasn't sure about going back to the scene of combat at Miss Aunt Lucy's house.

"I wouldn't go so far as that," drawled Professor Bellbuckle.

Aunt Lucy was fuming outside the ticket office when the professor and Rab arrived at the railway station in Grimethorpe. They would have been there long before the dogcart if they hadn't argued over where they should leave the motor car. Professor Bellbuckle said they should leave it at the train station since that was where they were going. Rab thought they should take it to the police station and hand it in like lost property. They compromised by leaving the horseless carriage stuck in a hedge, two miles outside the town; the professor had swerved off the road, and they couldn't get it out.

Aunt Lucy gave them a look of withering criticism. "Our train is waiting at platform four," she said. Rab could tell she was mad at the professor.

The train was bound for London. Lal Singh had brought the luggage in, arranged for a boy to take Ernest and the cart back to the village and settled Emmaline and Purnah inside a carriage with hot drinks and many cream cakes. He smiled as the professor tottered in, his glasses broken and his collar twisted.

"Afternoon tea is served, Professor Bellbuckle." Emmaline thought that the tall Sikh liked to see the professor make a fool of himself.

Aunt Lucy was not at all pleased. "I'm not at all pleased," she declared. "This is no way to start a nice restful holiday. Violence! Assault on a servant of Her Majesty's government. Attempts to lie to someone bearing the lawful authority of the crown!"

She stopped and broke into a grin. "And that was just me!"

Emmaline wasn't certain whether her aunt was amused or mildly hysterical. Aunt Lucy continued in a more sober vein. "Our plans have changed. I had hoped that we would sneak out of the country with a minimum of fuss so that the government — by which I mean that silly man and his department — would simply decide to forget about Princess Purnah. I mean, as long as she's safe and warm and not kidnapped by Russian agents, why should they worry? But today's, um, disagreement may have changed their views. Mr. Botts might well be capable of using the telephone to speak to his superiors, and they will put all sorts of obstacles in our way. Purnah, I do wish you hadn't spoken quite so freely."

Princess Purnah frowned, her brows knitting together. "What you meanish, Auntilucy?"

"I mean that when Emmaline said that she was you and you were her, it wasn't absolutely necessary to tell the truth." Purnah glowered. Emmaline knew that whenever Purnah had behaved rashly she became angry if anyone mentioned it. "In particular," continued Aunt Lucy, "it wasn't helpful that you told Mr. Botts we were bound for the sunny shores of Italy."

"Is warm! Ice cream! Gladiating! Trikk!"

"Of course it is, and now we can no longer go there. In fact, I seriously doubt we will be able to leave England by any of the southern ports."

Professor Bellbuckle started. "You think they'll be looking out for us?"

"Indeed, Ozymandias. I believe that within hours every police officer, every ticket agent and every steamship porter in southern England will be looking for a short, rotund woman, three unrelated children, a small dog, an Indian butler and a very handsome and distinguished scientist from the United States."

Professor Bellbuckle blushed.

"Meanwhile, we need to make alternative plans. That is why we will be leaving this train before it gets to London." Rubberbones started. "You mean — jump out?" That would be champion, although he couldn't see Aunt Lucy throwing herself from a moving carriage.

"Actually, I was thinking of changing trains at Leeds."

The man who picked up his letters under the name of Samuel Soap was interested in the case his contact had given him. Actually, he was interested in the bank draft for a hundred pounds (a huge sum) and the promise of a bonus when the business was complete. He was a ratty little man, all whiskers and teeth, and he worked with his wits. If he was to ask questions about these two kids — Emmaline and Robert, it said — he'd need to look the part.

He selected a tweed coat and a bowler hat from his extensive wardrobe, which ran from clothes a banker might choose to garments a tramp would reject. He combed the bushy mustache above his lip, a real one he'd grown since he'd last been known as a clean-shaven jewel thief called Emerald Ernie. He pulled the hat brim across his brow and stood up straight. The mirror told him he'd got it right, even if he was short for the part. A police inspector looked back at him.

The "inspector" paraded before a mirror, chest puffed out, eyes goggling fiercely. "Allo, allo, allo!" he declaimed. "What's all this, then?" he demanded. He glared into the glass, daring it to argue with him. Oh yes, Soap was impressed by his impersonation.

He could be on the case by lunchtime if he caught the first train north.

———

They changed trains at Leeds, which was half an hour's journey. The ticket seller at Grimethorpe Halt would have told the authorities that the short, rotund woman in question had bought tickets to London, so it was crucial that the train arrive in London without them. Rab thought that there might be detectives waiting for them, and they'd be "foiled." He liked that word. It was in all his favorite tales.

The railway station there was always busy; it was not the sort of place where people remember strangers. Emmaline went to buy tickets. There had been discussions as to whether she could be disguised as anything other than a gawky fourteen-year-old girl, but she refused Rab's sug- gestion that she impersonate a magician's assistant or a Canadian Mountie. Aunt Lucy sent telegrams, and Professor Bellbuckle devoted himself to making sure that Princess Purnah didn't catch an express train accidentally. "Get down off that roof, young missy! I mean right away, Your Majesty!" chided the professor. Stanley yipped. Purnah huffed, but climbed down.

Emmaline bought two tickets, third class, to Manchester. Professor Bellbuckle, impersonating a one-eyed Irishman with a limp (although not convincingly, as Emmaline noticed) bought three for the boat train to Dublin. Lal Singh bought two tickets to Podgemout Parva.

"Where's that?" asked Rubberbones.

"Shh, somebody'll hear us," replied Emmaline.

Rab thought of his choices when they'd all put in suggestions where to go. They weren't going to the South Pole (even though it was nearly summer there) or the jungles of the Congo, or even Birmingham. They weren't going anywhere by boat from the south coast. Where, then? He could overhear Aunt Lucy complaining to the professor. "Italy would have been ideal. Or Greece — I wrote down Greece as one of my suggestions — or the south of France. I think Emmaline's ideas all had to do with flying machines. But now our only choice is —"

"It won't be too unpleasant, Lucy dear. It's a lot less crowded in winter."

"Of course it is, Ozymandias. There's a reason for that." Then Aunt Lucy called everyone together.

"Right! Here's the plan. We'll split up and head off in different directions. We won't go as far as the tickets permit, but get out before our destinations and take another train to Edinburgh, Brighton or Little Piddlecombe. Then we'll all meet at our final destination. The adults know where it is. You, Rab, must take Stanley and go with Lal Singh; you must handle the luggage, I'm afraid. Princess Purnah will accompany me. Emmaline, you'll be in charge of — er, you'll go with Professor Bellbuckle."

"I wuntings go with perfessurr! Or Errand Boy!"

"I don't think that would be a good idea, Purnah my dear." They'd broken into pairs, one youngster and an adult. Aunt Lucy felt responsible for Princess Purnah, and Purnah would listen to her, at least a little. Rubberbones and Lal Singh were fast friends, and the Sikh wouldn't allow his young companion to do anything foolish. Emmaline's job was to supervise the

professor, who was very likely to do something foolish. "Come on, Professor Bellbuckle. We are going to, er,

Manchester." They'd handed out the tickets like drawing straws. "But we don't actually have to go there. We'll get off the train and wander about a bit."

That cheered the professor up. "There's a fine hill near there where we can fly kites," he suggested.

"Excellent plan," said Emmaline as she clapped him on the back. Good Lord, she thought to herself. I'll have to make sure Aunt Lucy tells me where we are going. The professor wants to fly kites.

"Good-bye!" called out Aunt Lucy, bundling Purnah onto the train for Podgemout Parva as it began to pull away.

"I'll see you all in —"

Emmaline couldn't make out that last word amid the sound of the train picking up speed. The professor knew, of course. At least, she hoped he did.

The Collector sat back in a leather armchair, long legs twined beneath him, a snifter of brandy in his hand. It had been a mixed sort of day. One of his subjects for study, theman who claimed to travel through time, persisted in his refusal to give his name. This was inconvenient since it was vital that the Collection was properly arranged. Today he'd decided simply to file him under "T" and had him flung into a cell with Nikola Tesla, the electrical genius, who was pining for his own laboratory and refused to eat.

But he'd had a telegram from London where the two primitive brutes he employed had located and persuaded Professor Cavor to accompany them. He'd wanted to procure Cavor for the Collection for quite some time. Cavor's new metal alloy that defied gravity might prove an entertaining toy, although far too dangerous to be allowed to develop. People didn't need to know about that sort of thing. So, another victim caught in the web.

Lastly, he'd received a report by telephone from Samuel Soap. The ratty little man had acted immediately, traveling to a seaside village called Fishwick, where he interviewed the boatmen. One of them recalled a girl with a kite, although clearly the old sailor had been drinking as he'd also mentioned dragons and rockets. Soap had interviewed a retired colonel who threatened him with a shotgun when he asked about the girl. Soap would go next to Lower Owlthwaite where both Miss Cayley and young Master Burns lived. His prey would soon be caught. It was proving surprisingly easy.

Of course, the Collector hadn't yet seen the newspaper reports about an incident at that oddly named village.

⇒ CHAPTER 3 ⇐

A Chapter for Train Timetable Enthusiasts

Rubberbones was full of admiration for Lal Singh.

They'd been left to deal with the baggage after everyone had gathered clean socks and toothpowder for a few days. It was a mass of trunks, crates, suitcases and hatboxes; Aunt Lucy believed in taking her comforts with her.

"We'll never carry all that!" said Rab.

Lal Singh smiled. "Why would we be wanting to?" he asked. "The railway company will do that for us."

"Aye, but if all them folks is looking for us, you can't just walk up and send it to wherever we are going. They'd spot it and be waiting for us when we arrive."

Lal Singh was writing an address label. Rab read it. "The Reverend Chasuble, 'The Larches,' 34 Hanover Rd, Frinton, Essex."

"You're sending all our stuff to the vicar?"

The Reverend Chasuble had been the parish priest at Lower Owlthwaite for thirty years. Stanley was his dog. The vicar had retired this autumn and was staying with his spinster

sister in Essex. She didn't like dogs — or, at least, didn't care
for Stanley — so he'd become Rab's constant companion.

"The Memsahib has sent a telegraph to the vicar. He is to
be forwarding these baggages to another address under the
name of Mrs. McTavish. I shall be collecting them for Mrs.
McTavish at the appropriate time and place."

"Who's Mrs. McTavish?"

"She is a fictitious personage of my own inventing," said
Lal Singh.

"What if there's a real Mrs. McTavish?"

"I suspect that will be the least of our difficulties. Now, if
you would be finding a boy to carry things?"

Rubberbones reasoned that the porters at Leeds would
remember Lal Singh — who was, after all, a very tall brown
man with a turban and a beard — but not a small boy with
a certain amount of grime all over him. He'd get another
grubby boy to help with the luggage — there was one waiting close by.

Which he did, for a penny, and everything went as Lal
Singh said it would.

"Podgemout Parva!" called out the ticket inspector as the
train lurched to a halt. Princess Purnah watched as Aunt Lucy
woke up with a start. She peered around her in confu- sion,
then jumped up to pull her bag down from the rack above the
seats. "Hurry, Purnah! Time to get out. I'd meant to get off
at an earlier station!"

Purnah grinned. She was always glad to see a grown-
up get flustered. "Hooty-hoot!" she chuckled, and skipped
onto the platform as Aunt Lucy struggled with her luggage.
Podgemout Parva was quite unlike Leeds. It was an idyllic
railway station, the kind that small boys with train sets
owned. It had a single platform and an office-cum- waiting-

room. That was it. There was one person on the platform, a smart young man with a monocle and smooth, shiny hair. As Aunt Lucy handed down the bag, he stepped forward to help. Princess Purnah thought he was very handsome.

"Lady Flagstone? And this would be your ward, Marie-Thérèse!"

Aunt Lucy looked at him and at the policeman who had appeared in the office doorway. The constable, who was holding some sort of paper, peered at her, at Purnah and at the paper once again. She decided that she was, indeed, Lady Flagstone.

"Charmed! Charmed, dear lady. My name is Lancelot Stilton, and I've got the jolly old cart to take you up to the castle."

The constable mumbled something deferential as the young man swept his two charges away from the platform. "Yes, I'll pass your best wishes on to her ladyship," said Mr. Stilton.

Then they were in a carriage, trotting through the Shropshire countryside, Princess Purnah pointing at sheep, as Mr. Lancelot Stilton — "Call me Stilters, everyone does!"

— talked smoothly about relatives and plans for the weekend and —

"You do know I am not Lady Flagstone, don't you?" said Aunt Lucy. "I just wanted to get past that policeman."

The young man smiled. "Of course. Lady Flagstone telegraphed, care of the station, to say she'd been delayed for a week. I was wondering what to do next as I desperately need a Lady Flagstone today. You are the two ladies who biffed that jackanapes and stole his motor car, aren't you? I didn't want P.C. Squelch to reach that same conclusion."

———

Emmaline decided that she would not permit Professor Bellbuckle to stop and fly kites. Today was not the time for that. He'd told her where they were going, but she had only the vaguest notion of how to get there. They sat in a third-class carriage with tickets for Manchester.

"This island. Professor — stop playing with your watch a moment, if you don't mind — this island is completely devoted to scientific experimentation?"

"That's right, my dear. Mad scientists gathered like seals on a beach. So many you cain't but fall over 'em."

"And it's off the coast of Scotland?"

"Uh-huh. Catch a boat from Nochtermuckity."

"And where is Nochtermuckity?"

"Dear girl, I have no idea."

Emmaline thought that was a minor obstacle. There'd be

maps at the next station and timetables, and all they had to do was get a ticket.

"Professor Bellbuckle, did Aunt Lucy give you money for the fare?"

"Ah, lemme see. She did say something, but —"

He put his hand in his pocket. Rather, he put his hand through an enormous hole in his pocket. The professor's clothes were thirty years behind the fashion and showed signs of explosions past.

"No," he said.

Another minor obstacle. The train went on as far as Liverpool. Emmaline's knowledge of local geography was slim, but she did know that Liverpool was a port. There'd be ships there, and since they were going to an island, a ship might be a useful thing. They'd just stay on the train until it got there. If a ticket inspector appeared, they'd simply hide.

Samuel Soap informed Mr. Peel that he was Inspector Trout of Scotland Yard. The ancient bell-ringer at St. Cuthbert's Church, Lower Owlthwaite, told the detective in return that young Rab Burns had — for reasons he didn't understand but considered vaguely immoral — jumped off the church tower attached to a complicated sort of kite. Yes, that Cayley girl and her mad aunt were mixed up with it. And the vicar (now retired) had agreed to it, which was also immoral. Inspector Trout nodded in agreement as the man griped about the vicar and his dog, and privately told himself that the Reverend Chasuble must have been a saint to put up with Mr. Peel for thirty years. But Mr. Peel did have some information that the Inspector did not have.

"You know they all ran off today? Some business about stealing a horseless carriage. I don't hold with motor cars. Sinful, they are. Jesus never stole a motor car."

Inspector Trout cursed and rushed to buy an evening newspaper. There might be something about the stolen car.

Rab bought an evening paper as soon as he could when they changed trains. There it was, on the front page:

OFFICIAL ASSAULTED WITH UMBRELLA MOTOR CAR STOLEN

So, the incident at Lower Owlthwaite was in the headlines. "It is the motor car, Rab-Sahib. There are as yet few of them, so the thieving of one becomes of considerable importance to public interest. And many an ordinary person would feel gratified that a governmental man should be smitten down by an irate citizen."

Lal Singh was right. But did it mean that other governmental men would want revenge against the attackers?

These were listed as "Mrs. Lucinda Butterworth, widow of Major Butterworth, Indian Army; a man, described as thin, aged fify to sixty, with white hair and a small beard; and three children."

Rab rather resented that. "Three children"? Aside from the fact that he was nearly thirteen, and Purnah and Miss Em were even older, the newspaper didn't give any descrip- tion at all.

"This is helpful to us, although less so for the Memsahib," said Lal Singh. "You are unidentifiable. I am completely absent from the account."

Which was true. There was no mention of the man who drove the dogcart, and that must surely help. If they weren't looking for a six-foot Sikh, there was no need to worry about Lal Singh's distinctive appearance. Maybe Mr. Botts and his cousin hadn't seen the butler. Maybe they thought he was just a servant; Rab knew that the upper classes seldom noticed servants at all.

"In that case," said Lal Singh, "we have no need to take this boat-train to Dublin, which I understand to be a fine city but unhelpful to our purposes. Instead, we will travel to a place by the name of Nochtermuckity, about which I will find out more."

"Nock-ter-muck-itee?" said Rubberbones.

"In Scotland," replied Lal Singh as he headed for the ticket office. "Our friends will be meeting us there soon. Then we shall go to Urgghh."

"Urgghh?" echoed Rab. Did Lal Singh have something caught in his throat?

◢ CHAPTER 4 ◣

Unpleasant Characters and a Parrot

Aunt Lucy studied a different evening newspaper. The lead story was similar, with the colorful addition of the words "INSANE GRANNY IN BRUTAL BROLLY BRAWL." It also

gave her name, her address and her age as seventy-six. "Ruddy cheek!" she said. "They just made that up."

"Sorry about the local paper," said Mr. Stilton. "I only get it for the racing results. Would you like tea? Cakes? Crumpets?"

Princess Purnah agreed to take a few delicate bites, shouting "Eeky-oo! Chocolate cake!" Lancelot Stilton rang a bell. Within moments, a butler shimmered in with a tray.

"Thank you, Strand."

They were in something called the morning room, in somewhere called Podgemout Castle. It was a grand old house covered in ivy with towers and buttresses and lots of castlelike features.

"My aunt will be home shortly," said Mr. Stilton. "She has never met Lady Flagstone — or you, Marie-Thérèse — but

she's passionately interested in your field of accomplishment."
Aunt Lucy leaned forward. "My field of accomplishment.

What would that be?"

"Why," replied Mr. Stilton, "you are a spirit medium,
invited here for a séance, to see if Uncle Fred will drop by
and chat."

"Does he usually drop by and chat?"

"Not since his death in 1874. A roof tile fell on his head.
He's been silent since then."

"And yet?"

"And yet my aunt, Lady Agatha Stilton, has spent the past
twenty years trying to communicate with the dear departed.
She has spent a good deal of cash and — more importantly
— energy on bringing every cheat, trickster and lunatic here
to Podgemout Castle to get in touch with Uncle Fred. Lady
Flagstone — the real one, not your good self — is simply the
latest in the line. She's a dotty high-society woman. She has
pots of money, so she probably won't steal the knives and
forks, but she is no more likely to contact the spirit world
than she is to fly."

"I can fly," said Purnah, "whenever I gets the chances!"
Mr. Stilton ignored this rather odd remark. "I want to get
Aunt Agatha to forget all about this ridiculous spiritualist-
séance-what-have-you. What you can do, if you don't mind,
is preside over a séance so grotesquely false that even Aunt
Agatha recognizes it as fakery. In the past she has believed in
people who were transparent swindlers, who used wires and
trick devices and all sorts of obvious things. You'll have
to be very bad indeed."

"I'm sure I could be completely incompetent," admitted
Aunt Lucy. "I have no experience in contacting the dead, so
that's already in my favor."

"I'd be immensely grateful. And, in return, you can stay
here until the newspapers stop mentioning your name and

the search ends. It's not as if you were accused of murdering a dozen people and burning down a cathedral. You smacked a government-Johnny with a brolly and borrowed his motor car. They'll have forgotten you by next Wednesday."

Princess Purnah thought that Aunt Lucy had a devilish look in her eye. "By George, we'll do it!" she said.

"Jolly good show, Lady Flagstone. And Marie-Thérèse, of course. Oh, young M-T, I ought to mention that you are a deaf mute. Stone deaf, can't say a word. That won't be a problem, will it?"

"Glekk!!" said Princess Purnah; then she shut up, after raising three fingers and indicating three cream cakes. As long as that was understood, she didn't have to say anything.

———

Five strapping men dressed as merchant seamen climbed into the railway carriage at Manchester. They were on their way back to their ship and had celebrated with enough ale to make any ticket inspector leery of questioning them. They weren't unfriendly, just boisterous, like very large puppies who'd been at the brown ale. The biggest, oldest, beardiest, reddest-faced of them addressed Professor Bellbuckle. He had a huge, funguslike mat of hair sur- rounding his face and a parrot on his shoulder.

"Avast there, old matey. Off to the 'pool, then?" "Eh?" said the professor. "What pool?"

"Liverpool! And then on a fine jaunt up the Scotch coast and across to Ireland. Tramp steamer, the Saucy Emmaline! Arr!"

"Arr! Shiver me timbers! Saucy Emmaline!" squawked the parrot.

"That's my name!" said Emmaline before she thought about whether she ought to be starting a conversation with a drunken sailor and his parrot. Her mother would have fainted at the thought.

"Luck! There's luck!" called out the shortest, palest of the sailors, and each of them pulled a bottle out of their reefer jackets. "Drink!" One of them waved his bottle in front of Emmaline's face. "Drink! Arr!" squawked the bird.

"No! Thank you, but I'm too young for, er, whatever that is." The professor also refused a swig. "I have abstained from alcohol since an unfortunate incident in Paris and some ill-judged words to a policeman —"

Emmaline cut him short. "Did you say Scotland?" she asked the first sailor.

"Up and down the coast. Oban, Skye, the Outer Hebrides — the bigger islands."

"Do you know a place called — what is the island called, Professor?"

"What island, child?" The scientist had a dreamy, faraway look on his face.

Emmaline almost shouted in exasperation. "The island with the experimental facilities! The place we are trying to get to!"

"Ah. Um. Oh. Urgghh," replied the professor.

"Are you all right?" she asked, concerned. Had he forgotten how to speak?

"No, that's the name of the place — Urgghh."

The sailors grinned at one another. "That's where all the loonies go."

The beardiest sailor leaned forward. "Don't listen to them idle lubbers. If you want to go to Urgghh, stick wi' us. We'll get you close enough to get a local boat to the island. You'll just have to come aboard the Saucy Emmaline."

"Won't the captain mind? I mean, we don't have any money to be passengers," asked Emmaline.

The red-faced man laughed. "Nah! I be First Mate, and I can take on extry 'ands if we need 'em. If you'll shove yeer 'air up under a cap, you can work your passage as crew."

One of the seamen finally fell off his seat, turning a sickly green as he did so. The man next to him said, "Blimey, looks like Bert won't be fit for galley duty tonight. He's our cook. He'll be in 'is bunk for three days. Beer don't agree wiv 'is constitution."

The First Mate turned to Emmaline and the professor. "One of yer will be cook. One be deck 'and. Decide atwixt yerselves."

"Arr!" agreed the parrot.

Lal Singh bought tickets for Nochtermuckity with the money that Aunt Lucy had given him, which he hadn't lost. They'd have to change trains at Glasgow and Strathcarrot. It was at Strathcarrot that the trouble occurred. It was really none of Rab's business, but he couldn't just stand by.

He and Lal Singh had just climbed down from the train as Stanley made a flying leap onto the platform in sheer exuberance. You couldn't blame the dog. He'd been cooped up for hours.

You couldn't blame the porter, either. He was hardly older than Rubberbones, and he was hauling a huge steamer trunk on a handcart. The steamer trunk was piled with smaller bags. The porter couldn't see where he was going. Of course, where he was going was exactly the spot Stanley had chosen to jump. The lad stepped, the dog yelped and all the luggage hit the stone surface of the station platform. A flying suitcase skidded to a halt at Rab's feet where Stanley was cowering in fear. The little dog yelped again and ran to hide behind Lal Singh. The big trunk tumbled in the air and caught Rubberbones square in the chest. This ought to have hurt. But Rab shrugged it off. You had to try harder than that to hurt young Master Burns.

The porter scrambled to his feet, patting his cap back into place. He was freckle-faced and nervous.

"Sorry!" Rab called out. "My dog. I'll 'elp you wi' them cases."

Out of the station dining room burst two men. One was a huge brute of a fellow, flat cap jammed low on his brow, fists formed into balls. The other was tiny.

It was the tiny one who addressed the porter.

"You bloomin' idiot! Them is our employer's luggages. Wotcher throwin' 'em abaht for? I'll show you wot for!"

But it was the giant thug who showed every indication of showing the porter "wot for." He seized the boy by the sleeve and smacked him across the side of the head. It was a vicious backhander, and the porter dropped to the ground like a felled tree.

Rubberbones was crouched over the trunk, trying to lift it, when he saw what was happening. He stood up and waved a fist. Not a very big fist.

"You lay off 'im, you big bully! It weren't 'is fault!"

The little thug, who seemed to be in charge of the talking duties, shouted out, "So, 'oo's fault was it then, you cheeky little monkey?"

Rab's cheeks flushed. He was nobody's cheeky monkey. "It were just an accident," he replied. "You could 'elp 'im wi' the bags yerselves, 'stead of stuffing your faces."

Which was probably not the most tactful thing to say. The little bruiser had brown sauce stains on his collar while the big brute was idly chewing the butt end of a sausage.

"Why, you —" the small man began. His tone was nasty. The giant — who was closer to seven feet than six and had hands like haunches of pork — lurched toward Rab in a threatening fashion.

"You have a question for my young friend?" said Lal Singh. He had stepped silently alongside Rab. Stanley snarled at the big man, but kept close to Lal Singh's legs.

The little bruiser eyed Lal Singh, evaluating him. The huge fellow stopped his advance. Lal Singh was motionless, smiling, standing like the soldier he'd been. He held his hands in front of him, fingertips together. The tiny thug recognized the Sikh as a very dangerous adversary.

"Come on, Titch. Let's get anuvver cuppa tea. You, lad" — he gestured at the porter, who was clutching his ear — "get them bags sorted out. Our guv'nor ain't going to like 'is property bein' damaged."

"Right, Hercules," replied the giant. His voice was a whisper and surprisingly high in pitch.

Rab and Lal Singh helped the young porter with the trunks. They were marked for "Invermisery House, Nochtermuckity."

"Isn't that where we are going?" asked Rab. Lal Singh smiled grimly, but said nothing.

—————◦∞◦—————

The Collector had spent the afternoon peering through his telescope. From his study window in the tower he could view the cliffs of the island, high above the channel. Everything was very gray and cold, and few of the entertaining people who lived on the island were out and about. In summer the place was alive with scientific persons building strange devices and testing their odd inventions. Every so often he spotted someone with potential, and observed him as a possible candidate for his collection. He was extremely selective in his choices.

It was just before dinner when Foglamp brought a pair of telegrams. The first was from the Soap man. The two potential specimens had slipped away.

"Fools! Why do I employ imbeciles?" the Collector screamed venomously, raging around the room, long legs and arms scratching at the walls.

Foglamp handed over the other telegram. It was brief and to the point:

Will trade information in return for item of lost property. State time and place for immediate meeting. Malvolia Wackett, Headmistress, St.Grimelda's School for Young Ladies.

CHAPTER 5

Not Much at Nochtermuckity

It was pouring rain when the train dropped Rubberbones and Lal Singh at the tiny stop on the West Highland Railway. There wasn't much to see at Nochtermuckity. It was smaller than Lower Owlthwaite. There was a hotel at the station imaginatively named the Station Hotel. There were also a post office, a church, a few shops and a pub. Boats were drawn up at a wharf. Across the narrow inlet (known as a sea-loch) lay the island of Urgghh. Rab knew this from a map, but you couldn't see it in the rain. There was a place called Invermisery a few miles up the road. And, up a hill past a few hangdog cottages was the home of the McGinnis.

The McGinnis was head of the clan McGinnis, or at least the ones around Nochtermuckity. He was the laird, which was the same as a lord, only said with a Scottish accent.

"We must make arrangements to go over to the island," said Lal Singh. "The McGinnis owns the island. He owns all the houses on the island. He owns the boat that goes to the island."

"Does he own everything else?" asked Rubberbones. "He must be very rich."

"I am imagining you can own a great deal of property in these parts without being very rich," replied Lal Singh.

Rubberbones watched the rain running down the steep little high street while Lal Singh hired the man with the station cart to take them up to Hard Knox House, the seat of the McGinnis.

The housekeeper was a thin woman who had the expression of someone who has received a lot of bad news over many years and resents it. "Ye can aye come in and sit doon. I'll see if the laird is receiving."

The McGinnis was happy to receive people who might want to lease a cottage in winter. Rubberbones understood that sensible people who had a choice probably didn't want to live on a windy island in cold weather. December was just over two weeks away.

The McGinnis was a stout man of middle years, solidly built, with stumpy legs that meant his kilt almost reached the tops of his socks. He sat in his parlor, account books in front of him and a plate with crumbs at his side. "Ye'll already have had your tea!" he announced. It wasn't a ques- tion. Rab thought about food and wondered when he'd get some again.

Lal Singh passed a letter to Mr. McGinnis. After spending a few minutes reading it, rubbing his mustache at the same time, the laird looked up. "So, ye'll be Mrs. McTavish's butler? Indian fella, nae doot. She says that she wants accommodations on the island for six persons in all, wi' facilities for scientific experimenting. Naturally, there'll be a charge for insurance; my inventing gentlemen do have a habit of causing damage to my property. Ye'll also under- stand that Christmas is a very popular time so naturally prices are a touch higher."

Lal Singh smiled. "I find the second part of your last sentence truer than the first."

The McGinnis looked at him severely. Rab could tell that Lal Singh didn't believe what the laird had to say. Nobody came to spend Christmas on Urgghh.

"Mrs. McTavish says that ye're to see what I have available and select the best," Mr. McGinnis trumpeted. "As if all my properties weren't of the highest standard."

Lal Singh said nothing. Rab knew the Sikh well enough to know that he'd keep his opinions to himself.

While Mr. McGinnis mumbled through a list of cottages with prices and additions and alterations clearly calculated to make the costs increase, Rubberbones peered forward at the letter from "Mrs. McTavish." Had Aunt Lucy written this? Or had Lal Singh created the document, as he had made up the imaginary Mrs. McTavish whose luggage would be arriving at the station shortly?

"Now, let's be takin' the boot over tae the island and decide on a cottage. Time is money," said the McGinnis.

Rubberbones wondered why were they taking a boot to the island. He always wore two. Maybe it was a rubber boot, so they wouldn't get wet crossing the water. It must be pretty shallow. Maybe two boots weren't available. Maybe they'd have to hop, taking turns. That'd be champion.

Aunt Lucy was practicing her spiritualist skills. Since she didn't have any, this was easy. She just pretended to be as mystical as possible. This was working well so far. She and Lady Stilton had become instant friends. They'd met an hour before on the terrace overlooking what was probably a fine rose garden in the summertime.

"As two souls! I can see the true gift in you, Lady Flagstone."

"I see what I see, Lady Stilton. If the spirits choose to speak through me, I'll let 'em chat away."

"Oh! They come so easily, do they? Many of the spiritualists I have met previously seemed to have so much difficulty contacting the other side," said Lady Stilton. She was an elderly woman, stooped and very shortsighted.

"Easy come, easy go," said Aunt Lucy, trying to behave as much like her cheery Gypsy fortune-teller friend, Madame ZaZa, as she could. "You've got to welcome them over. It can be hard work for them, having no bodies an' all."

"Yes!" exclaimed Lady Stilton, impressed. "How true. No bodies!"

Princess Purnah was about to add that the dear departed had no feet to walk about with either, but she remembered that she was supposed to be a deaf mute. She hadn't decided what deaf mutes were supposed to do with their time. Did they have hobbies? Mr. Stilton caught her eye as if to remind her to be still. That was probably for the best. She held up a finger in what she felt was the universal sign for cake.

Lady Stilton leaned forward. Purnah could understand how she had been fooled by frauds in the past. She couldn't see past her own nose. You could put a dancing marionette in front of Lady Stilton and she'd believe it was her late lamented husband. "We'll have a séance the day after tomorrow. That will give you time to build up your powers. The journey here must have been tiring to someone of your sensitivity."

"Anytime you like, ducks," replied Aunt Lucy. Her efforts to behave like a mysterious Gypsy — or perhaps a silly member of the nobility pretending to be a Gypsy — were a little strange. Lady Stilton didn't notice.

"Oh! Lady Flagstone! You have such a radiant soul! A cheery spirit!"

"I like to think of myself as a happy medium," replied Aunt Lucy.

It was lucky that Princess Purnah didn't understand the joke because she'd have laughed, and that would have spoiled everything.

"Tarnation," observed Professor Bellbuckle. "Criminy. This sure is one ugly boat."

"Arr!" agreed the parrot. The Saucy Emmaline was a rusty tub of a vessel that sat low in the water as if it were about to sink. The crew hadn't sobered up. If Emmaline had been worried about whether the captain would accept a fourteen-year-old girl and an elderly American inventor as members of the crew, she needn't have been. The captain was the drunkest of the lot. In fact, she hadn't seen him at all; he'd not left his cabin, but the sound of his singing indicated that he was still alive and conscious — sort of. She couldn't make out a word of his song.

At the moment Emmaline was acting as the look-out. This was a job that demanded no nautical skills whatsoever. It simply required that she stay awake and notice large vessels passing by or rocks and cliffs that might prove a nuisance if the vessel ran into them. Emmaline could do this. She was neither drunk nor hung over, so she could probably do this better than anyone else on board.

There was heavy fog in the Irish Sea. Emmaline thought that it was like looking into cold gray soup. The raw wind made her pull her collar up higher. The First Mate — who called himself "Blackbeard," even though his beard was clearly brown — had taken her to what he called the "slops box" and let her rummage through smelly blue coats known as reefer jackets and dirty canvas trousers. The ones she'd chosen were the best fit, which was still shapeless and baggy. The whistle of the wind didn't drown the noise of the ship's engines. Emmaline was not familiar with how they were supposed to sound, but she was pretty sure it wasn't like a rumbling stomach that had eaten a bad meat pie

washed down with beer. It sounded very uncomfortable.

The last time Emmaline had been this close to the sea was just a few weeks ago. She'd been about to crash into it as the "birds" of St. Grimelda's ripped her improvised flying machine apart and Professor Bellbuckle fired homemade rockets to add to the unpleasantness. It seemed like ages ago, yet the sea looked as bone-chilling and dangerous as it had that day in October.

Look-outs aren't supposed to get lost in their own thoughts, so it was lucky that Emmaline was brought back to reality by the massive blast of a horn and the sight of a vessel. "Good grief, that thing's moving right in front of us!" It wasn't as close as she had first thought, but that was only because the vessel was very big indeed; huge, in fact — as high as a cathedral and twinkling with row upon row of lights. Emmaline realized it was an ocean liner. It made the

Saucy Emmaline seem like a bathtub toy.

. She grabbed a speaking tube. She hoped that the First Mate was on the bridge. "Mr. Blackbeard! There's a ship in front! And a bit to the right. Do something!"

"Bow, lass, bow! Not the front, the starboard bow!" came a disembodied voice.

"No time for lessons, Mr. Blackbeard. Hard astern or something! Jibber the mizzen! Luff the mainbrace!"

"Arr!" It was the parrot talking into the tube. "Arr!" added Mr. Blackbeard.

The massive horn of the liner blared again. Emmaline gripped the handrail in fear. She was meant to build flying machines, to discover principles of aeronautics. She was not meant to end her life in a stinky sailor suit on a rusty tub full of drunken seamen who recklessly drove their boat smack into the pride of some luxurious shipping line.

The Saucy Emmaline turned slowly, and the massive ship passed safely by.

"Well done, lass!" called out the First Mate. "Most of the lads would never have spotted that ship!"

The fog closed in again.

≈ CHAPTER 6 ≈

Urgghh

Rubberbones looked up at the sheer cliffs rising from the foam. The sea lashed against the rocks relentlessly, swirling white. The little boat bobbed against the driving waves, lurching forward between the blows. It had an engine that made a dreadful smell but didn't seem to be able to compete with the might of the North Atlantic. The boy was trying to keep his lunch inside his stomach. Stanley whimpered at his feet. "It's a pleasant day oot," said the McGinnis. "Sometimes the sea gets rough at this time o' year. Ye're lucky this afternoon." He steered toward a sheltered cove and pulled the

boat up against a stone jetty. "Urgghh!" he announced. "Urgghh," said Lal Singh, looking at the windswept

chunk of rock.

"Urgghh!" said Rubberbones, clutching his stomach. "Been in my family these thoosand year," said the

McGinnis. "O' course, we've never seen any reason to actually live on it."

Rab could understand that, as an Arctic blast struck him when he stepped out of the boat.

"But we kept sheep here. Excellent wool, ye understand. Thick. But now we keep yon scientist fellas. They can be pretty woolly, at that." Mr. McGinnis seemed to consider this an excellent joke.

"Please be showing us these cottages," said Lal Singh, who didn't.

"There's a couple o' fine houses, and a shop and a public house just here by the jetty. They call it the Village, although its real name is —" At this point Mr. McGinnis made a noise in his throat that sounded as if he was trying to spit up a small reptile. "But most of yon scientists are English, and they canna speak the Gaelic tongue."

They walked into the howling wind across a cobbled yard to a cottage built of stones piled one on top of another, as if by a giant child. "This ane's vacant."

Lal Singh surveyed it from the outside before ducking through a low doorway. Rab followed. It was two bare rooms with a narrow staircase leading upward. The windows were tiny and closed, yet freezing air swept in gusts through the building. Rubberbones looked to see if the door was still open. It wasn't. He heard a low whistling sound. Putting his ear to the wall, he was treated to a blast of icy wind blowing through gaps between the stones. The place was like a colander.

"I don't think this is being suitable for our needs," announced Lal Singh.

"The previous gentleman didnae mind it!" said Mr. McGinnis, offended.

"The previous gentleman left in July. And he for extra blankets often asked." A new voice cut in. A firm female voice, possibly foreign. Rab turned to see a woman, a round, motherly figure in thick tweeds and sensible boots. "If our new tenant is a lady, she vill not vish this pigsty. Do not harass these persons with your cheapness, Vilhelm. Take

them to the large new cottage, and do not overcharge them, as is so often your vay. I can see that this boy needs a nice cup of cocoa. And schokoladekuchen. And this fine dog — find him a bone!"

"Yes, dear," replied the McGinnis. "Right away."

The woman beamed at Rab, patted Stanley and gave Lal Singh a look of appreciation. "You vill not mind my husband. Let me know ven you are settled in. I must now be attending to my scientific gentlemen, for they are as kleine kinder — little children — and need a vomanly management."

Rab noticed that she said "vill" and "vomanly" instead of "will" and "womanly."

Mr. McGinnis shook his head. "That's Mrs. McGinnis, ye'll ken. She's a mite German. I expect ye'll see a lot of her." He shook his head again. "To the large cottage, then. I was going tae show it next anyways. I didnae really think —"

He waved his arm at the crumbling hovel, but the wind howling through the wall drowned him out.

Princess Purnah was enjoying Podgemout Castle. It was the sort of palace that she ought to own. In Chiligrit, the royal dwelling was a mud fort with thick walls and towers from which to drop things on your enemies. Which was good, of course. Podgemout Castle was very short on facilities for dousing your foes with boiling oil, she'd noticed. And the walls probably wouldn't withstand much in the way of cannon shot. She'd told Mr. Stilton about this problem when they were together in the garden and she didn't have to be deaf or silent.

"You are quite right, my dear. The castle is not a real fortress at all. It just has a few medieval-looking bits. My great-great-grandfather had it built about a hundred years ago, when there was no chance of meeting marauding knights.

Real castles are dark and cold and have appalling lavatory arrangements. He wanted something that looked like a castle but had proper modern facilities."

Yes! That was it, thought Purnah. None of her late father's palaces had anything resembling "proper modern facilities." There wasn't a flushing toilet in the whole kingdom, or in any of the nearby kingdoms. The palaces of Chiligrit were also short on rose gardens and cream cakes. One day she'd remedy all that.

"About the plan for tomorrow night ..." said Mr. Stilton. Purnah knitted her eyebrows in a scowl. "Not likings! Glekk!"

"What is it you are not — that you don't like?"

Princess Purnah wasn't about to admit that she simply didn't understand the scheme. It was all madness. The strange old lady thought that she could speak with her dead husband by sitting around a table in the dark. Everyone in Chiligrit knew you contacted the dead by smearing your face with the grease of a fat-tailed sheep and wailing for hours at the old shrine under the waterfall — still, these English people were odd. This plan was odder still. Mr. Stilton wanted, somehow, to mess up the "séance" so that his aunt could finally see that it was all a fraud. She'd never spotted a fraud before, so why should she do so now? And — this was the part that concerned Purnah — somehow most of the messing up bit was left to her. It was as if people expected her to mess things up. Porok! That was an insult!

"It is an insult!" she announced.

"There'll be cream cakes," said Mr. Stilton.

Princess Purnah smiled. Cream cakes! Excellent! Pingg! But she still wasn't sure about the plan.

"I sits at the table. Then lightings goes out. Much flickery candles. I slips under tables and makes banging noise. Then I speaks out loudish, saying, O, I is dead husband, all is good here on Other Sidings —"

"The 'Other Side,' dear."

"Yes, Other Sidings, and not to worry about me, there is lots of beautiful maidens attendings on me, but no wine or beerings because that is sinful. But much chocolate."

Mr. Stilton looked a bit startled. "I'm not sure Aunt Agatha will like the beautiful maidens, my dear."

"All the better," said Aunt Lucy firmly. "I think Princess Purnah will suit our purposes admirably."

Emmaline was tremendously glad that the ship named after her (well, it wasn't really named after her) hadn't struck an ocean liner in the fog. Mr. Blackbeard had congratulated her for spotting the giant vessel and calling out a warning to prevent an accident. All the crew had patted her on the head and called her "shipmate." They had also presented her with a huge tin mug of rum.

"I don't drink. I'm not old enough. I'm only fourteen," said Emmaline.

"Arr!" said Mr. Blackbeard. "I were drinkin' rum when I were ten."

"I were eight," said the engineer.

"Six!" proclaimed the cook, who had returned after two days in his bunk. Emmaline didn't think he was sober; he was simply standing upright again. The replacement cook, Professor Bellbuckle, was now free of duties in the kitchen — the galley, as it was called — and could do other things, which worried Emmaline. He was a terrible cook, but at least when he was on galley duty he couldn't get up to any- thing else.

"Drink up!" commanded the First Mate. "Arr!" agreed the parrot.

Emmaline took a tiny sip. It was like fire. It was like a

fist in the face. It was like something you'd use to clean the engine with.

"Blecchhh!" she said.

"I told you she'd like it!" said the Second Mate. "Din' I say so?"

———

The Collector left his lair only for the most important of reasons. He was irritable elsewhere, away from his Collection and his comforts. Foglamp had arranged a private room at an inconspicuous hotel in a northern town. Now the old man sat facing Mrs. Malvolia Wackett, vast in her bulk as she crushed a sofa beneath her. My goodness, he thought, what a massive creature. And so baleful in her glare. But Mrs. Wackett did not scare him. He was simply fascinated by her as a specimen of her type. If he collected headmistresses, he'd have snapped her up.

"You mentioned an item of lost property," he said. His voice was deliberately small, quavering as he spoke. It gave a false impression of mildness.

"Indeed, Mr. ... Smith. Not so much an item as a person. A young gel known as Purnah, who was taken from my school some weeks ago. She was placed in our care by important people, and we want to ensure her safe return as soon as possible."

"A runaway schoolgirl?" asked the Collector.

"Nobody runs away from St. Grimelda's!" thundered Mrs. Wackett. "She was abducted against her will."

The Collector knew the headmistress was lying. People lied all the time, in his experience. He did it himself, quite often. Not that he cared about this Purnah person. "I see," he replied. "I assume the Cayley girl abducted her?"

He watched as Mrs. Wackett's eyes grew small and suspicious. He wasn't supposed to know about Emmaline's involvement. Actually he didn't, but her reaction told him what he needed.

"The Cayley gel, yes," hissed Mrs. Wackett. "I don't want her back — just Purnah."

The Collector thought that Mrs. Wackett very much wanted to get her revenge on young Miss Cayley — but that she'd forego that pleasure if this Purnah child was returned. Interesting.

"I think we can do business," he murmured.

⚔ CHAPTER 7 ⚔

The Cunning Inspector Pike

Rubberbones thought the cottage was champion. It had proper plaster on the walls and, more importantly, the wind did not blow through. You could even take off your coat inside if you got the fire going. Lal Singh had done so, and Stanley was settled down before the flames. There was room for everyone (if they didn't mind being cramped) and a shed for the professor's experiments. Mr. McGinnis had made all the arrangements with Lal Singh. He'd make sure the luggage all came over for the imaginary Mrs. McTavish. Rab hadn't really listened to the details; he was more inter- ested in the cottage, and the island.

There was a nautical chart tacked to a wall; Rab liked to look at maps. Urgghh was about three miles long and two wide, and shaped like a kidney. (Rab hated kidneys, even when fried up with bacon.) It was at the mouth of a sea-loch; there were smaller islands nearby, home to sea birds and seals. Maybe walruses. Rubberbones wasn't sure whether there'd be polar bears, but he hoped so.

Urgghh was high and flat on top except for a single steep hill and the sheltered cove at the harbor. There were no trees whatsoever. Rab thought it must be very windy. He was anxious to explore.

"Tomorrow," said Lal Singh. "It is far too late in this day to be going to unknown places."

"It's only afternoon," protested the lad. "What time is it?" "It is half past the hour of three, which is later here than you are accustomed to."

Rab didn't really understand what Lal Singh meant. But when he went to the window, he saw the sun sinking in the west.

———◦◦◦◦———

"There is a visitor for Lady Stilton," announced Strand. Princess Purnah was impressed with the butler. He was smooth and silent, and she wanted one for her palace. "A gentleman from the police. Inspector Pike."

They were in the small morning room, which was about the size of Belgium. Lady Stilton was not present.

"My aunt is resting," said Mr. Stilton. "But I'll see the chappie. Show him in!"

Princess Purnah thought that Aunt Lucy appeared nervous. Mr. Stilton must have seen this as well because he said, "Stay here. I shall do the talking."

A ramrod-stiff man with glittering eyes and a fierce mustache strode into the room. His bald head shone in the gaslight.

"Pike! Scotland Yard! Mr. Stilton, I assume!" he barked. Lancelot Stilton responded by crossing his legs in a slow, lazy way. "Do take a seat, Inspector, and tell us how we can help you."

Inspector Pike sat down, looking suspicious.

"We — at the Yard — received a report about two persons

being seen at Podgemout Parva Station. Suspicious persons. Persons of interest to Her Majesty's Government for reasons of public interest."

"What reasons, Inspector?"

"Reasons as wot I'm not obliged to tell."

"But I'm a member of the public. I'm interested. Tell!" Inspector Pike moved uneasily in his chair, which squeaked. He glared at Princess Purnah, then at Aunt Lucy. "These two ladies 'ere. You know 'em?"

Lancelot Stilton gave an easy, carefree laugh. "Know them? Would they be in this room drinking tea if I didn't?"

"Ah, right," admitted Pike. "And 'oo would they be? Beggin' your pardon, sir, but 'oo are they?"

Mr. Stilton laughed again. "Let me introduce Lady Flagstone, the well-known spiritualist, and her ward, Marie-Thérèse."

Lady Flagstone, Aunt Lucy, glared at the detective as if at a trespassing woodlouse. "Mmm. Inspector Pike, you say? Mmm. You have a negative aura."

Princess Purnah glared at the officer in her best "off with his head" manner.

Inspector Pike was not intimidated. "Are these the ladies you met at Podgemout Parva Station?"

"I met them off the train, Inspector. As arranged with my aunt, weeks ago. You may ask her, when she is available. Lady Flagstone is a medium. My aunt is most interested in communing with the dear departed. We have a séance arranged for tomorrow evening. "

Pike changed his expression. Princess Purnah could tell she was facing a deceitful man. A cunning man. He reminded her of her Uncle Bakistabbo, who had slain her Uncle Stabbibakko, treacherously, at bathtime.

"Oh yes, sir. I'm most interested in spiritualism myself. Bit of a hobby. Is there any chance that I might be permitted

to attend the séance? Purely as a spectator, you understand."
Princess Purnah knew that the séance was meant to be a disaster. All the same, it was a bad idea for this man to be there. Aunt Lucy must say no, surely.

"I don't see why not," said Aunt Lucy. "The more the merrier!"

No! No! Princess Purnah knew this was a mistake. Men like this should be strangled by loyal servants as soon as was convenient. But Marie-Thérèse was supposed to be a deaf mute, so Purnah said nothing.

———

Emmaline felt dreadful. The muffled thumping of the engines and the appalling stench below decks combined to make her feel nauseous. She could still taste the liquor they'd made her take a sip of to celebrate not hitting the ocean liner. It was disgusting.

"Rum," she mumbled. "Never before, never again."
"Oh," said the Second Mate. "Sorry about that. It was the cheap stuff. We use that for cleaning the engines."

He was bringing food, but Emmaline didn't want it. Even if she'd been well, the cook wasn't much better than Professor Bellbuckle, whose meals were hideously, unbeliev- ably bad. Aunt Lucy bad. She slipped out of the bunk.

"I'm going up on deck for some fresh air," she announced.
Professor Bellbuckle seized her by the arm as she climbed up a ladder. "Emmaline! Amazing discoveries! Come with me!"

The first amazing discovery was that the engineer had passed out from drinking the cleaning rum. Emmaline thought he might have finished the mug that she'd been given. The second was that Professor Bellbuckle was taking the engines apart, piece by piece. There was nobody to stop him. "You've heard the noise this thing makes? No wonder!" The professor was excited. "Hasn't been serviced in years. This part here is held together by an old belt. There's a pair of boots jammed in over there, too — I have no idea why.

There's a leak that needs fixin', and a few adjustments that need adjustin' and —"

If Emmaline had felt better, she might have tried to stop him. Instead, she just said, "No fireworks, Professor. No explosions. No rockets. Please?"

Which did not seem like a lot to ask.

Samuel Soap had received a telegram from his employer concerning the foreign schoolgirl and the headmistress. This was fortunate, as Soap had completely lost track of his prey. The papers were full of news about Princess Purnah but said nothing about the Cayley girl or young Burns. Everyone was looking for the princess and old Mrs. Butterworth. So, if he could latch on and follow Purnah and Mrs. B., that'd do the trick nicely.

Scotland Yard would want to catch Purnah and return her to the school. The school wanted her back as soon as possible. The best way to find Miss Cayley and Master Burns now was to follow Purnah and the dear old biddy to see if they met up with the youngsters. The best news in the telegram was that his employer was willing to double the reward if he caught Princess Purnah as well as the two sci- entific children. That was a bonus!

This meant two things to Samuel Soap's devious mind. First off, he'd have to get close to the fugitives. He'd have to trust that the authorities would find them, of course, but they had policemen patrolling, posters everywhere and notices in the papers. Someone would report an eastern princess and a plump woman traveling together. Then he'd race to the scene, disguised as the Spanish ambassador, a toothless old granny or a largish sheep. Whatever caught them off their guard would do.

That brought to mind the second thing. If Soap was to follow the pair to a rendezvous with Emmaline Cayley and Robert Burns, he'd have to make sure that nobody else caught them first.

Soap twiddled with his mustache and snorted thoughtfully as he packed his bags.

⚔ CHAPTER 8 ⚖.

Two Dogs, Three Cakes and One Explosion

The morning was fresh and clear. Rubberbones thought it was just the weather for exploring without having to worry about being blown off a cliff by the Atlantic winds. He strode out of the cottage while Lal Singh went to see about the luggage. Stanley bobbed about Rab's feet, sniffing new sniffs and worrying tufts of grass he'd never met before. The high plateau of Urgghh was a barren blend of rocks, knee-high bracken and faded heather.

"Champion!" said Rubberbones. He threw a stick for Stanley. It was really part of an old packing crate, as Urgghh was low on actual sticks. He did this more than once as they walked, until one hurl too many took the piece of wood over the edge of the cliff.

"Oh flippin' 'eck! No, boy!"

Stanley was bounding toward the edge, the end of the world, with gusto and abandon.

"Heel!"

The dog ignored him.

"Heel!" commanded another voice. Stanley stopped dead in his tracks. It was Mrs. McGinnis. She had her own dogs on leashes; one, a tiny — yet fat — brown dog, the other a massive black and tan monster. One looked as if it wanted to play with Stanley. The other looked as if it was considering whether Stanley would be one big mouthful or two smaller bites.

"You must be careful. The ground falls directly downward in a most alarming manner," said Mrs. McGinnis. "Your dog is impulsive. Like Fang, here."

Fang grinned, with her tongue out. She was the tubby little dog.

"The Duke is more circumspect. He does nothing vithout considerable thought. Except ven he is surprised or on guard or dislikes someone. Then he is less ... cautious in his ways."

The big dog perked up, as if he knew he was being spoken of. He cocked an eye toward Stanley, then Rubberbones and back again. He did not seem impressed.

"But you are exploring the island? You are proper voollen undergarments vearing? You require sandviches? Also fruit and biscuits?"

Mrs. McGinnis pulled a waxed paper bundle from her bag. "I bring lunches to some of the scientists. Many of them fail to eat sensibly, out of excitement and forgetfulness. Can you eat two?"

Rab could definitely eat two, and took the packages gratefully before he walked off over the field. Mrs. McGinnis had suggested he climb the hill, known as the "Cuillin," which she pronounced as "Ku-link." "You can see much from the summit, but avoid gustiness or tragedy might incur."

He could indeed see much from the summit. There was a cluster of buildings below, and he watched Mrs. McGinnis and the dogs moving toward them. In the other direction lay the cottage and the track down toward the harbor and village. The island was surrounded by a deep and turbulent sea. Across the loch was the mainland, rocky and stark. An old gray house, high above the water, stood out. It had a single round tower with a big window near the top. He saw the flash of a reflection. Rab peered carefully. It was a telescope, looking back at him.

"I wasn't thinking. I am sorry," said Aunt Lucy. "I thought that detective would be suspicious if I said he couldn't come. Now I realize that he'll spot us for fakes as soon as we turn down the lights. He tricked me. Now he'll know we aren't in touch with the other side."

Mr. Stilton tried to reassure her. "Well, it won't be a complete disaster if you can't mess up the séance as we discussed. My aunt has seen all sorts of incompetent spiritualists, and she never sees through them. She'd probably not even notice how terrible you were, anyway. Just do the best you can."

"That's the problem. The best I can do is the same as the worst!"

Princess Purnah ate her third cream cake of the morning and thought deeply. She had to pretend to be unable to talk or hear anything. Then she was supposed to make knocking sounds under a table, wailing noises and maybe even the voice of a dead Englishman. But — and this was very confusing — she was supposed to do this all very badly, so nobody believed her.

Only now, she was expected to get it right, and make noises and wailings and perhaps dead men's voices so that everyone believed it was truthyful. Glekk! She didn't know how to talk to the dead. She had enough trouble talking to the living.

In Chiligrit, life was easier. You had to watch your aunt in case she decided to poison you. You noticed whether your cousin appeared for supper with six large "friends" you hadn't met before. You might have to help your uncle over the edge of a cliff if he seemed unwilling to jump. But this was all different.

Purnah scowled as she took another bite and got cream over her nose where she couldn't lick it off.

Emmaline awoke at the sound of a massive, jarring noise that rocked the steamer. The sudden shock of it drove her splitting headache away. Adrenaline surged through her. She tore away the scratchy blanket and leapt from her bunk. As she pulled on her shoes, the scientific Cayley brain analyzed the information it had so suddenly received:

Rickety old ship — defective engines — drunken engineer — Professor Bellbuckle loose in the engine room — "No fireworks, Professor!"

The lunatic inventor had caused an explosion.

Emmaline ran through the rusty old vessel shouting "Fire!" She wasn't certain whether there was a fire — she'd really prefer that there wasn't one — but it was the right thing to yell in hopes of waking the crew. It was simpler than "probable explosion!" or "failure to adequately maintain engines!" Even the most drunken sailor understood what fire was.

She ran down the line of cabin doors, banging frantically. "Get up! Emergency! Fire!" The First Mate stuck his head out of his cabin, eyes bleary and confused. He wore a stylish one-piece undergarment. "Arr!" he said, but his heart wasn't in it. "Arr!" trilled the parrot with greater enthusiasm. "Shiver me timbers!"

"There's something wrong with the engines," said Emmaline to the parrot.

It took a moment for Emmaline to remember that there was no point in discussing marine safety issues with a talking bird. She seized the First Mate by his prodigious beard and tugged. He simply screamed in response, but the pain grabbed his attention.

"There's been an explosion. Wake up the crew, and I'll go below!" shouted Emmaline. Then she ran for the ladder down to the engine room, leaving the First Mate to rub his sore chin and — she hoped — do what he could to save the ship.

"Abandon ship!" croaked the parrot.

Emmaline leapt down the steps two at a time. "Professor Bellbuckle!" she shouted. "Professor?" He must be down here. The ship lurched and heeled over at an angle. Water sloshed around her ankles. It was dark, and a strong smell struck her lungs as she reached the lower deck. As she turned a corner, she saw flames. The engine room was on fire.

A figure staggered into Emmaline, knocking her against an iron bulkhead and almost into the icy water. "I apologize, young sir," said an American voice. "Please excuse my clumsiness. I am somewhat preoccupied by the gosh-darned boilers, which have carelessly blown up."

"Professor Bellbuckle!" shouted Emmaline. "It's me! Let's get out of here!"

She could see the professor's face through the flaring yellow of the fire. He seemed to be thinking about it. "Yes, we probably ought to do that."

A second figure appeared, flailing wildly at the flames with a towel. It was the engineer, just awakened from his rum-induced slumbers. Emmaline sloshed toward him and grabbed his arm. "Up the stairs!" she commanded. "To the lifeboat!"

As she followed the engineer up the steps, with the professor in tow, Emmaline hoped fervently that the Saucy Emmaline's lifeboat was the kind that floated. But that might be too much to expect.

She shoved the engineer through the hatchway just as another explosion went off below decks. The ship rocked once again, and juddered to starboard (or "the right" as Emmaline still thought of it). The cook dropped a big pot of something appalling over the side and fell backward into the Second Mate.

Mr. Blackbeard grabbed the professor and pushed him into the hands of other sailors already in the lifeboat. Emmaline hauled the engineer — who'd begun to stagger off — into the Second Mate's arms, and jumped in after her friend.

"Abandon ship!" announced the parrot once again. It was good that somebody was in charge.

———◦◦◦———

It was a stroke of luck that Foglamp had overheard the two bruisers talking in the servants' hall. He'd popped downstairs for a moment and glimpsed those disreputable characters swilling down tea. They had abducted a new specimen for the Collection and were cock a' hoop over their triumph. The big one, known as Titch, was listening as the little one — called Hercules, as some sort of joke — talked of a boy they'd encountered while changing trains the day before. Something about a porter dropping a trunk on him. The lad ought to have been hurt by such a heavy piece of luggage — it contained a full-grown scientist, after all — and yet hadn't been. Titch agreed it was uncanny. Hercules said the boy was almost rubbery in the way he'd bounced back from the impact of the trunk.

Foglamp thought about that as he returned to his study.

A rubbery sort of boy. That rang a bell.

ᴁ CHAPTER 9 ᴂ

Shipwrecked!

The sea was the color of iron, the mist a shade lighter; Ireland or Scotland, or possibly Morocco, lay ahead of the lifeboat's bow.

Emmaline was shivering in wet clothes while the parrot squawked, the cook paddled a frying pan in the water and the Second Mate explained that "summat 'd turn up, no fear."

"Arr!" said the engineer. "Someone'll have 'eard the explosions."

"Big bang!" squawked the parrot.

Professor Bellbuckle was huddled in the bottom of the boat, but he stuck his head out from under a tarpaulin when he heard the talk. "Yes, it was a gosh-durn fine explosion, wasn't it?"

Emmaline thought that it probably had been, if you liked explosions, and wanted one just after breakfast. What mattered to her was that the Saucy Emmaline, which had been a slow and creaky old tub, was now mostly submerged in the middle of the Irish Sea. The bit at the back — the stern, as Mr. Blackbeard called it — was still sticking out of the water at an angle. Probably it'd disappear in a little while.

Blackbeard seemed annoyed. "Four hours from port and

we blows up. What caused it?"

The engineer shook his head. "Dunno. Engines was all right when I checked 'em."

Emmaline knew this was a lie, because the engineer had

been unconscious. She knew also that what had caused the explosion was surely — must be — had to be — something to do with Professor Bellbuckle. She could tell from the look on his face.

"Professor, you absolutely promised me there'd be no fireworks or rockets!"

"No, no. None of those blessed instruments of progress was involved. I just modified the pressure in one of the boilers — well, two of 'em, really — and it was then I found out why the third one didn't work at all," whispered the Professor.

"Why was that?"

"Because it was disconnected from the engine and used as what they call a still. It was filled with that vile rum. That's where they made the stuff."

"I tasted it. It was horrible."

"It was combustible, as it turns out. Right explosivible — is that a word?"

Emmaline was pretty certain it wasn't. But she under-stood the idea. The professor had caused one of the "improved, repaired, renovated" boilers to blow up, and the rum had burst into flame with it. It was a wonder they weren't all dead. Although the parrot was a bit singed.

The parrot didn't seem to mind, though. He began croaking his way through a shanty, and the crew joined in, and after a while, Emmaline did, too. It was a jolly song about a ship that foundered and survivors who ate one another, one by one, as their lifeboat drifted across an endless ocean.

Samuel Soap liked using the newfangled telephones. He could easily impersonate anyone he wanted. He rang Scotland Yard in London.

"Hello there! Superintendent Flatfoot, West Yorks Constabulary here. I'm calling about the missing princess. No luck! The trail has gone cold. Who is handling it for the Yard then? Yes, I know Pike. Good old Pikey! I do have some information that he might find useful. Is he there now? No? Where can I reach him then?"

Soap was always amazed — and pleased — that nobody ever doubted he was who he claimed to be. The only problem was that he actually did know "good old Pikey." Inspector Pike knew Samuel Soap as well, from some old dealings in which the policeman had almost collared Soap (under another name, of course) over the matter of some jewels that the original owners wanted back.

All this made things more complicated, but Samuel Soap was a man who throve on challenges. Next time he used a telephone he'd pretend to be an old Chinese laundress. With a limp.

Lal Singh hadn't come back when Rubberbones returned to the cottage. But there was an apple pie on the table and a dozen slices of a type of sausage Rab didn't recognize. The boy went to find a knife and a plate; while he was doing that, Stanley jumped on the table and ate all the sausage.

"Bad boy!" shouted Rab, but only half-heartedly, because he would have given the dog most of the sausage anyway. Stanley obeyed Lal Singh but nobody else, really. He was more a playmate than a loyal hound. Rab offered him some pie crust.

Most of the apple pie later, they ambled down to the harbor. "Let's 'ave a poke around," said Rab. "And no pinching food!" — as if that meant anything.

There was strange, quavering music emerging from the first cottage they came to. Rubberbones tapped on the door, and it opened under his touch. He was met with flickering electric light, brightening in waves with the music.

"Mornin'! Anybody in?" called Rab.

"Come in, come in!" replied a voice from a strange apparatus at the far end of the room. "I can't stop now. I'm building up the batteries."

Rab stepped forward, and the lights went out. Then all was bright suddenly, and the boy found himself eye to eye-socket with a skeleton. "Cripes! Ruddy 'eck!" He recoiled as the voice laughed. The skeleton grinned at the joke, clacking its jaw.

"No, that's not me. That's Arnold. He's been with me since I was at university. I'm over here!"

The cottage was full of strange equipment, most of it like a huge weaver's frame, but there were boilers and pipes, too, and a thing akin to a concertina on wheels. The windows were covered in black drapes.

Shaking reflexively but pretending not to be afraid, Rab advanced. The music welled up louder and faster.

"Welcome, guests! My name is Smoot. Aloysius Smoot, Ph.D., M.A., et cetera, et cetera. Would you like to help me for a moment?"

Rubberbones had learned to be wary of opportunities to help people he didn't know. "Erm. What d'you want?" He craned forward to see a small man inside a framework of wheels, sitting at a narrow desk that was holding constant position among whirling treadles. The man was writing at the desk, but his penmanship was shaky owing to the fact that his legs were pumping away at pedals much larger than his feet. A reading lamp lowered over his paper flickered disruptively as he wrote. The light reflected on his half- spectacles and bald forehead.

"I've almost finished this letter. Would you mind pedaling the device for a few minutes while I toddle to the post office?"

It didn't seem like a lot to ask. Rubberbones was accustomed to riding a bicycle, and this didn't seem a lot different.

"What am I doing exactly?" he asked.

"The energy created by the treadmill serves to fill galvanic batteries, which then operate the lights, the electro-victrola — playing Beethoven today, so dignified — and the analytical engines, which will monitor the moon rocket."

"Moon rocket?"

"Potential moon rocket. Moon rocket I haven't actually built yet."

Rab was interested in a potential or maybe imaginary moon rocket. So he began pedaling, and Stanley helped, too. Dr. Smoot scuttled out of the cottage.

Of course, he didn't come back.

———

"Coconuts," said Mr. Stilton. "You bang the two halves together. It makes a noise like horses' hooves."

"Is useful when talkish to dead 'uns?" asked Purnah, puzzled.

"Perhaps not. Unless the dear departed gallop from the other side to contact us."

Aunt Lucy had provided a selection of bells, sticks and odd kitchen utensils to see if any of them had otherworldly potential for the séance that night. Purnah waved a spoon around and knocked on a table top with it. It sounded like a spoon rapping on a table.

"Wail a little, Purnah dear," requested Aunt Lucy.

That was something Purnah was good at. She let out a howl that any banshee would be proud of.

Aunt Lucy shushed her. "Not so loud! Sorry about that, Mr. Stilton. I should have realized the princess would make so much —"

"Worry not, dear lady. My aunt is out, and the servants are all in on it."

"They are?"

"Of course. We couldn't manage without them. Strand and the staff are as sick of Aunt Agatha bringing in every trickster in the country as I am. I told 'em you'd end all this silliness for good. They'll help however they can."

Princess Purnah had enjoyed her howl. Now she was practicing her impersonation of the late Fred, fourteenth Earl of Stilton. She pitched her voice low, like an elderly man, or an unhappy cow.

"Hall-ooooh! I is dead Fred, and I is happy, so happy, to stick my head out of the other side for minutes to wish good cheers to my missus. Hall-oooh, missus! I is fine too-day! Quiet life after death. Much chocolates. Not being no bee- ootiful maidens servings me wine and ice cream here — oh torkkipish! Hofful!"

"No talking Chiligriti, dear," coached Aunt Lucy.

Mr. Stilton sighed. "We were better off when we wanted it to be a disaster."

Purnah scowled again.

CHAPTER 10

Meeting the Madmen

It was not a jolly party in the lifeboat. After a few shanties and tots of rum — Mr. Blackbeard had loaded vital supplies of rum, biscuit, rum, water and rum before the boat was launched — the mood had turned ugly. Even the captain, who never said anything, looked surly. The boat simply bobbed along. As far as Emmaline could tell, nobody had bothered to provide it with oars for rowing.

The Second Mate blamed Emmaline. "Ah, 'tis unlucky to have a woman aboard. I always said that, didn't I?"

Nobody remembered him saying that, and Blackbeard pointed out that Emmaline had prevented the ship from colliding with a huge ocean liner only yesterday. And she'd just saved them from a fiery doom. The crew looked annoyed that he should even mention it.

Then the engineer chimed in. He'd fallen asleep, as anyone might, and the next thing he knew that ruddy American had blown the boiler up.

Emmaline knew this was true, but she defended Professor Bellbuckle. "You were drunk! It was your responsibility, and your fault!"

"The engine was poorly maintained," said Professor Bellbuckle, "and I decided to make some small repairs." Emmaline thought he probably shouldn't have mentioned this. The engineer decided that this was fighting talk and stood up. "I'll sort you out!" he shouted, and advanced toward the professor.

Emmaline was so angry she didn't call out that he was about to fall overboard. He stepped forward, swayed and disappeared over the side with a splash. Nobody else noticed this. The parrot was swearing loudly, and Blackbeard was arguing with it.

"Who pushed me in?" spluttered the engineer. He seemed to believe that it was somebody else's fault. Emmaline and the professor pulled him out of the sea. The drenched man spat out seawater and forgot about punching anyone.

"Ship ahoy!" squawked the parrot. Fortunately, someone was looking out.

"Can ye come alongside?" shouted a Scottish voice from out of the mist. The Second Mate remembered that the lifeboat did have oars, hidden under all the casks of rum, and between them the crew managed to row toward the fishing boat that steamed forward to the rescue.

The trawler picked up the crew of the no-longer-floating Saucy Emmaline and brought them into harbor.

As the fishermen pulled the castaways aboard, Emmaline apologized to Mr. Blackbeard for all the trouble. She did feel that perhaps if she'd kept a sharper eye on the professor — "Never mind, dearie. It's just another vessel; we'll steal a new one in a week or two."

Emmaline realized that Blackbeard and his crew were actually pirates.

"We'd had the Saucy Emmaline for ages, really. Pinched 'er in Denmark in June. The cap'n was with 'er then, and we just kept 'im with us. Don't speak a word of English, even when he's sober, which is never. Very convenient all round. I 'spect we'll make 'im captain of our next ship, too."

Rubberbones was an agreeable boy, but he wasn't a fool. After fifteen minutes he stopped pedaling Dr. Smoot's treadle device and went to find him. Experience with Professor Bellbuckle had taught Rab that if a mad scientist told you he'd be gone for a few minutes, that might mean anything.

As soon as he stopped pedaling, the music slowed to a whine and the lights dimmed.

"Not much flippin' use," he told Stanley. "Only works when some poor beggar's doing the 'ard work." In this case, the poor beggar had been him. So, annoyed, Rubberbones walked out of the cottage briskly, before he was plunged into darkness again.

Rab came across a larger building nearby that had a sign over the door.

The Royal Society of Experimental Science and Invention, Established 1855.

He went in. It was a reception room — a bit like the hotel he'd visited in London — with a long desk, a thick book and a bell. Rab rang the bell.

A fat man in evening clothes scurried in. He looked sweaty, although it was quite cold outside. "Yes! Yes! Who is it? What's the emergency?"

He glared at Rab, and at Stanley. Rab knew he was about to say "No dogs!" or "No small boys!" Instead, he said, "Bless my soul! What's he got in his mouth?"

Stanley had a bone in his mouth. It was the hand and upper arm from Dr. Smoot's skeleton.

"Erm …" said Rab.

"It's Arnold! Oh, this is a lark! Your dog's got Smoot's skelly!" He was laughing now.

"Sorry," said Rab. "I'll put it back. I can glue it. Or use string. I'm good wi' string."

Two more men, one with a monkey on his shoulder, had appeared from a rear doorway. They were grinning as well.

"This is priceless," said one.

"Priceless!" Rab was mortified. He'd thought it was just an ordinary skeleton, as you might find anywhere.

"No, not like that. I mean, it's funny. Every one of us has walked into Arnold in the dark at one time or another. Old Smoot thinks it's a terrific joke. None of us has ever thought of pinching a few bones to get our own back. I'm Sneed, by the way. Oxford. Gargoyle College."

"Grockle, University of Edinburgh," said the man with the monkey. "This is George."

"And I," said the man with the evening clothes, "am the secretary of the Royal Society of Mad Scientists, although we have a more formal name on the door. You can call me Mr. Secretary. Who are you?"

Rab gave his name, and Stanley's as well, and explained that he was looking for Dr. Smoot. The secretary waved off that information, and asked, "What Mad?"

"Sir?"

"What mad scientist are you affiliated with? I know you aren't Smoot's assistant, and you wouldn't be on this blessed cold lump of rock if you weren't associated with one of our members. It isn't somewhere anyone comes for the bracing air and seaside views."

Rubberbones understood. "That must be Professor Bellbuckle."

The three men stared at one another, and at Rab, and burst into laughter. "Bellbuckle! He's the maddest of the lot!"

Then, debating the relative madness of inventors they knew, the scientists took Rab into the inner halls of Mad Science, where lunatic schemes were hatched, and ordered cocoa all round. A servant who had an oddly sheeplike expression took the instructions and retreated to the kitchen. The room was a cozy parlor, Rab noticed, although it had pictures of inventors rather than distant cousins, and strange bits of machinery rather than potted plants. Also, there were scorch marks on one wall. The servant brought the hot drinks with a little comment that sounded like "Baaa." It was good cocoa, and Rab decided to stay there until Lal Singh arrived. The scientists evidently thought he was a servant boy himself, and he didn't tell them he was a pioneer aeronaut. It was best to keep that quiet for now. He didn't mention Emmaline, either. The three men sat in armchairs, smoking pipes, and chatted about their colleagues. They thought Dr. Smoot was out of his mind. They talked of Professor Bellbuckle, although — looking at Rab — they hummed and hawed over the details of what they knew. Rab thought they might be leaving out stories that were too scandalous, criminal or demented for the professor's twelve-year-old helper to overhear. Grown-ups did that, he'd noticed.

They joshed each other about a chemist called Griffin who had worked on a formula for invisibility. "Haven't seen him in ages," declared the secretary, and they all laughed. Then Dr. Sneed spoke, in grumbling terms, of a Dr. Moreau who had lived on the island some years previously. He'd been a brilliant but difficult colleague.

Rubberbones remembered the name from somewhere, but before the discussion went any further, Dr. Smoot burst in.

"My lights! Out! My batteries! All depleted! I left a boy in charge, only gone a few minutes —"

Dr. Sneed reached out with the bony hand of the skeletal Arnold and tapped the newcomer on the shoulder.

"Need a hand, old man?"

"He seems 'armless enough," added Grockle.

Rab tried to hide in the armchair, which was hard to do, but Dr. Smoot clearly didn't recognize him as the same boy he'd left in charge. He went out, muttering bitterly, the bones tucked under his arm, brushing against Lal Singh coming in the other way.

"I would appreciate help with provisions and sundry supplies," said Lal Singh. "Good day, gentlemen."

———◦◦◦◦———

It was the first time Princess Purnah had visited the library. She saw bookshelves and a table that had been brought in with chairs for this evening's séance. There were refreshments and a plate of cream cakes. Mr. Stilton had told her that if everything went well tonight, Purnah could eat as many cakes as she liked.

"It was my late husband's favorite room," said Lady Agatha. "So it seems the appropriate venue to contact him. All his mementos are in here."

Purnah had no idea who or what "mementos" might be, but she saw much that excited her. On one wall was a map showing the lands beyond the Himalayas and the Pamirs, known as "The Roof of the World." The princess's education had been lacking in many areas, but she could read a map of her homeland. There was Rootitooty, full of jackals, and Yargarwar, home of dolts. Unclean Hoolgar sat in its valley, close to the bandits of Deepo, all stabbed with colored pins like arrows. And there, like a beacon of goodness among the thieves and savages sat Chiligrit, celebrated with a red topped pin.

Next to the map was a display of weapons — pistols, swords and a shield with a scarred face. Purnah's eye was drawn to a dagger. She knew that design. It was Chiligriti handiwork. The stylized carving of the leaping sheep on the pommel was the mark of Sharposwishi the Toothless and his kin. Sharposwishi was the finest blade-maker in the kingdom. He'd stabbed all the others to demonstrate his excellent work. Uncle Fred had been to Chiligrit. "Eeeky-ooo!" she said, but only to herself. She remembered that she was supposed to be mute.

Purnah didn't have time to think any more about the late Lord Silton's travels because just then the rest of the party came in.

Aunt Lucy was dressed in outlandish "spiritualist" clothes that one of the housemaids had stitched for her. In purple robes and with tangled hair, she looked like a for- tune-teller from a penny-a-seat theatrical production. She wore bangles and bracelets and a huge red jewel around her neck. Purnah knew that all this had been bought at a bric- a-brac shop in Podgemout Parva. She wasn't sure what "bric-a-brac" meant, but she thought it might mean "rub- bish" in some foreign language.

Lady Stilton entered, as shortsighted as ever. Mr. Stilton with his monocle and well-cut black suit. Two old ladies, friends of Lady Stilton. The cunning Inspector Pike and the friend he'd brought — the man called Botts, who beamed vacantly all around him through his spectacles.

Gloppit! Peep! thought Princess Purnah. She hoped he didn't recognize her or Aunt Lucy. Yet, why was he here if not to identify them? Purnah noticed that Aunt Lucy's face had gone pale. Perhaps she should grab Sharposwishi's dag- ger and — no. She was thirteen now, too old for stabbing her foes in the carefree manner of a Chiligriti childhood.

Purnah composed herself and tried to appear even more deaf and silent than she had before.

⚔ CHAPTER 11 ⚔

Dead Fred Is Speakish

"Port Haddock!" Professor Bellbuckle was excited. "They've brought us to Port Haddock!"

Emmaline wasn't sure why this news was so astounding. The trawler surely had a home port, and of the many gray stone ports along the coasts of the Irish Sea, one seemed much like another.

"I have an old friend in Port Haddock!"

This was good news, since Emmaline was acutely aware that she had no money or dry clothes. It was lucky that she and the professor were already traveling light and completely penniless; it meant that fewer of her belongings had gone down with the ship.

The crew of the late lamented Saucy Emmaline were in the best of spirits. They'd lost everything but didn't seem to care. "We've got to find a tavern! Arr!" announced Mr. Blackbeard.

"Arr!" agreed the survivors.

Professor Bellbuckle stood on the stone pier, allowing the sound of the parrot to fade into the distance. Emmaline thought this was a good idea. She'd had enough drunken yo-ho-ho. "Where does your friend live?"

The professor didn't know. "I just remember a letter from Port Haddock."

"We should ask at the post office. Or the police station." Emmaline wondered whether it was safe to go to the police station. She had been party to an assault, theft of a motor vehicle and possibly piracy so far this week. And it was only Tuesday.

———

Foglamp thought about what he'd overheard. A rubbery boy traveling with a tall man in a turban. That wasn't something you came across every day. Why were they traveling, and where to? It was too late in the year for most visitors who came for fishing and shooting and to see the fine scenery. The only outsiders Foglamp could think of were the lunatic inventors who wasted their time experimenting on Urgghh, across the water from his desk.

Foglamp hadn't mentioned any of this to his employer yet. Once the secretary could gather more information about this boy, he'd bring the dossier to his master. Titch and Hercules were all well and good in their brutish way, but Foglamp wasn't about to entrust a delicate mission to them. No, he'd have to contact his friend on the island. The Collector had a spy living on Urgghh, long ago having bribed one of the mad scientists to watch out for promising specimens. Now Foglamp could discover whether the boy was the Robert Burns his employer was seeking. It seemed to be an unlikely coincidence. But after all, the Collector had bought Invermisery House precisely because it was so close to the Island of Mad Scientists.

He carefully wrote out a note in a complicated code involving substituted letters: "A" was "R," "B" became "S," and so on. Then, in the second sentence, "A" became "S" and "B" was translated as "T." In the third sentence, the letters changed again in a logical progression. Foglamp enjoyed these sorts of complicated games with words. It took a while to complete a message, even with the ciphers written out on a grid for translation. Then again, it wasn't as if he were planning on writing out his shopping lists in code. Anyway, Foglamp paid the fellow enough to spend a few minutes decoding messages.

Foglamp went to a window where there was an electric light that would summon a messenger to carry the dispatch. The secretary had rigged the lamp to flash a little pattern in Morse code, which he considered more appropriate than just leaving a light in a window. It appealed to his sense of mystery. Subterfuge. Espionage. After all, if he didn't care about secrecy, he could send a postcard.

Aunt Lucy, speaking in her most mystical voice — quite unlike the one Mr. Botts might recognize, Purnah thought — demanded that the lights be turned out as soon as every- one was seated.

"It's the ectoplasm. Can't be holding up the ectoplasm."

Purnah understood that "ectoplasm" was a nonsense word that believers in spiritualism used.

Everyone held the hand of the person next to her — or him. Purnah sat in between Aunt Lucy and Mr. Stilton, so when she slipped under the table, nobody was any the wiser. "It's getting colder in here," announced Aunt Lucy. "A spirit draws nigh."

"Brr!" said Mr. Stilton helpfully. "I wish I'd worn my fur stole." The two old ladies shivered in response.

Princess Purnah hadn't noticed it getting any colder, but she did note that somebody's feet smelled like cheese.

She was supposed to knock on the table. Once for "no," twice for "yes." Or was it the other way round?

"Is anyone among us? Is there a visitor from the Other Side?" asked Aunt Lucy.

Purnah knocked once on the underside of the table, experimentally.

"That means no," said Lady Stilton.

"It can't mean no," argued one of the ladies. "It can't tell you it's not there."

"Might be a mischief of some sort," observed Inspector Pike. "An occult joke."

"Two knocks for yes," said Aunt Lucy, very loudly and distinctly. "Is anyone there?"

Purnah knocked twice.

"A spirit! A messenger! Have you a message for someone here?"

Two knocks.

"Is it for … Mr. Stilton?" One knock.

"Is it for my ward, Marie-Thérèse?"

This was clever on Aunt Lucy's part, for she was pretending that Princess Purnah's other self was still seated at the table. Purnah smiled to herself, and delivered a particularly loud rap to the woodwork.

"For Lady Stilton?" Purnah knocked twice.

"And the messenger, the envoy from the ethereal realms — would that be her late husband?" Two knocks.

"I knew he'd come!" Lady Stilton was agog with excitement. "Frederick!"

"Agatha!" came the reply. It was a deep, moaning voice, and appeared to come from under the table. As, of course, it did. "Agatha! My love! My turtle dove! My owwwwn!"

"It's him!" cried Lady Stilton.

"Nonsense!" declared Inspector Pike. "It's a trick of some sort."

"You think I don't know my own husband?"

"I am not disputin' whether you recognize your husband's

voice. I, er —" spluttered the detective.

"I am certainly glad of that!"

Purnah heard one of the old ladies whisper to the other "Impudent young whippersnapper!" Normally that was what people said about her.

Aunt Lucy cleared her throat loudly. She was the spiritualist, after all. "We must not break the thread between our world and the next."

Purnah decided to wail a bit more.

"Ayeeeeeeeeee!!! Is here in paradises, very nices, three meals a day, plus cake. Wish you was here!"

"Oh, Frederick!" "Stuff and nonsense!"

"Don't you insult my aunt, Inspector," interjected Mr. Stilton.

"Mr. Pike, settle down!" This was Botts, the battered bureaucrat.

"Is all floaty about on cloudings. They got bee-ootiful maidens here" — then she remembered that Lady Stilton would not want to hear about her late husband associating with attractive young maidens — "but I tells 'em to pish off and leaves me with my newspaper!"

Purnah was enjoying herself, until one of the old ladies decided to take her shoes off. This meant pulling at boots and reaching and wriggling; Purnah took a kick between the shoulders.

"Oww! Glekk! Porok! Watch you selfs!" she shouted. "Oh!" Lady Stilton nearly swooned. "It's definitely Frederick. He called me that — Glekk Porok — sometimes. He said it was a term of endearment in one of those foreign places he visited!"

"Trikk!" Princess Purnah couldn't stop herself. She knew what it really meant.

"It's all a trick, yes!" said Inspector Pike, slamming his fist on the table. Purnah hammered back on her side of the tabletop.

"Ah, I don't know what that means," said Aunt Lucy, confused by the raps. "Are you still with us, Lord Stilton?" Purnah was about to bang the woodwork twice when a foot kicked her. It was a smelly foot, all sweaty socks and no shoe. "Ecch!" She tried to get away from it and banged into another pair of legs. The legs shuffled and dropped something.

A glop of cream dropped onto her face. Someone was eating her cakes! "Is all minings!" she muttered resentfully. "There's someone under the table!" shouted one of the old ladies.

"No there's not!" snapped Mr. Stilton. "My Frederick!" wailed his aunt.

"There is something there!" said Mr. Botts, dropping the rest of the cake he'd helped himself to. I think it's — ouch!"

Purnah had bitten his leg.

"A disturbance in the ectoplasm! A spiritual, erm, emanation through the void," announced Aunt Lucy, with desperation in her voice.

"Let's 'ave a look," said Inspector Pike. "Turn the light on, and we'll see."

He seized the edge of the table and upended it.

The lights did not come on. Instead, the voice of Mr. Botts rang out. "Help me! I'm being attacked."

"No you aren't, you fool!" said Mr. Stilton. "You've run into me. I'll find the lights."

The lights remained off.

"I'll have them in a minute," said Mr. Stilton. "Get off my lap!" This from one of the old ladies.

"It's Frederick! I feel his presence on my knee. He's lighter now, being wholly spiritual in form," explained Lady Stilton.

"Errko Eep!" cried Purnah.

Then the lights bathed the room in bright electric whiteness. The table was tipped over. Aunt Lucy sat in repose,

her hands clasped as if nothing was wrong. Mr. Stilton stood by the light switch. Mr. Botts was clutching his leg, cream cake smeared over his suit. Inspector Pike pointed pointlessly at the carpet, which was curiously lacking in criminological interest. The old ladies appeared shocked, one of them in buttoned boots, the other without. Lady Stilton had a rapt expression on her face, murmuring, "My Frederick!"

Princess Purnah was sitting in her original chair, with a plate of cream cakes.

"What's all this, then?" demanded Inspector Pike.

"It's a séance, Inspector. Except that you've messed it up completely," said Aunt Lucy. "The departed has, in fact, departed."

"They don't like a lot of trouble," said one of the old ladies. "I expect that was what he was trying to tell us when he ran over my lower personage."

"Not right," mumbled the other. "Scaring the dead like that."

And it seemed as if the whole thing had gone amazingly well. But then Inspector Pike looked right at Princess Purnah. "You 'ad something to do with this, young miss." "Oh no," she replied. "I is completish deaf and does not

spikk never no words. Nothing to do with mees at all."

Purnah realized this was a mistake even as she uttered the words.

She hurled a cream cake at the inspector, and as it splattered across his shining forehead Mr. Stilton turned the lights out again.

The door flashed open and three figures ran through it. "Glekk! Porok!" yelled the smallest of them.

"My Frederick," said Lady Stilton, softly. "He always called me that."

⇴ CHAPTER 12 ⇴

A Scottish Automaton

The constable at the police station gave Emmaline and the professor the directions they needed.

"Och, yes. The inventor. The furrin gent." He narrowed his eyes at Professor Bellbuckle. "A friend of yours?"

Emmaline had expected this. The "furrin gent"— a Mr. Vasilieff — was clearly seen as a suspicious character. Which meant that she and the professor would also be seen as suspicious characters. She wanted to simply be an ordinary girl once again. An ordinary girl who invented flying machines.

"We hardly know him at all," declared Emmaline before Professor Bellbuckle could open his mouth.

The address was one of a row of identical houses. Maybe Mr. Vasilieff wasn't an inventor who needed the privacy of an isolated place to blow things up without frightening anyone. Perhaps, thought Emmaline, he preferred to blow things up in close proximity to his friends and neighbors. She cut her eyes toward her own friendly mad scientist.

The door was opened by a slender figure in a tweed jacket and kilt. "Hello, Angus," said Professor Bellbuckle. "Is Vassy at home?"

"Greetings, Professor," replied the figure. "Please enter. Your companion, also."

Despite the kilt and matching plaid stockings, Emmaline knew that Angus wasn't a Scotsman. He wasn't even human. His face was polished brass, and his neck was a long steel spring. She followed him into the house.

———◦◦◦———

It was fully dark by the time Rab and Lal Singh had stacked the baggage in the shed and put the groceries in the pantry and their own belongings in a cupboard.

Lal Singh produced spices and herbs (strange things that Rab had never heard of) from the just-bought provisions. Aunt Lucy always made strange dishes such as stewed nettles and fungus, but since she was absent the Sikh was able to make the dishes he actually enjoyed. Lal Singh chopped pieces of chicken, onions and peppers with amazing speed, stirred them rapidly over a flickering gas jet and shook aromatic powders over the sizzling mixture.

"This is champion, this is!" announced Rab. "It's like food, only better."

Lal Singh smiled. "I prefer chicken curry to anything involving slugs."

After they'd eaten, Lal Singh brought out two letters. The first was from their friend in London, Mr. Holmes.

221B Baker St.
London WC
November 17th, 1894

My dear Lal Singh and Rab:
I received the letter that you sent from Glasgow, in which you apprised me of the difficulties of the situation — both yours and your companions. I was, of course, aware of the incident at Lower Owlthwaite — top marks go to the professor for stealing the motor car — and of the India Office's pig-headed insistence that Princess Purnah be returned to that insufferable school. I have made discreet inquiries of my own. These are my findings:
The India Office people believe that Princess Purnah has been kidnapped. One must suppose that, having done nothing to prevent the actual attempt to kidnap her a month ago, they are now convinced that they must forcibly retrieve her from her friends.

The ports are being observed carefully, and the police are vigilant. Fortunately, no photographs exist of Princess Purnah — that ghastly school never took class photographs, it seems — and if any exist of Mrs. Butterworth, I suggest that you ensure they remain hidden.

The case is being handled by an Inspector Pike of Scotland Yard. I understand that he is a determined officer, as tenacious as a bulldog in tracking the subjects of his investigation, and not unintelligent by the standards of the Metropolitan Police. He was disappointed in his last major case, the pursuit of a gentleman jewel thief known as Emerald Ernie, and his failure to apprehend that individual may add to his determination not to fail again.

I have taken the liberty of describing Princess Purnah to the authorities as being some six inches taller than I believe she actually is, with straight brown hair and green eyes. I have also arranged for certain of my associates to report seeing her and an elderly woman (I hope that Mrs. Butterworth does not mind some necessary exaggeration as to her age) in places as different as Paris, New York and a tea stall outside Westminster Abbey. I trust you will not hold this small deceit against me.

I would suggest that you continue to use my address for any communication in this matter; should I hear from Mrs. Butterworth or Miss Cayley (from whom I have received nothing) I shall pass it on.

I trust that, with care and patience, these matters will be resolved.

Yours,
Sherlock Holmes, Esq.

Rab read it carefully, for Mr. Holmes used words that were complicated to understand. Still, he got the meaning of it. He'd been so excited to arrive at Urgghh that he hadn't really considered whether his friends were in danger. What could he do about it? He realized that the answer was "nothing at all."

———————

Princess Purnah ran down the hallway with Aunt Lucy a step behind. Mr. Lancelot Stilton, shouting "Come back, you charlatans!" helped them through a doorway, where the stately figure of Strand awaited. "This way, ladies," said the butler. "We'll have you on your way as quickly as possible." He had their baggage in hand, together with railway tickets and a packed supper. Mr. Stilton shouted to Inspector Pike, "The blighters have given me the slip — I'll show you to the
   telephone!"
   Purnah giggled, because she knew that Podgemout Castle had no telephone and that Mr. Stilton would simply lead the inspector all round the corridors.
   Strand led them down the servants' staircase. Two carriages waited. "Stay here, please."
   Purnah didn't. She crept up behind Strand as he told the driver of the first carriage to leave and return in an hour. "The two ladies suggested you might like to visit one of the many fine taverns in the locality." The butler handed coins to the man. "Enjoy a four-course supper."
   The driver gargled his thanks and drove off. Strand moved to the second carriage, which had a passenger inside. Purnah moved around to see. The man in the coach wore a police uniform.
   "Ah, Constable! Inspector Pike wishes you to join him immediately. Please go in through that door over there." Strand pointed at a distant entrance. The policeman obeyed instantly, as if the smooth servant were the inspector himself.

As soon as the constable left, Strand addressed the driver. "Billiam! Inspector says you aren't needed again tonight.

Please take these two ladies to the station!"

"Oooarrh," agreed Billiam. Purnah noticed he wasn't a policeman. He was probably the village cabbie, running to and fro from the railway station.

"And hurry up. The next train for London goes in fifteen minutes."

"Ooarrh!" As Aunt Lucy and Purnah slipped inside the carriage, Strand gave Billiam a handful of coins. "Oh, ooarrh!"

"Thank you for your efforts, dear ladies," whispered Strand as he shut the door. "Alas, the mistress believes what she chooses to believe. Good luck!"

Billiam shouted something to the horse, and the carriage jolted forward.

Samuel Soap didn't simply walk into the police station at Podgemout Parva disguised as Inspector Trout of Scotland Yard. There was far too great a risk that he'd run into Inspector Pike, and Soap was not going to risk recognition. Instead, Soap went to the Pig and Whistle, a pub opposite the police station. He was dressed in a giant cowboy hat and a buckskin jacket he'd stolen from the props room at a theater. In this costume he was "Lucky Luke Lariat, the Texas Cattle King." Soap reasoned that people would be excited to meet someone called Lucky Luke Lariat and would readily answer anything he asked. Also, he liked to say things like "Whoopie-tie-eye-oh" and "Git along little dogies." It was likely that a policeman coming off duty might very well want a pint of beer and a chat with his mates before toddling homeward. And, as Samuel Soap knew well, an off-duty copper is much freer with informa- tion than when he's working the beat. He would certainlytell all to impress a real cattle baron of the wild west.

But he hadn't considered exactly what would happen if everyone else in the pub wanted to make friends with Lucky Luke, as they obviously would. Just as he was surrounded by a fascinated group of dairy farmers (all asking searching questions about the Texas ranching industry that Soap hadn't thought to find out the answers to) a policeman rushed in, laughing uproariously, and announced that Inspector Pike had just suffered a blow to his reputation.

"So, Pikey's down at Podgemout Castle at one of them séances and about to nab the girl and the old lady 'e's come for. Then the lights go out, they do a runner and Pike's lost in this country 'ouse, crashing about in the dark. The girl and the old lady scarper for the station and take the first train out before anyone knows what 'appened. Pikey's livid, I tell you. He's been on the telephone to all the police stations between 'ere and Grandchester, but it won't be 'im that gets the credit if them two gets captured."

Soap announced, in a desperately fake Texas drawl, that he had to "hit the trail, pardners" and raced back to the railway station. Too late! He'd missed his quarry while he was telling lies about driving herds of longhorn steers to Dodge City. "Doggone it!" he cursed.

"The master is out," said the ... what? The metal man? The mechanical servant? The automaton?

"Angus! Long time, no see!" Professor Bellbuckle was excited. "This is Miss Cayley. She's an inventress. Emmaline, Angus is not actually human."

Emmaline tried not to roll her eyes. "Really!"

"No, Vasilieff and I put him together some years ago. I taught him to count."

The automaton fixed his round, glassy eyes on the professor.

"Yes, we played cards. Double or nothing." He spoke with a rasping, flat voice. Sometimes he wheezed and steam came out of vents at the top of his head. Emmaline thought Angus sounded like a talking shirt-presser.

"Yes, so you could learn mathematical probabilities," said Bellbuckle.

"Double or nothing. Over and over. I won." "Streak o' luck, Angus."

"Perhaps, Professor, but you still owe me sixty-four million dollars, legal American currency, no Confederate dollars, no IOUs, no credit."

The professor slumped a little. "Gosh-darn it, Angus, I was hoping you'd have forgotten that by now."

The Collector rubbed his hands in dissatisfaction. There had been no news from Soap since the man had sent a brief and cryptic telegram about following a lead halfway across the country in pursuit of "the object in question." The private detective could at least have given some idea as to where he was going.

There was no news about the two real "objects in question" that the Collector wished to possess so avidly. The Cayley girl and the Burns lad. They could be at the ends of the universe by now. It was very frustrating.

If young scientists of no real reputation could avoid his grasp, how on earth would he ever manage to kidnap the likes of Thomas Edison? Or the Benz chappie from Germany? Oh, he'd love to catch them in his web!

Sometimes he almost wished he'd stuck with collecting stamps.

⚓ CHAPTER 13 ⚓

The Last of the Cream Cakes

Rab opened the second letter carefully. It was from his mother. Mrs. Burns had beautiful handwriting, all curls and scrolls.

> *Dear Robert,*
> *It was grand to see you on your recent adventure in London — imagine, our lad mixed up with foreign agents and Mr. Holmes! How proud your dad would have been to see you!*

She went on about what a fine young man he'd become. She talked about his brother, Danny, and the three girls. Danny was nine, and the next child down from Rab; Tess was eight, Susan was six and Annie, the youngest, was three. Their father had been gone for more than a year, to seek his fortune. Mr. Burns hadn't written in all that time. Danny thought he might be in the goldfields of South Africa, or on a pearl-diving trip to the Pacific. Tess and Susan cried a lot. Rab was afraid that his father had simply abandoned the family. But his mother would never say that, and Rab wouldn't, either. He'd become what people called "the man of the family" before his twelfth birthday.

That meant staying in Lower Owlthwaite with his gran, working and sending money to help his mother. Mrs. Burns had taken the family to London where she had relatives. Rubberbones had believed that the address in Bethnal Green where he sent his letters must be a pleasant cottage in a clean-swept street. "Old Nichol Street" — it sounded cheerful. Instead, he'd found it a dirty slum. His mother kept the cramped rooms spotless, but the yards and alleys were places of filth and squalor. Rab had managed to make some money during his adventure in London, and there had been a reward for his efforts in foiling a villain.

> *I thank you for the money that you gave to Danny, and also for the sum Mr. Holmes delivered. He explained the services you had done, and how brave you had been. I shall put most of the money by for a rainy day, but I will spend a little on a proper Christmas for the family. Perhaps we'll roast a plump goose from Smithfield Market.*
>
> *I'll say good-bye now.*
>
> *All my love to you, and kisses from your sisters,*
>
> *Mother*

Rab sat back on the bed, thinking of his mother and Danny and the three little girls. One day he'd get them out of Old Nichol Street. One day there'd be roast goose for all of them.

The train rattled northward through the darkness. Aunt Lucy — dressed in widow's black — was snoring with her mouth open. Princess Purnah looked out of the window and saw nothing but her own reflection. Or rather, the reflection of a lady's maid, with a neat white cap and apron over a sober dark dress.

The costumes were the work of Strand and his efficient staff at Podgemout Castle. Inside the traveling bags he'd provided were a set of clothes, a railway timetable, a wallet of crisp banknotes and some unpleasantly vegetarian food for Aunt Lucy, and what Purnah suspected might be the last cream cakes she'd see in a while.

Purnah decided that it was folly to let the cakes rest in their bag any longer than necessary. As she crammed the first one into her mouth, she thought about the events earlier that evening. They'd caught the London train. Aunt Lucy announced that they'd be changing trains at Chipping Piebury, to connect with an express for Scotland. The train they were on stopped at a lot of places. Aunt Lucy would have preferred it otherwise, but people running away from the law have to catch whatever train is available.

What had impressed Purnah was the smooth way they'd been spirited out of the castle and onto the train. The princess had always been the kind of girl who relied on loud curses and threats of violence to get her through life's little difficulties. All her relations in Chiligrit did that, using sharp swords and small bits of artillery to handle the stum- bling blocks of day-to-day living.

She thought about it. There were wicked and cunning persons — uncles and cousins mostly, and some aunts — who employed poison and assassins with daggers, but Purnah had never before come across anyone who used clever tricks for a good purpose. Yet tonight she had seen it! Turok! Mr. Stilton had pretended to be chasing them when he showed them the way out. And Strand, sending off the police-ling on a false instruction, and sending the other driver to drink himself asleep! Excellent! And with a bag of disguises already made up, too. As if they had seen into the future, as Aunt Lucy — Purnah had already forgotten her assumed name — was so lamentably unable to do. Spigg!

Purnah resolved to use her brains "more cunningish" in the future. All the same, she ran her fingers over the sharp Chiligriti blade, made by the gifted Sharposwishi the Toothless, that she had stolen from the library wall.

Mr. Vasilieff was dressed in kilt and tam-o'-shanter cap, like a Scotsman in a pantomime. "Och, Bellbuckle, laddie!" he said. Emmaline thought he spoke like a Russian pretending to be Scottish. Which was clearly the case.

"McVasilieff, now, Bellbuckle. Blendink in with the locals. Not drawink attention to mysel'. Livink a quiet life as a highland gentleman. Naebody kens I am a Rooshian. Och the noo."

Emmaline felt this was probably not true. Mr. McVasilieff seemed to have been dressed by a cut-rate theatrical costumier in clashing plaids of garish colors. The kilt was a violent purple with checks in green and orange that seemed to hate one another.

Even the professor seemed surprised. "Er, good to see you, Vassy. I hope you don't mind us calling unannounced, only we've been unexpectedly shipwrecked."

McVasilieff waved that away, as if shipwrecked visitors were a daily occurrence. "Hass Angus made you at hame?"

Angus had already clanked in with a tray of tea and shortbread.

"Sure has, Vassy. And he said something about supper, once you came home. Oh, by the way, this is Miss Emmaline Cayley. Like ourselves, she is an experimental scientist. Miss Cayley specializes in the field of aeronautical research on a practical basis. In short, she builds flying machines."

"Most admirable, lassie," said McVasilieff. "Ve need a muckle mair o' girls inventink things as needs inventink."

"We are on our way to Urgghh," explained Professor Bellbuckle.

"The island." "Yessiree."

"It iss not far from here. I vish I could accompany you but, alas, I canna. Many experiments at vital stages of development. Crucial processes."

There was a crashing noise from upstairs. "Like that. I'd better see vot it voss. Possibly a chemical reaction of some sort. Or squirrels. Angus vill be servink dinner, so go ahead and eat."

Angus, true to the strangely artificial Scottishness of the house, announced that the haggis and boiled turnips were ready, if the guests wanted to seat themselves.

"Oh Lord," Emmaline whispered to the professor. "Haggis. I've never eaten it, but I know what goes into it." What goes into a haggis is mostly bits of a sheep's inner parts, of all sorts, boiled in its stomach with an onion and a carrot for variety. She'd heard her father speak of facing it when dining with the officers of a Scottish regiment in India. He'd thought it was a punishment.

"It's a mistake to inquire too closely what goes into a meal," replied the professor wisely.

"How fast can you get me to Chipping Piebury?" asked Samuel Soap, still dressed in full rancher costume. "Can you get there before the train that's just departed?" He didn't even try to sound like a Texan.

"Ooarrh!" Old Billiam replied. "Oi can take the old Coddleton road and turn off where Widow Parsley's cottage used to be, 'afore it fell down, then oi can —"

Soap snapped, "I don't care about the widow's cottage! If I give you this much money," — he brandished a fistful of banknotes — "can you get me to Chipping Piebury before the London train gets there?"

"Ooarrh!" Billiam reached for the wad of money. Soap snatched it back before the village cabbie could get his fingers on the notes. "It's the slow train. Makes three stops before it gets to Chipping Piebury."

Soap shouted, "Go on then, man!" and vaulted into the cab.

⚔ CHAPTER 14 ⚔

In Which Martians Are Discussed

Aunt Lucy awoke with a start. "Good grief, Purnah! Why did you let me fall asleep like that?" she demanded. Her tone was sharp. Purnah looked back at her with surprise.

"Why you shoutingly at me thus so? I is ready for all eventualings! Hrikk!" The princess pulled out her latest weapon, the Chiligriti knife. "Ho for merry slicings!"

"I'm sorry to be short with you," apologized Aunt Lucy. "It's my fault. I intended to stay awake so that we could change trains at Chipping Piebury Junction. It doesn't do to stay too long on one train when the authorities are after you. Especially a slow train that stops at every little station along the way." She looked at her watch. "It's almost nine o'clock. We must have passed through Chipping Piebury five minutes ago. If the police were waiting for us there, they'd surely have nabbed us already."

Purnah thought back. The train had stopped a few minutes ago at one of these trainish stations. It had stopped at other stations before that. She'd looked out of the window, but it was dark. Was that Chipping Piebury? Was it five minutes ago? Purnah was vague about minutes. In her homeland, nobody measured time in tiny snippets. Chiligritis knew when it was time to take the goats up onto the mountain, time to lie in wait for your nearest neighbor with a big musket called a "jezail" or time to throw your cousin into a ravine. Plus dinnertime. That was important.

But thinking about dinnertime wasn't so important that Purnah's ears didn't catch the sound of heavy footsteps coming along the corridor. Her hearing was as keen as the tiny Lesser Himalayan Smikkyl, a sort of gerbil whose ears were larger than its whole head.

And now the corridor served as a way to bring men with heavy footsteps along the train, from one coach to another.

The haggis was every bit as disgusting as Emmaline had expected, mouse-brown and squidgy, but she picked at it anyway. It was no worse than anything Aunt Lucy had offered her. Not much, anyway. Well, quite a bit, really.

McVasilieff's house was horrible. It smelt of cabbage and tobacco and chemicals. Angus had been built — so the professor said — to be a general servant, but his skills were limited; the window ledges had been dusted to the point that the paint had worn away, but the bookshelves had never seen the swish of a cloth. The furniture was a mixture of old chairs, packing crates and soggy mattresses. There were photographs of bespectacled men with fierce beards; Emmaline thought that they must be Russian.

There were pieces of machinery, oily or rusty, on all the chairs. Mechanical rubbish lay on every shelf. She swept the cushion of her chair with the back of her hand, knocking a handful of bolts onto the carpet. But the haggis was served with silver tongs on Chinese porcelain, and Angus knew the details of proper table service. Emmaline was impressed to see that he had pulled on a black-tailed coat to serve dinner. He had a bow tie around his springy neck.

Mr. McVasilieff appeared after a few minutes. "It voss squirrels, hoots mon. They nest in my greatest invention, a boon tae all mankind, but involvink a muckle great brass dome ideal for the hibernations. Ah gie 'em a squirt o' steam and they run for the rafters, curse the wee beasties." "What does your greatest invention do, Mr. Vasil —

McVasilieff?" asked Emmaline.

"Many things!" replied the Russian Scotsman. "It iss big, and hass a whirry thing on top. I devised it for polishink carrots and for playink lullabies, but it performs many valuable services. If I remember to put coal in it every mairnink it might perhaps be able to contact Mars. Angus forgets. The device makes a beepink soond that ah dinna recall tellink it to do. That could be Martians telegraphink back."

"Or mice," suggested Professor Bellbuckle. His friend shot him a dirty look.

Emmaline noticed Angus shuffling squeakily from one mechanical foot to the other. She had the impression the automaton didn't want to hear about Martians and mice. Could a machine be embarrassed? Or scared of small rodents?

"The squirrels would drive away the mice," she announced. "So it's probably the Martians." Angus gave her a look that suggested gratefulness.

The professor wondered whether, if what Emmaline had said was true (and he seemed to think it likely), the Martians might also be deterred by squirrels in the machinery.

"Och, no," replied McVasilieff. "The messages purely consist of interplanetary transmissions. The actual Martians vould be millions of miles away, on their red planet. They vould not be troubled by the squirrels in person."

"I bet Martians are bigger than squirrels, anyway," said Emmaline. She thought that this whole conversation was a dead end. It was a topic for lunatics. Professor Bellbuckle and his friend could choose to debate the relative size and ferocity of Martians in a contest against a nest of squirrels, but she wanted to talk about more important things.

"Mr. McVasilieff, we have no money and we need to meet our friends on the island of Urgghh. I understand that your contributions to the progress of humanity keep you busy, but —"

"Can you lend us ten pounds for a couple of weeks?" The professor finished the request for her. He was accustomed to borrowing money.

"I'll dae better than that, laddie. Ye can add it to the, erm, substantial sum you already owe Angus."

Angus coughed, with a spray of steam.

"Sixty-four million and — ten pounds at a conversion rate of one-to-four — forty dollars, United States currency," said the automaton.

Emmaline was not surprised that the iron being was good at arithmetic. "And no checks, either," Angus added. Careful, too.

"Tell you vot," said McVasilieff. "I'll let Angus go wi' ye tae the island. You can borrow him for a month or two. He'll be of considerable help in your scientific endeavors." The professor spluttered, which might have been thanks.

Or might not have been, thought Emmaline. Angus had a look of steely determination on his brass face.

Emmaline knew what it meant. Angus wasn't going to let a man who owed him sixty-four million and forty dollars get away again.

Which might be a problem, but not tonight's problem. The haggis was tonight's problem, and it wasn't getting any more appetizing as she pushed it around, cold and congealing, with her fork.

Samuel Soap had reached Chipping Piebury just as the train pulled into the station. Shoving banknotes into Billiam's fist (not quite as many as he'd shown the cabbie before they started the breakneck journey), he raced for the platform, one hand holding his giant ten-gallon hat in place.

"Hey, you!" shouted the ticket inspector as Soap vaulted the turnstile and hauled himself into the last carriage just as the whistle blew. The train started to roll forward as he slammed the door behind him.

A few minutes later he was sneaking along the corridor — it was hard to sneak in pointy boots with spurs — peering into each compartment as he went. The old woman and the girl were on this train. In a moment or two, he'd find them. Soap had not advanced far along the train when he heard the distant sound of policemen's boots. He'd recognize it anywhere. While he had stepped onto the train from the rear, a party of police officers must have started at the front end. It was likely the coppers would find them before he did.

It was time to make sure the police did not catch their quarry.

After all, it wasn't as if anyone who knew him expected him to be a good citizen.

The sound was definitely policemen's boots, thought Purnah. They were noisy, unlike her own choice of ballet shoes, which were also "prittee," as she'd tell anyone. The princess prodded her companion and made the gesture that means "Shush!" in all languages except Deepo (where the finger-to-mouth action means "All our goats are loose in the attic"). Aunt Lucy had been riffling through the pages of the big book of railway timetables, looking to discover when the train would reach the next station that might offer a connecting train to somewhere else. Anywhere else. Aunt Lucy hadn't heard the sound of boots yet, but she knew that the clump of policemen's feet must surely be part of her evening if she stayed on this train.

"Oh, dear!" whispered Aunt Lucy. "Better do something!"

"We foolings them with our disguises!" replied Purnah. "I don't think we'll fool anyone. They must know that we caught this train. Can you hide, do you think?"

Purnah looked around the compartment. The new railway carriages had all the doors on the corridor side; you climbed into the carriage through doors at each end, and walked down the little hallways looking into each compartment for an available seat. The compartment had no door to the outside world. Purnah considered the window. She could open it and climb through, but Auntilucy certainly couldn't. She could climb onto the luggage rack and pretend to be a suitcase, but even to her wild imagination this seemed unlikely to persuade the most shortsighted of constables. There was no space under the seats. They were done for. Aiieeee!

"No," declared Aunt Lucy, setting her jaw in an expression of firm resolve. "We aren't captured until they get the handcuffs on us!" She had been reading her cowboy novels again. She liked cowboy novels. "Let's vamoose before the posse hunts us down. You first, Purnah. Let's gallop down the corridor ahead of those ... ah ... gosh-durn varmints!" She looked at Purnah fondly. "Take your coat and scarf, Your Royal Majesty. It's cold outside."

Princess Purnah needed no further instructions. She slid back the compartment door and ran. Behind her, Aunt Lucy waddled as fast as she could. Purnah reached the end of the corridor, and wrestled with the door to the next carriage. A voice rang out from behind her, some distance away. Purnah knew it was a policeman, because he called out, "Hey, you! Stop in the name of the law!"

She ignored him, because she was a princess, and princesses don't obey anyone's laws but their own.

≋ CHAPTER 15 ≋

Purnah Misuses a Tea Trolley

Emmaline had managed to eat perhaps a quarter of the haggis. She was accustomed to dreadful food from living with Aunt Lucy, but this was appalling even by the standards of her aunt's jellied snails and centipede soup. With every mouthful it got worse.

The haggis had been followed by a dessert made from root vegetables mashed up and boiled with milk and sugar. Angus had served it in little glass bowls. "This is very nice," declared Emmaline, which was almost true. It was certainly tolerable, and contained no sheep intestines at all. Angus smiled a mechanical smile. "Radish, turnip and parsnip pudding. I get a big tub, put the vegetables in it and dance on them all."

He lifted a leg to show his flanged iron feet. Then, with a wiggle, all the little metal plates in each foot moved rapidly up and down in a chopping sequence, like steel teeth dancing. "Aye," said Mr. McVasilieff. "One foot iss peelink and the other iss choppink. It's an amazink labor-savink device.

I make him vash his feet first, ye ken."

Emmaline thought she should turn the conversation to practical matters. "How do we actually get to this island from here?" she asked. "Is there a train or a boat?"

Mr. McVasilieff pondered the question, as if it were a surprising problem that he'd not considered. "Actually get there? Hmm —"

Professor Bellbuckle peered though his spectacles as if he expected his colleague to say something brilliant. Emmaline rolled her eyes. These scientific gentlemen were completely lost when it came to ordinary things like getting from Place A to Place B (unless they could stop on the way at Place C to blow something sky high). Even so, she was surprised by the answer.

"It iss not a question of how you vould get there, och nay. It iss a question of avoiding the Collector."

"Who is the Collector?" asked Emmaline. "And why must we avoid him?"

"For the same reason that I never leave this village," replied McVasilieff, in the sort of hushed whisper that suggests a conspiracy at work. "Because he collects scientists — he kid- naps them — and they are never seen again."

"I've never heard such nonsense!" declared Professor Bellbuckle. "I've not heard of him. Why in tarnation would he want to do such a thing?"

"As the English poet Tennyson wrote, ours iss 'not to rea- son why.' I do not know who this Collector iss. I only hear of him from other great scientists like myself, some of whom are fully disappeared like the puff of smoke, och the noo. He only desires to capture the most brilliant of thinkers. Then he sets hiss trap and catches hiss prey. There iss no name for this person, only iss 'the Collector.' Five scientists to my knowledge are vanished within the last two years — four of them close to the island. This iss natural, for Urgghh iss the center of experimentation and attracts many brilliant persons. So I remain here, for undoubtedly a man of my dazzlink intelligence would be a jewel in the collection."

Professor Bellbuckle snorted at this last statement. McVasilieff's eyes narrowed. "Perhaps you should not vorry so much, Ozymandias."

Purnah ran down the corridor. Behind her, Aunt Lucy stumbled along the narrow hallway. The train had not been designed for a person as wide as she was tall to race from one carriage to another. It wasn't going to work.

"Purnah! You run, and I'll hold them off!"

"I not leavings you!" replied the girl. "You good subjects!" Aunt Lucy thought about that for a moment but decided not to debate her status with the Chiligriti princess. "Now look, Purnah. I can't run fast enough to escape. You can. Take this money and find your way to Scotland, to an island called Urgghh. Lal Singh and the professor will be waiting. Can you remember that name?"

Purnah nodded. It was a strange name, but so were all the other names in this country. Who could say "Cricklewood," after all?

"Now go, and I'll fight off the policemen. I wish I had my brolly with me." Aunt Lucy was deadly with an umbrella. Purnah opened the nearest carriage door, where two business travelers snoozed soundly. She reached inside and turned back to her protector. "Here is weapony for smitings, Auntilucy. I go now. Slay thee many policishes with mighty blows of umbrelly!"

"It is rather a nice one," said Aunt Lucy, admiring the umbrella.

Just at that moment a police constable burst into the carriage, and Aunt Lucy broke the stolen umbrella over his helmet. He went down in a heap. "Oh, this is such fun!" she announced. "I'm sure this is illegal!"

Purnah had already hauled the next doorway open and stepped into the corridor beyond. She knew that she must flee and that Auntilucy would fight gallantly in what the newspapers called a "last stand." When Purnah took the throne of Chiligrit, she would award a medal for this courageous act. She deliberately didn't turn around when she heard a deep voice yell out, "Steady on there, madam, I only want to — aaaaagggh!" before a repeated thwacking noise stopped the flow of words.

It was lucky for Purnah that she didn't turn, because a device was approaching her, a boiler on wheels with steam gushing from the top. A large woman followed behind, steering the fiendish contraption. The woman was chanting something.

"Tea! Who wants a nice cuppa tea, then?"

Purnah realized that the machine was not some form of mad invention. She'd spent far too much time with Professor Bellbuckle. It wasn't an experimental weapon. But she could make it into one.

The carriage door opened behind her, and the unmistakable sound of policemen's boots echoed on the floor.

Swiftly the princess ran forward and slid back the doorway to a compartment about halfway down the carriage, beaming broadly as the tea lady approached.

"Do you want tea, lovey?" asked the woman.

"No, not tealings for me," replied Purnah, flashing her most winning smile. "You go past, yes?"

A voice from behind Purnah muttered, "I might want a cup of tea!" An elderly man sat in the corner seat. "Come in 'ere and let the cold in an' saying I don't want tea —"

Purnah half turned and addressed him over her shoulder. "You shuts up! Gettings no tea, and be grateful for your life, wretched subject!" she whispered. She didn't want the tea lady to hear. Of course she did.

"That's very rude of you, Miss Hoity-Toity! Of course the old chap can have his tea." She glared at Purnah, then faced the elderly passenger. "How'd you like your tea, then, dear?" The man mumbled something about sugar. The tea lady stepped close to listen to his wheezy voice, and Purnah seized the opportunity. Dodging behind the woman, the princess grabbed the handles and launched herself and the cart forward along the corridor.

There were two men up ahead — one in uniform, one in plain clothes. The detective, in front, was poking his head inside a compartment, oblivious to what might be coming. The constable, bringing up the rear, saw his fate clearly. His face turned red, and he began to stutter. "Superintendent! She's got a tea trolley!" The senior officer, hearing this bizarre shout of alarm, pulled his head out of the doorway to see the onrushing cart, with cups and saucers dancing madly on their tray. His eyes widened as the trolley crashed into his solid bulk and the gleaming brass urn that kept the tea at a perfect, near-boiling temperature, toppled onto him. He shrieked — the urn was almost as hot outside as inside

— and the spigot poured tea over his shirtfront. The cart fell forward, and all the cups smashed around his feet. Except for one, which Purnah had taken.

She threw it, and the terrified constable ducked back behind the carriage door as the cup knocked his helmet off. Purnah instantly remembered the day that Professor Bellbuckle had tried to teach her to play baseball. "Eeee-strike!" she announced, then turned and raced down the corridor. The tea lady, open-mouthed, stepped aside to let the maniacal lady's maid run past.

Purnah flew down the length of the carriage, laughing wildly. She'd shown them! Now she'd escape those villainous police-ish men by outpacing their flattish tackety-feets. It was an excellentish plan! The train was heading up a hill, slowing down, so Purnah had the advantage of running downhill toward the rear.

She looked around. More policemen were crashing their way down the corridor. Suddenly a man in a ridiculous hat and jingly boots stepped out of a compartment, right into the path of the constables. There was yelling as they all fell down in a heap. Purnah laughed, because they were too far behind her to catch her now. All she had to do was run, fleet-footed as a mountain goat across the ridges of the Himalayas.

Purnah hadn't been on a lot of trains.

She reached the end of the next carriage. There was, as previously, a door at the far end. It was locked. Purnah tugged and pushed and jiggered with the handle. "I commandings you openings, O door!" she shouted in her most imperious royal voice. The door took no notice. She pulled out the dagger and tried to pick the lock. No luck at all. She'd reached the end of the train. The only door Purnah could use was the one designed to open onto the station platform.

She did what any self-respecting Chiligriti princess would do. She flung open the door, and although there was no station platform, hurled herself out into the darkness.

The train was traveling at thirty miles an hour.

———◆———

Samuel Soap was no longer a happy man. True, his "accidental" stepping in front of the onrushing constables had prevented any chance of the coppers catching up with the girl. The police had been pretty decent about it, given that one of them needed to have his head bandaged. Soap had claimed that he'd simply stepped into the corridor to stretch his aching legs. They were concerned in case the visiting Texan cattle king had been injured himself. Indeed, he'd stabbed himself in the leg with one of his spurs. It hurt. Still, he was able to chat with the wounded policeman while other constables explored the train for the princess.

"Who is this durned filly who vamoosed so pronto?" he asked, using words he'd read in a tale about Buffalo Bill.

"It's that foreign princess what's been in the papers," replied the bandaged officer. "Her and some old lady. We've got the granny — she's a demon with an umbrella, that one — but the girl's taken off down the train. They'll catch her, though — there's nowhere to go, is there?"

Samuel Soap agreed that there was nowhere to go. This was a problem, since there was no chance he could somehow wrest her from the custody of half a dozen burly constables. Even so, when the policemen who had checked the whole train announced that there was nothing to be found but a flapping carriage door, Soap knew that his trail had, once again, gone cold.

Emmaline was stretched out on a workbench. Angus had moved all the half-finished experiments that had covered the bench and had even mopped up the patches of oil. He had also found blankets and a pillow.

Just as helpfully, Angus had provided her with a book of railway timetables. It was easy for Emmaline to work out how to get to Urgghh. All they needed to do was take a train from Port Haddock to somewhere called Cape Porridge, then a ferry to Invercrockery, another train across a mountain chain to a place called Nochtermuckity and a short boat ride to the island. Her guess was that it was perhaps twenty miles away, and would take no more than a day and a half to get there. Her friends would be waiting, and they must be worried about her and the professor. Surely they would be the last to arrive after their catalog of misadventures?

⊰ CHAPTER 16 ⊱

A Very Fine Cat Indeed

Rubberbones was up before the sun had risen. Since they were in Scotland in November, this didn't mean it was early at all. Lal Singh had breakfast ready — naan bread and something with spicy potatoes.

"This is good, this is!" announced Rab, mouth full and spitting food.

The butler didn't correct this lapse of manners. "Today, I must collect more necessities from the railway station. You may accompany me or explore this place most further."

Rubberbones enjoyed spending time with Lal Singh, but a trip to the railway station didn't seem all that exciting. Besides, he'd thought about the incident with Dr. Smoot and the skeleton. He had, after all, promised Dr. Smoot that he'd keep pedaling away on the inventor's strange device, and he'd abandoned the task before he was supposed to. And Stanley had behaved badly toward the dead. Rab knew that his gran would expect him to go and say how sorry he was about the whole thing.

He pulled on his boots, buttoned his coat and told Lal Singh he had something to do. The Sikh smiled. "Then do so, and if you are returned in time for dinner, there will be curried mutton in the style of my country. While the Memsahib is absent, I will ensure that no insects or things found in ditches become ingredients in our meals."

Rab replied that this would be "Champion!" He tugged his cap down over his ears and went out into the blustery Scottish morning.

Princess Purnah hadn't enjoyed spending a whole night at the bottom of a railway embankment, but at least none of the policemen had followed her off the train. Purnah thought about her decision to jump. On one hand, she was impressed that she'd managed to leap from a speeding train without suffering any broken limbs; her friend Errand Boy would admire this feat. On the other hand, she had spent many hours in complete darkness, miles from anywhere, dressed in the stupid maid costume that kept her shivering through the November cold.

She gave thanks to Klanggo, the Goddess of Falling Objects. The ancient Chiligriti religion had gods and goddesses for things that most faiths had not seen fit to celebrate, and since Chiligrit consisted mostly of sheer ravines and steep mountains, a deity in charge of climbing accidents was a bit of a necessity. Klanggo had, in this instance, provided an old mattress abandoned beside the railway tracks that had served the leaping princess well.

The first rays of the morning sun revealed a landscape of derelict railway wagons, sacks, pipes and a hundred different kinds of useless rubbish. Purnah decided that she might as well get up and head toward Scotland. It could take all day to walk there. But she had no idea of directions, and was wondering whether simply walking along the tracks was her best choice when something mewed at her.

It was a mew of strong opinions, and Purnah looked around to see where it came from. A tortoiseshell cat slunk out from an old iron pipe and looked back at the princess. Purnah beamed in delight. It was one of those kittikat creatures that she liked so much. She'd never had one of her own and didn't know a great deal about them. "Here, O kittikitti!" she called out. "Come gettings nice furling coat all stroky!"

The cat tiptoed along the top of the pipe it had emerged from, then turned and meowed in commanding fashion. It jumped daintily onto an old wheelbarrow and vanished over a pile of junk. Princess Purnah followed, taking a longer path around the heaped rubbish.

For the second time in a few hours, a voice called out and asked her an important question: "Do you want a nice cuppa tea, my dear?"

Purnah turned to identify where the voice had come from. A wizened old man sat beside a wrecked carriage, poking a fire into life. His wrinkles were stained with a layer of dirt. A shapeless hat perched on his matted gray hair, and his beard had apparently not been cut since before Purnah was born. She liked him immediately. He looked like her grand- father, who although a royal personage in his land, hadn't much bothered with soap or scissors.

"They call me Harry Hawkes," announced the man. "I'm a tramp."

"They calls me Purnah," replied the girl. "I is a princess."

"Two spoonfuls of sugar, Princess Purnah? I've only got enough milk for Maisie."

The tortoiseshell cat reappeared as the tramp poured the last drops from a milk bottle into a tin plate. She held her tail up high as she began lapping in a businesslike way.

Princess Purnah agreed she didn't need any milk in her tea. She was delighted to watch Maisie. One day, when she was returned to her rightful throne in Chiligrit, there would be royal cats by the dozen, all lapping yaks' milk from golden saucers.

Samuel Soap knew that he'd lost the trail yet again.

The old lady had been taken to the police station in Grandchester. Soap had no doubt they'd have to release her; she was elderly, and the police would not want to stand up in court to testify that she'd soundly thrashed several constables with an umbrella. For Soap it was a question of what to do next. He could simply follow the old biddy, since he had no doubt that she'd meet up with the Cayley girl and that boy. But he was being paid to catch both them and the foreign princess, and he was dashed if he was about to throw away a fat reward for a silly girl who'd jumped out of a train.

She'd probably broken her ankle, so she couldn't have gotten far. If he couldn't catch Princess Purnah, his name wasn't Samuel Soap —

He frowned at that thought, because his actual name was something else entirely. It certainly wasn't Lucky Luke Lariat, whose hat, jacket and spurred boots had been left in a waste-basket.

———

Emmaline had difficulty getting Professor Bellbuckle away from Mr. McVasilieff's house. The two mad scientists had begun what looked like was becoming a long debate over the merits of a clockwork potato peeler. They watched intently as the device whittled a perfectly good spud down to nothing at all. Bellbuckle thought that just a little gunpowder would improve the mechanism. It might cook the potato as well ... maybe.

"We have to go now, Professor," Emmaline insisted. "There's only one train each day, and it goes in half an hour." She hated to nag the old fellow, but there were limits to her patience. Angus was ready for the journey, dressed in tweeds and a knitted scarf. He carried a bag that Emmaline feared might contain the remains of the haggis, now cold, for a picnic on the way.

By the time Professor Bellbuckle was finally torn away from his discussion — now on the likelihood of Martians enjoying ice cream — the train was due to go in twenty minutes. Luckily, Port Haddock was a tiny place, and with Angus leading the way at an impressive mechanical pace, the three travelers arrived at the station with time to spare. Emmaline walked up to the window and asked for three tickets to Nochtermuckity.

"That'll be five shillins an' ninepence," announced the man behind the counter. He was stationmaster, ticket seller and porter at this tiny railway station. "That includes the ferry across from Cape Porridge."

Emmaline was about to hand over the fare when Angus whirred up to the window. She had hoped that, muffled under his tam-o'-shanter and scarf, the automaton would not be noticed as anything but a rather stiff human who walked oddly. The mechanical man had other ideas.

"I should travel at the rate designated for children, och aye. The notice clearly informs the traveling public that persons under the age of fourteen years are eligible for half fare. I am only three years old. Hoots mon!" He said all this in his flat, metallic voice. Emmaline winced and turned away in exasperation.

The stationmaster was old and wore thick spectacles, but he was no fool. He leaned forward to examine this odd passenger who claimed to be an infant. He had seen many a fifteen year old claim to be thirteen to save fourpence. None of these attempted fraudsters had ever told him they were three years of age, but he had an infallible way of checking the truth.

"So, laddie wi' the funny mask on, whit's yer birth date, then?" That always caught them out, in his experience. They could never do the arithmetic fast enough.

"August 26, 1891," replied Angus. "My master oiled me and connected the driving rods to my interior gears, adjusted the piston and sent me to bake a chocolate cake." There was nothing the stationmaster could say to that, so he told Emmaline that the tickets would cost four shillings and tenpence halfpenny, thus saving almost a shilling. Angus insisted on spending this on two pieces of walnut cake and a currant bun, all made fresh this morning by the stationmaster's wife.

The Collector's spy was astounded by the coded message he'd received from Foglamp. Was it possible that the small boy he'd so recently met was not (as he'd assumed) some sort of servant to the mad inventor Bellbuckle but an actual scientific experimentalist himself? And furthermore — his thoughts raced, because there'd be a cash bounty in it for him — that this boy was listed for the Collection?

That would be most ... gratifying. He'd do all he could to place the boy into the Collector's hands. He'd make sure that he, himself, got the credit for it. He didn't want to share a reward with those grubby thugs Titch and Hercules. A hundred pounds would buy a great deal in the way of experimental equipment for his own research.

☙ CHAPTER 17 ❧

A Tramp, a Train, a Lunatic

Rubberbones and Stanley staggered through the howling gale toward Dr. Smoot's cottage. Stanley didn't seem to mind at all, but he had the advantage of being low to the ground. Dr. Smoot answered the door after Rubberbones had rapped for some considerable time. "Oh, it's you, is it?" said the scientist. "You were here yesterday, weren't you? You and that — creature!" He pointed at Stanley. Rab didn't like the sneering tone in the man's voice. Still, he

needed to apologize.

"Er, I wanted to say sorry about yesterday. The pedaling an' the skeleton and all."

Dr. Smoot peered at him. "You may very well apologize. I left you for a few seconds to nip down to the post office, and when I returned all the lights were out. And then I find that your horrid little dog had mutilated Arnold!"

Rubberbones didn't think this was going very well. He preferred it when he could just say how sorry he was about breaking a window or falling through a ceiling; the apologee would then pat him on the head, say "Boys will be boys" and all would be forgiven. Dr. Smoot was still listing his grievances. They seemed to be grievances that he'd stored up and that were completely unconnected with Rab and Stanley's misbehavior the day before. His eyes had become glazed, and he babbled softly to himself.

"Left out in the rain all night — my brother sold it to a scrap-merchant — eaten by pigs — told me never to come back —"

"Er," said Rubberbones, interrupting the flow of unhappy scientific recollections. "We'll make it up to you if we can!" Dr. Smoot appeared to come to his senses (such as they were) and peered sharply at the lad. "Well, yes, no doubt! Come on in! And your fine little dog!"

Then an odd look passed over his face. "Have we met before?" he asked anxiously.

Rab had nothing to say to that. He stepped inside.

Princess Purnah knew right away that she could trust Harry Hawkes. As a member of the Chiligriti royal family, it was important to learn — and learn early — whether a stranger could be relied on, and whether your cousin was about to push you into an icy Himalayan crevasse. Hawkes treated Maisie as if she were his child, for one thing. That was a good sign. He didn't ask a lot of questions either, which was another.

"I've got a bit of bread and cheese," announced the tramp. "You are welcome to share it with me and Maisie. We are heading toward London, but there's a rather fine old Norman church I'd like to see at Chudleigh Underdown. One never knows when one will have a chance to see an original eleventh-century chancel and nave, does one?"

Purnah looked at him blankly.

"I'm sorry, my dear. Old churches are my passion. My plan is to see as many examples of medieval church architecture as I can while I am still spry enough to wander the length and breadth of the country. If you would like to accompany myself and Maisie, you are more than welcome. I notice that you wear a maid's uniform. I know nothing of your situation — and you don't have to tell me anything that you don't want to, of course — but I assume that you are in no hurry to resume your position in domestic service."

Purnah had forgotten that she was dressed as a lady's maid. "Ekk!" she said. "No! I quits!"

"And you did so in a most impressive fashion, dear young lady. I assume that you simply jumped off the train as it slowed down going up the hill?"

"Oh, yess! Trikk! I sez I no care about buttoning dresses and pinnings of hair-up. Ook! I telling missus, I —" (Purnah tried to remember the correct phrase) " — I gives notices immediately! And I tosses myselfs out of carriage to show her I means businessings! Porok!"

Purnah flashed a huge grin, for she was pleased with this version of events. It wasn't true, even a little bit, but it was an exciting tale in which a princess was working as a maid but resigned from her position.

"Good for you!" exclaimed Harry Hawkes. "Now eat some breakfast!"

Purnah liked this man more and more. But her conscience told her that she shouldn't have made up the story of her career as a mutinous maid. If he was as trustworthy as she believed, she'd have to tell him the truth.

Suddenly Maisie's ears pricked up, and she jumped onto a pile of old crates. She'd heard something. Purnah leapt to her feet and peered in the direction that the cat was scanning with her green, almond-shaped eyes. Glekk! It was men in blue coats and helmets, scouring along the railway line. They were still distant — beyond the range within which Purnah could, on a good day, strike a passerby with the hurled egg of a Fhnorkk bird. Yet, the policemen would find her soon.

"Thankly you, but I gots be leavingish now," she told Harry Hawkes. "Must hurrying find new job as lady's maid right soons! All good jobs gone if I am lately. Turok!"

The tramp smiled brightly. He'd spotted the constables as well. "Well," he replied, "I'm sure you know best, but if you'd like to climb into this broken goods van behind us, I can certainly tell those policemen that I have never seen you. I've been here all night, and you haven't been here at all."

Purnah grinned at him once again, and Maisie mewed a sharp cry of agreement.

———————

Emmaline sat with her back to the engine as the little train (much smaller than the one her friend had recently bailed out of) chuffed out of Port Haddock. Nobody else had boarded, and there seemed to be few passengers traveling the line. Angus was a happy automaton after his successful battle for a half-price ticket, and the professor was doodling on his shirtcuffs. Some valuable invention that would prove a boon to humanity, thought Emmaline. Possibly an exploding pudding whisk or a combined hedge clipper/beard trimmer.

They were almost there now. Almost at this island with the bizarre name that sounded like the noise you'd make if you had a brussels sprout lodged in your throat. A place where experimental scientists could create, test, research and blow up without causing inconvenience to the tax- paying public. It sounded demented. It sounded perfect.

Even though it was almost winter and hardly the best time for launching flying machines.

She thought about Mr. McVasilieff and his strange fears. Something about a man who collected scientists. Surely it was all nonsense ...? The Russian was a madman. He was probably some sort of exiled revolutionary — perhaps an anarchist or some such — who lived in fear of the agents of the emperor in St. Petersburg, the Czar as he was known. Many of Professor

Bellbuckle's friends were not the sort of people her mother and father would have welcomed at dinner. There were his American friends, like Butch Cassidy, who robbed banks and trains. There were men from eastern Europe, all bushy beards and guttural accents, whose political views were expressed with gunpowder. Indeed, with chums like these it was no wonder that Aunt Lucy had taken in the professor as a sort of fixer-upper project.

Still, Emmaline had encountered some of the people who worked for the Czar, and she hadn't liked them at all. If Mr. McVasilieff was scared of Russian secret agents finding him, despite his cunning new Scottish name (and adoption of much plaid), she could understand that.

All this guff about a "collector" was clearly his imagination running wild.

Foglamp had received a reply from his man (well, the Collector's man) on the island. The fellow had indeed met a boy but — assuming him to be merely an odd-job lad — had not bothered to ask his name. He had also received word from an informant at Port Haddock that a young girl, accompanied by an older man of eccentric appearance, had visitedthe Russian madman Vasilieff who was under regular surveillance. So Foglamp tapped on the study door, ready to divulge all he knew. As he thin voice from within wheezed "Come in!" the efficient secretary shivered a little.

He went in.

Dr. Smoot ushered Rubberbones into his cottage. The boy had his hand firmly around Stanley's collar to ensure that the dog did not repeat his trick of running away with bits of Arnold. The cottage appeared different from the strange place that Rab had visited the day before. Dr. Smoot had taken down the black curtains from the windows. There was no weirdly strangled music playing. The single room was still crammed with the strange equipment, but the treadles that surrounded Dr. Smoot's desk had been pushed against the wall. Arnold was still hanging there, tempting any dog of spirit. Papers were laid out on the floor in a muddle of diagrams, doodles and dirty footprints.

"Er," said Rubberbones. "Er, you've took down the pedaling machine."

"Indeed I have," replied the scientist. "That device suffered from a key problem. Despite my provision of the Smoot Galvanic Storage Batteries (Model 1893), it was clear that once the operator ceased the pedaling action all the subsequent desired activities ceased — to wit, the lighting, the heating and the playing of music."

Rab nodded. He understood that, put in straightforward terms, Dr. Smoot meant that none of it worked unless you were pedaling at that very moment. If you stopped to, say, make a cup of tea or visit the lavatory, you'd do so in complete darkness and silence. Which would be a problem. "I may try to use the same principle on a smaller scale, employing teams of trained hamsters," declared Dr. Smoot, as if this were the most normal idea in the world. "But for now, I shall leave that aside. Indeed, I fear I am not as far advanced on the Smoot-to-the-moon project as I would like."

"How far have you got?" asked Rubberbones. "Nowhere at all. But, on the other hand, I'd only started

on it thirty minutes before I met you yesterday. That's really quite satisfactory. A complete failure in half an hour is a massive improvement for me. Often I have spent periods of months or years working toward complete failure."

That was sad, thought Rab. To work on something, to not give up even when people said you ought to, and then to find out that they'd been right all along.

"This is what I'm working on today!" announced Dr. Smoot. He flung himself down among the untidy papers and picked up a diagram that looked like a game of hangman that had been left unfinished. "It's the most brilliant development in the field of transportation since ... the bicycle! No, the steam engine! No, the —"

While the inventor was considering which of humanity's most important inventions his diagram would surely trump, Stanley lunged into the pile of papers and shredded a couple of sheets, purely out of exuberance. Rab seized the dog's collar, and Dr. Smoot gathered the surviving papers and clutched them to his chest.

Rubberbones knew that he'd ruined any chance of making it up to Dr. Smoot. So he was surprised when the scientist said, "So, will you help me with an experiment?"

Of course he would.

Samuel Soap had decided there was no way he could find Purnah until morning. So he had spent the night at a hotel in Grandchester then risen at five. Dressed in old brown tweeds with rubber-soled boots, he gathered binoculars, handcuffs and a flask of coffee, for he expected a long day in rough country. If anyone asked, he was a bird-watcher. He'd have to retrace the railway tracks to where the girl had jumped out. Soap recalled that it was on a hill where the train had slowed down as it steamed up the incline. A map told him that this hill was five miles to the west, between Grandchester and Chipping Piebury. So, hiring a cab, he explained to the driver that he was looking for a briefcase that had, inexplicably, fallen out of a train window last night.

"I can't get any closer to the railway line, sir," announced the cabbie. "There's waste ground between here and the tracks, full of old wagons and broken stuff. I'll wait here, but you'll 'ave to walk if that's where you lost your case."

Samuel Soap strode off toward a fence painted with the words "Keep Out — No Trespassing." With a leap he was over the fence and scanning the ground in front of him. He took cover at the sight of two policemen scouring the junk-yard. They must be looking for the girl themselves. He pulled out his binoculars, an expensive pair of German- made field glasses that he'd stolen from a duke the year before. If the Purnah child broke cover to run from the coppers, he wanted to see which way she went.

⚔ CHAPTER 18 ⚔

Fictional Kittens

The policemen were within egg-shot, if Purnah had possessed any eggs, and if she had been willing to use those eggs as missiles instead of breakfast. She didn't and wasn't, so she slunk low inside the abandoned goods van and peered through a gap in the wooden slats.

"Allo, allo! What's all this 'ere?" demanded one constable. He was fat and looked as if he had never once missed breakfast. "Good morning, gentlemen!" replied Harry Hawkes. "I am just pouring tea. I can't start the day without a nice cup of Darjeeling."

"Yes, well," said the constable. "I'm 'ere on official business." "I'm doing nothing wrong, officer," said Harry. "I am just a wanderer o'er this green and pleasant land, Maisie and I. You don't have any reason to tell me to move along."

"No, it's not that. We are looking for a girl. She's some sort of escaped foreign princess." He pulled out his notebook. "Princess Purnah, it says here. From somewhere I can't pronounce. Anyway, she's evaded her legal guardians and scarpered. She jumped out of the 8:45 to Paddington last night somewhere along this stretch of track."

"That seems most ill-advised of her," replied Harry.

The second policeman had been poking around some bags of old newspapers, but now something had caught his eye. Purnah pushed her face closer to the gap between the planks to see what had attracted his attention. It was a tin mug.

Harry had poured two mugs of tea. The constable pointed to it. "Two cups, old man?" he barked. Purnah didn't like him immediately. The princess spotted Maisie, now perched on a broken barrel. The cat's expression suggested that she felt the same way.

"I poured that when I saw a constable approaching," said Harry Hawkes. "I didn't spot that there were two of you. Sorry, but I've only got the two mugs. You'll have to share. Or toss up for it."

The fat policeman — who was older, and probably senior — grinned and picked up the tea. "Very kind of you, Granddad." The other constable snorted.

"I hope you find your lost princess," said Harry. "If I see her, shall I tell her that people are worried about her?" Purnah tried hard not to laugh bitterly. She had to jam her knuckles between her teeth.

"Just report it to the nearest bobby," replied the constable with the mug of tea. His colleague, tea-less, wasn't prepared to let it go at that. "What's in this old van?" he demanded.

"I wouldn't go in there," answered Harry Hawkes. "Why not, you old tramp?" The policeman made toward the van.

"Kittens," said Harry simply. "Maisie is very protective of her kittens. Two weeks old, they are. Mother cats can be extremely ferocious where their offspring are concerned."

Maisie had left her post on the old barrel. Purnah spotted her again, scrabbling up onto the roof of the van.

The younger constable sneered, and said, "She'll just have to put up with it for a minute." He strode toward the open doorway. Another step and he'd be able to see inside, where there were no kittens at all but simply one eastern princess pressed up against the wall.

Porok! Purnah tried to flatten herself into the shadows.

There was a bloodcurdling howl as Maisie flung herself down off the roof. She landed squarely on the constable's helmet, knocking it askew. The policeman staggered backward as the chinstrap dug into his throat; he lost his balance and stum- bled into the sacks containing old copies of the Chipping Piebury Advertiser. He got up, embarrassed and angry.

Maisie stood in the doorway, her fur on end and her ears slung back. She emitted a long, threatening wail that could have curdled fresh milk.

"Lucky she didn't take your eye out," announced Harry cheerfully. "I've seen that happen."

The fat policeman laughed. "Come on, Len. Have a swig of this tea, and we'll keep looking." Len gave Harry a dirty look. He gave Maisie an even dirtier one, but her expression was far more ferocious than any young copper could be expected to face. Len slunk away, following his colleague. Purnah watched them go, grinning broadly as she peered through the narrow slit.

"Ho ho, fierce catlings! Drives off poky policishes! Get medal for this!" she announced.

"I think she'd prefer a nice sardine," replied Harry Hawkes. Maisie mewed in agreement.

Dr. Smoot had a variety of interesting experiments that he was anxious to show Rubberbones. The boy got the strong impression that the inventor had demonstrated these to a lot of people before, and that most of the viewers had been completely uninterested.

Rab was interested. I mean, who wouldn't be interested in a pocket egg poacher? That'd be dead convenient, for one thing. Although the formula for dried bathwater (just add water) seemed to miss the point. But what did he know? He was a twelve-year-old boy with half an education, and Dr. Smoot had been to many universities and colleges. There were scrolls and diplomas hung in a corner of the cottage, partly hidden behind the parts of the machine that Dr. Smoot wanted to set up.

Rubberbones thought it must be the same device that Dr. Smoot had spoken of a few minutes before. It would, for reasons that the lad could not fully comprehend, dip any sort of livestock in strawberry jam.

"I don't think I'd want to eat a cow that'd been dipped in jam," said Rab. Even if beef and strawberry preserves sounded tasty (and, honestly, it didn't), surely you wouldn't dip the whole animal in the fruity sauce, would you? Rubberbones had an idea that medieval kings went in for cooking whole oxen on spits, and they might have wanted a bit of a change sometimes.

Dr. Smoot stared at him. "Good grief, no! We aren't eating these beasts. We are simply finding a way to dip them in jam before they return to, um, chewing grass or whatever it is they do with their time!"

That shut Rubberbones up. The man was a lunatic. Rab thought he'd stay a little longer.

The spidery old man had listened to Foglamp's account of a boy who might, or might not, be the much desired Robert Burns, aged twelve, of Lower Owlthwaite and of a girl seen visiting a known mad scientist in Port Haddock. He glowered, revealing his fanglike teeth. The secretary shrank into his chair. Had he wasted his employer's time with a handful of irrelevant details that added up to nothing?

Then the Collector smiled thinly. "You've done well," he rasped. "If it is the boy in question, then the girl may very well be along in a little while. Perhaps we should send Hercules and Titch — a stupid name, but I've forgotten his real one — to greet her before she arrives at the island. They can be very welcoming, in their way!"

He considered the other part of the problem. "And we'll have to find some way to get hold of young Burns." He smiled once again, with that fang-revealing grin that always repelled Foglamp. "It might be such fun to trick the boy into visiting us of his own free will. Yes, I'd enjoy that."

⚞ CHAPTER 19 ⚟

Dr. Smoot's Telescoping Stilt Shoes

After the constables had left, Purnah emerged from the abandoned van. She was careful to look around for more policemen, but Maisie's observation post on top of the old barrel gave the cat a perfect field of vision; she'd let them know if other intruders appeared.

"Thankings to Maisie for pretendly to have kitteneses!" said Purnah.

"She's a clever one," replied Harry. "And she protects her friends. Sorry about your tea, but I can make toast if you like." He'd cut up the bread and cheese and was holding the slices over the fire with a piece of bent wire.

He didn't mention the police or the tale about the missing princess. Purnah understood that the tramp knew that she must be the lost royal personage in question. Since Harry Hawkes didn't ask any questions, Purnah told him the whole story, with her usual dramatic impersonations, and some improvements to the duller bits. Not that there had been too many dull parts, even by Chiligriti standards. She emphasized the difficulty of pretending to be mute, and the enjoyable qualities of cream cakes. Purnah described her recent adventures on the train — especially the part with the tea trolley, and Auntilucy's heroic last stand — with so much vigor that Harry told her to climb down off the roof of the van and stop throwing things.

"They'll hear you, dear young lady, if you scream like that!" he said. "Even the average police officer will notice a girl who yells — what was it? 'Glekk! Porok! Takings that!' — while dancing on top of an elderly railway vehicle in a field."

Purnah saw that he had a point.

As they ate the toast and cheese, Harry asked, "My dear princess, you say that you have to get to an island several hundred miles from here. You've no experience of traveling alone in this country, am I right?"

Purnah was about to argue until she remembered that all her solitary travels in Britain had involved getting badly lost in small woods, or jumping into coaches she had mistaken for taxi cabs but that turned out to belong to master criminals. "Ekk," she conceded. "Is rightlings."

"And the police are after you, and your description has been circulated?"

"Turok! Yess, is truthy."

"And, aside from your maid's outfit and an overcoat, you don't have any resources for this journey?"

"Has moneys!" announced Purnah, pleased at least to have something to count in the positives column. She brandished a wad of banknotes at the tramp.

"I'd put that away, my dear. You don't want people knowing you have it. Meanwhile, I think Maisie and I can spare a day or so to help you get to this Scottish island. We don't have to be home until the beginning of Advent, which is four Sundays before Christmas."

"Huh?" said Purnah. This meant nothing to her. "Advent is the season leading up to Christmas. It's a very
important time in the church year. And my own church expects me to be present for services."

Purnah tried to reason this out. She didn't know much about Christianity and its odd ways — she understood it was short of useful gods and goddesses and featured hardly any human sacrifices — but she hadn't realized that church ceremonies demanded the presence of a penniless wanderer. Although the annual Feast of Hlunchee, God of Eatings, required a pastry cook. Or it would, once she resumed her throne.

"Is church needings tramp-man?" she asked.

"No, the church needs its vicar — its priest. That's me. I'm only a tramp for a few weeks a year. It's my holiday. The rest of the time I am vicar of St. Bogwell's-in-the-Marsh, a small place, but restful."

"Is Maisie priest-cat, too?" The princess liked the idea of a holy cat ministering to the congregation.

"Oh no, she's much more important than that."

———

Samuel Soap smiled. He had watched the policemen stop and interrogate a tramp at his campsite. This wasn't very interesting in itself, but Soap's instincts were to stay hidden and observe. So, when the constables moved on, he remained still for a minute. Then he saw a small figure emerge from an abandoned goods van to join the tramp and — was that a dog? No, a cat.

He put his binoculars away and began to skulk forward silently.

———

It was a two-hour journey to cover nine miles, but Emmaline didn't mind the slow pace. She had nothing to read, so she passed the time thinking about better ways of designing a flying machine to cope with the problems of lift and drag under field conditions. As anyone might.

The train pulled into Cape Porridge exactly on time. From here, it was a short walk to where the ferry for Invercrockery was waiting. Emmaline could see it from the carriage window. Indeed, Emmaline could see the other side of the water. It wasn't far at all. So, a short voyage in a boat, and then another train to Nochtermuckity.

Maybe there'd be somewhere to buy sandwiches and a pot of tea.

Dr. Smoot enthusiastically continued showing Rubberbones his inventions. Most of them were simply sketches drawn on pillowcases or napkins and — Rab thought this was a bad idea — on the back of an otherwise perfectly good ten pound banknote. Other inventions consisted solely of the surviving broken parts.

One box contained a pair of shoes, the soles of which were on springs, with telescoping poles attached inside oversized rubber heels. "What's this?" asked the boy.

"Telescoping stilt shoes, my lad," beamed Dr. Smoot. "For those times when being taller is an advantage. Would you like to try them on?"

Rubberbones thought that he might.

"Good man! Let's go outside to see if they still work." Dr. Smoot rubbed his scalp as he said this. Rab wondered if the inventor was remembering an old bump on the head.

Rab took off his boots and laced up the experimental footwear. He stood up. Stanley eyed him quizzically, then retreated ten feet. "Right, Dr. Smoot. Shoes on. What do I do now?"

The scientist glowed with excitement. "Do you see the little metal catch on the instep of the left shoe? Can you kick it with your right foot? Not too hard, mind."

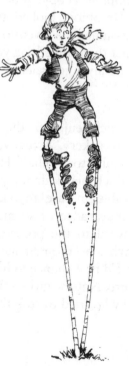

Rubberbones tapped the catch gently. A whirring noise started up. Rab found his feet bouncing gently on the springs as the soles revolved madly against the ground. Then, with a jolt, a metal pole shot out from under each foot, and the boy shot upward.

Stanley whimpered. Dr. Smoot clapped his hands and did a little hop. "Oh, bravo! Bravo!"

Rubberbones was standing on stilts, six feet above the

ground. He flailed his arms around in an effort to maintain balance. For an instant he was balanced upright. He could hold this pose for a moment, at least. It was excellent! Why, he could walk forward if only —

The left stilt retracted with a rattle and a swoosh. Rab lost his balance completely and tumbled to earth. He sat on the grass, one stilt extended to six feet, the other completely vanished inside the shoe. The sole whirled about like a deranged clock hand.

"Ah," whispered Dr. Smoot. "I suppose it would be better if both stilts maintained the same length for the same period of time."

Rubberbones grinned. "Aye, probably. Still, that were champion! People 'd pay money to try those out!"

Dr. Smoot looked at him uncertainly. Rab thought that he assumed his invention would be a great boon to mankind rather than something you might try out at a fairground for a halfpenny a go. Science was a funny thing.

———

Titch enjoyed the trip down to meet the ferry at Invercrockery. Actually, he enjoyed most of his journeys on the Collector's behalf. His spidery employer insisted that they conduct their kidnappings as far from Invermisery House as possible, in case anyone should think of investi- gating the disappearance of so many eminent scientists. Titch looked forward to the prospect of a bit of unnecessary violence. Maybe, he thought as he cracked his enormous knuckles, there'd be a chance to inflict grievous bodily harm in the near future. Not the girl — that would upset the boss. But anyone else who tried to stop them. Oh, yes.

⚔ CHAPTER 20 ⚔

"Thugs — Dangerous!"

"You need a disguise, my dear," said Harry Hawkes. "Is disguised!" replied Purnah. "Is servlingmaids!"

Harry shook his head. "Even if you were convincing in that costume — and you really aren't — people might wonder why a lady's maid is wandering the highways in the company of an old tramp and a particularly fine cat."

Maisie rode on Harry's shoulder as they trudged northward along a farm lane. She stretched and let out a small meow of agreement.

"But," he continued, "I expect that a fine day like today will offer a change of clothes. The Lord will provide."

Purnah understood that Harry was a devoted follower of the strange English faith of Gen-Taljesus Meekanmild and Christmas presents and dividing fish sandwiches up between thousands of hungry people. Purnah's view was that every god was worth taking notice of, just in case. Harry liked to sing songs about Him as he walked, and Purnah joined in as best she could.

"This is Hymn 298 from a book called Hymns Ancient and Modern," announced Harry. "There's a bit of a chorus after each verse."

So Purnah listened as the holy tramp's baritone voice sang out:

> *Fatherlike he tends and spares us,*
> *Well our feeble frame he knows:*
> *In His hands He gently bears us,*
> *Rescues us from all our foes.*

And, because Purnah was interested in rescue from foes, she helped the hymn along.

> *Hally loo ya! Hally loooo ya!*
> *Wildish yet Him's mer-cee flows!*

Which wasn't absolutely correct, but Harry roared with approval.

A cottage lay ahead, with a small walled garden. A line was strung across the lawn, laden with drying clothes.

"Behold!" said Harry Hawkes. "Indeed, the Lord hath provided."

———◦◦◦———

There was time for tea and sandwiches before the ferry got underway, as Emmaline had hoped. As they sat on a bench outside the café, Emmaline looked across the sea-loch to Invercrockery, a tiny hamlet nestled beneath a frowning gray mountain. Then, suddenly (and to her great surprise), Angus entertained her with an ability she'd never heard of before. Mr. McVasilieff had programmed the automaton to scan and analyze the features of human beings, as well as their dress and manners. Angus had been created by a man who thought that people were out to get him; indeed, some of them probably were. McVasilieff had attached a device that permitted Angus's calculations to be heard by means of a small brass trumpet attached behind the automaton's left ear.

"I can show how it works if you so choose, och aye," said Angus. There was pride in his metallic voice. "Touch the button below the trumpet."

Professor Bellbuckle, fascinated, reached over to do so.

"AMERICAN SCIENTIST — OLD — MAD!" screamed the speaker. The professor recoiled, mortified and deafened at the same time.

"There is a volume control, next to the button," said Angus. Emmaline reached over to adjust it downward.

"English girl — young — clever!" the speaking trumpet stated. Emmaline thought this was fair, if simple. But, clearly, you didn't need a full biography.

"Look around, Angus, and tell us who you see," she said. Professor Bellbuckle was still massaging his ears, but he nodded in agreement. Angus did so.

"Fisherman — old! Fisherman's wife — not as old! Fisherman's child — annoying!" Emmaline looked at the family over by a boat. She could see that Angus was correct, especially as the boy pulled a face at her.

Angus scanned a group of travelers who had arrived on the train from Port Haddock: "Train passengers — five — woman, man, man, man, woman — no danger!" They looked back at him; Emmaline could tell that they were very surprised indeed to see a mechanical being in a kilt and tam-o'- shanter. They poked one another and gestured, but none of them said anything. Probably they didn't want to be rude.

Angus was clearly pleased that this ability of his had proved entertaining to his new friends. He continued with it as they boarded the ferry, although Emmaline had to whisper "Hush!" as the metal man's speaker clearly announced, "Ticket collector — ugly!" as they handed over their tickets.

The ferry had an open deck with benches. As they took

a seat, Angus went on with his monologue. "Farmer — fat! Poet — bad! Shepherd — bored!" Emmaline thought that Angus was probably showing off for them. He didn't need to be so unkind. He just needed, she supposed, to be able to tell the postman from the bakery boy, and — if it ever came down to it — an agent of the Czar bent on murdering Mr. McVasilieff from an ordinary passerby who needed help with directions.

So, as the ferry pulled up to the jetty at Invercrockery, it was a shock when Angus scanned the dockside and said to Emmaline, in a confidential manner, "Thugs — dangerous!"

———

Samuel Soap cursed to himself as he followed the singing tramp, the cat and the girl. He dodged from tree to tree or kept to the hedges. It was hard work.

Still, that was what the reward was all about.

———

Mrs. McGinnis found Rubberbones and Dr. Smoot as they were gathering up pieces of the Telescoping Stilt Shoes. "I haff luncheon prepared for you both, together vith the other visitors to our island," she announced. "You must eat vell, for you do not look after yourselves. Good health!"

She tossed a piece of ham to Stanley. He leapt and caught it, wagging his tail.

Rab followed Dr. Smoot to the Mad Scientists' clubhouse. Mrs. McGinnis had covered a table with pies, stews, cold cuts of meat, puddings — the boy was enthralled at the sight!

"Eat! Eat!" Mrs. McGinnis ushered Rubberbones toward the table, as if he needed help. "Not you!" she told Stanley. "This bowl for you is. Dogs are not eating at the table. Most unhygienic!" She patted Stanley fondly and laid a huge bowl of ham, chicken and pie crusts down for him. Rab had never seen Stanley's tail wag with such vigor.

"You three!" Mrs. McGinnis addressed the secretary and two other resident scientists. They sat looking at the huge plates of food in front of them. "You do not eat properly ven I am not supervising. Dr. Grockle! You must eat another portion of the bread pudding before I vill let you leave the table. And I am not counting the bowl you fed to that monkey of yours. And you — Dr. Sneed — you must finish that excellent chicken leg before you have the desserts! Protein!"

The scientists gulped and obediently cleaned their plates. The monkey appeared from under a chair, licking a spoon. Rubberbones needed no instructions to tuck right in. He believed in three square meals, every meal. That was one thing he especially liked about Purnah. She could shovel down food as if she'd never eaten before. Rab wondered where she was today. He was thinking about that when one
of the scientists asked him his name.

"Robert Burns, sir. Most people call me Rab, or Rubberbones, 'cos I never get 'urt. I'm indestruckable, I am."

He had his mouth full, so it came out as "Hrobberbird surrmorspippulcormeraborrubberbordscuzayneverged-dirtaymindystruckibuliam."

≈ CHAPTER 21 ≈

A Valuable Lesson about Stealing Laundry

"Do you see the washing line?" asked Harry Hawkes. "Schnizz! Iz not blindings!" snapped the princess, then remembered that Harry was helping her. "I means, yess! Porok!"

"Do you see the shirts hanging up?" Purnah nodded.

"And do you see the coat and trousers as well? That's a stroke of luck. People don't often wash those; they just beat the dirt out of them and leave them to air out."

Purnah wrinkled her nose. That sounded unclean. In her country everyone washed all their clothes once a month, whole families jumping into a river fully clothed and beating one another against a rock. It built character, was good family fun and helped a little with the smell. Why was Harry telling her this?

"I'll go round to the front door and ask for a cup of water. You steal a shirt — no, two shirts — the coat and a pair of breeches. Hold them up against yourself to make sure they fit.

Then clip one of those pound notes you showed me to the line with a clothes-peg. That'll more than pay for the clothes."

Purnah followed his instructions, nimbly climbing the wall and stealing the clothes with the stealth of the snow leopards of Rootitooty. She didn't remember which of the banknotes were pound notes, so she left several of them pegged on the washing line.

In a minute or so Harry returned, with Maisie grinning on his shoulder. "Nice lady — seven children, can you imagine? And a very nice dog — huge, but gentle. Maisie liked him. The housewife gave me water, and some milk for Maisie. I think you should leave another pound note, if you don't mind my saying so. That will be groceries for a week for this family."

"Is leavings bunches of notelings," said Purnah. "Gots lots!"

"I am sure that's the right thing to do, my dear. It is very wrong to steal, and whenever I've had cause to take an egg or a loaf of bread in secrecy, I make a practice of paying more than the ordinary value of it. When one is a gentleman of the road, sometimes one has to resort to minor sins. And you need to be dressed as a boy."

Purnah had not realized that she needed to be dressed as a boy. She had disguised herself as Rubberbones in the past, although her impersonation had sometimes failed when she forgot who she was supposed to be and began loudly demanding to be treated as a princess. But Harry was right. If the police were after a girl, she'd have to stop being one.

———

Samuel Soap watched from a distance as Purnah crept across the garden. What was she doing? He focused his binoculars. She was stealing clothes. No — wait — she was leaving money pinned to the washing line. That was something he hadn't expected! Then he realized that the tramp and the cat had disappeared from view. Where had they gone? More importantly, did he have time to snatch the girl before they came back? He did not want to get into a scuffle on a country lane, and tramps were usually suspicious people. Just claiming to be a bird-watcher wasn't likely to work. Besides, simply following them would probably take him directly to the Cayley girl and the Burns lad.

Ah, the hairy old man was back in the view of the binoculars. So the kidnap plan wasn't on the cards anyway. As Harry Hawkes and Purnah set off up the lane again, Soap moved forward. There were banknotes on the clothesline, right there in front of him. He looked through the field glasses once again. From the colors of them, one

was a ten pound note. It would only take a minute.

Samuel Soap was only a shade less stealthy than the snow leopards of Rootitooty. Alas, as he reached the washing line the housewife stepped out of the back door to check her laundry. With her came a dog larger than any Soap had ever seen, part mastiff, part Doberman, part buffalo.

"What are you doing?" demanded the housewife. Soap's expression spoke of crime and fear. The dog, so recently described as huge but gentle, let out an ear-splitting bark and launched itself toward Samuel Soap. Soap turned. He fled. He ran with an impressive turn of speed.

Yet Samuel Soap (terrified) was slower than the dog (protective). As the man bent to leap the wall, a very large maw full of sharp teeth closed over his skinny, tweed- covered buttocks.

"They've come for me!" wailed Professor Bellbuckle. "They want me for this here dadblamed collection!"

"Pull yourself together!" said Emmaline through clenched teeth. "They may not have seen us yet. Angus and I will, ah, fend them off!"

She had no idea how they were going to do this. "Try to blend in with the other passengers." It sounded ridiculous as she said it. There were only eight other people on the ferry, and none of the others was dressed like Professor Bellbuckle, whose tailcoat and planter's hat showed obvious signs of explosions, fires and near-drownings. None of them had shiny brass faces either.

The two thugs pushed forward toward the edge of the quay. Emmaline saw that one was a hulking brute of a man, like an ogre in a fairy tale. The other was a tiny person with an unpleasant sneer plastered across his face.

There was nothing to do but step off the ferryboat. Emmaline jumped out first. She balled her fists and prepared for a fight. It was fortunate that in recent times her experience in fighting grown men had increased; she recalled the masked minion she had beaned with a copy of Professor Octave Chanute's recent book on aeronautics, and his equally masked comrade whom she'd wrestled with in one of London's nicer hotels. Still, she'd decided to slug the little one. The big fellow was clearly out of her weight class.

Angus whirred alongside her while the professor lurked behind. "Don't worry, Professor Bellbuckle," said the girl. "We'll see the rascals off!" She didn't believe it for a moment.

The little thug puffed out his chest while his friend glowered with menace. "A moment of your time, gen'lmen and young lady, if yer's not in a hurry." London accent, thought Emmaline. Before she could say anything, Angus bounced forward with a springy stride.

"Leave my friends alone. Begone! No door-to-door salesmen allowed inside! Away with ye!" said the automaton. Emmaline thought this was an odd thing to say, but everything here was pretty odd.

The tiny man (whom we know as Hercules, although Emmaline did not) grinned wider; it was not a smile of friendship. "Just a few minutes, please, then two of you can be on your way."

"You'll not take me!" wailed Professor Bellbuckle. "I'll have the law on you!"

"Nah, see, it's not you 'oo —" began Hercules, but he was interrupted as Angus whirred forward and smacked him with an open — iron — hand. Clearly the metal man was programmed to protect, and protect early, without waiting for all the idle chatter to finish. Angus took up the stance of a boxer, left fist forward, right in reserve. He bounced on the balls of his metal feet.

The little man fell aside and sat down hard, yelling "Get 'im, Titch!" Angus turned to face the massive bulk of his colleague. Titch was humongous. Angus sprang forward — literally — and delivered a flurry of punches to the man's chest and stomach. The automaton's boxing style was scientific, in the modern fashion. He jabbed. He hooked. He tried a right uppercut against the giant's jaw but — sadly — couldn't actually reach it. None of the punches seemed to make any impression on Titch. Or, indeed, connect with him at all.

Hercules rose to his feet. Snarling, he advanced toward Emmaline. The girl looked around and spotted a boat hook — a long wooden pole with a hook on the end for handling moored vessels. She remembered all that she had learned at St. Grimelda's. The school had not been helpful with her education in general, but the uniquely violent St. Grim's Ball Game had taught her some low tricks with a stick. Her only friend there, Josie Pinner, had shown her how to wield a hockey stick with crushing ferocity. Emmaline missed Josie quite often, but right now she especially missed the muscular girl's mighty sense of how damaging an opponent could be useful and, indeed, a lot of fun.

"This is for you, Josie," she muttered and swung the boat hook. It caught the tiny man higher than she expected and flung him along the quay. "Ouch!" yelled Hercules as he fell. All this time Professor Bellbuckle had been skulking behind Emmaline. Now he flung himself forward with a piercing scream that might, she thought, be the rebel yell that she'd read about in books on the American Civil War. Alternatively, it might signal severe constipation. In either case, the professor shrieked and rushed toward the giant. His arms were flailing and his knees worked like pistons. "You ain't gonna git me, you no-good varmint! I'll whup ya good! I'll —"

The professor cannoned into Titch, which seemed to surprise the huge thug. Titch knocked Angus aside with the back of one hand — the automaton's scientific boxing skills being insufficient to cope with the brute's sheer force — but he seemed unable to lay a paw on the leaping whirlwind of Georgian scientific fury. Bellbuckle poked, Bellbuckle kicked. Titch was too slow to lay a hand on him.

Emmaline heard the guard's whistle blow. The train for Nochtermuckity was about to leave. "Run!" she shouted. "Angus! Professor! Run for the train!" But Angus was determined to box, angrily springing up and dancing about, jabbing and punching. Professor Bellbuckle was like a tailcoated whirlwind, not exactly dangerous, but confusing as all get-out.

Then the little thug was up and rushing toward Emmaline. He yelled out something that made no sense — it seemed to be about catching her, when obviously he must mean the professor. She swung the boat hook again. It caught the man by his belt-loop, and the momentum of the swing lifted him off his tiny feet. Emmaline let go of the pole, and both boat hook and Hercules flew through the air. There was a splash. Emmaline didn't have time to look. "Come on!" she yelled, and tried to grab the professor. Like Titch, she could not place a hand on Bellbuckle.

Then Angus seized her around the waist and began to run toward the train. She tried to look back to see if the professor was following them. As far as she could see, Titch was actually trying to push Professor Bellbuckle aside to pursue them. Hercules was hauling himself out of the water, waving a fist. Professor Bellbuckle attacked Titch once again, screaming something about "low-down hornswogglers."

Angus moved fast on his spring-and-balljointed legs. But it wasn't fast enough. The train had picked up speed and was chuffing merrily away as the automaton reached the platform. "You'll never capture me!" shouted Professor Bellbuckle, dragging from Titch's shirttails as the giant advanced toward the railway platform. The little man ran forward, yelled something to Titch and pointed at Emmaline and Angus.

Angus's head swiveled around, making a bleeping sound as he scanned the landscape. "We must go up the mountain, for I am faster than they are while traveling uphill," he said. "Hold on tightly. Hoots! Auld lang syne!"

"But the professor!" protested Emmaline.

"We cannot help him now," declared the metal man. "We must save ourselves."

"I say, Smoot," said Dr. Grockle. "What are you and this lad working on? You've never had an assistant before. And a — what — 'indestructible' one?"

"How about that scheme that you said was the most brilliant idea of the century?" demanded his colleague Sneed. Dr. Smoot looked a little confused, and Rab got the idea that maybe he'd said that more than once. He had a cousin who said things like that.

"The catapult, Smoot! The Smoot Transatlantic Passenger Catapult!" said Mr. Secretary. "It was Smoot's big scheme a couple of years ago. Going to make him a fortune, it was! But stopped in its tracks by, what was it, Smoot?"

Dr. Smoot looked embarrassed, and mumbled something about his financial backers dropping out of the scheme.

"Of course they did," said Grockle. "They'd have lost their money on that one."

"Or they'd have been sued for every penny they had by the relatives of everyone killed in the experiment," added Sneed. Rubberbones didn't like this. They were making fun of Dr. Smoot, who was certainly a strange man, but he was a mad scientist; what could anyone expect? They weren't exactly examples of normal behavior themselves. "Er, what was this invention?" he asked.

Dr. Smoot blushed, but Mr. Secretary was happy to explain it.

"Imagine a really big catapult, large enough for a human being to be used as a missile. Aim the catapult at a prearranged spot in — where was it, Smoot? Newfoundland? North Carolina?"

Dr. Smoot muttered that he'd planned on several destination spots. The secretary overrode him as he continued, "Wherever this spot was, there would be a net. A really big net, you under- stand — old Smoot wouldn't risk anyone's life and limb! The passenger would don a padded suit, strap his suitcase to his back and be hurled bodily over a distance of three thousand miles to reach the American continent. Dr. Smoot often told us it would be far quicker and cheaper than one of those safe, comfortable steamships that most of us are forced to rely on." Sneed and Grockle laughed at this. Rubberbones disliked them more and more. So he said, "The suitcase should be sent separate-like, or at least strapped to the front. That way you could give the passenger a parachute to 'elp 'im land softly. And the catapult should not be permanently fixed on one target net, but adjusted every time to allow forwind and other weather conditions."

That shut them up. Rab smiled to himself. As he reached for another helping of apple crumble, he was glad to see Stanley leaping up to grab a sausage roll from Mr. Secretary's plate, upsetting it into the man's lap.

≈ CHAPTER 22 ≈

"We Walkings to Shott-land?"

Purnah stepped behind a tree dressed as a lady's maid, and stepped out again, one minute later, as a grubby sort of boy. Admittedly, she'd been unconvincing as a maid, but her male disguise wasn't a vast improvement. It depended heavily on wearing Harry's disgusting old hat and hoping that nobody looked at her shoes. Purnah had worn ballet shoes ever since she found an old pair in Aunt Lucy's attic, and she now refused to wear anything else. The shirt and trousers fitted well enough, but the jacket was two sizes too large. The Chiligriti dagger made by Sharposwishi the Toothless was stuffed in the pocket.

"Most tramplike," announced Harry Hawkes with approval. "You might want to roll in some dirt as fancy takes you."

"What I doings with maidly costume?" she asked.

"I'd keep the coat. You can only tell it's a woman's coat by which side the buttons are sewn, and it's cold in Scotland. Tie it on a stick and put anything else you have inside it. But throw the maid's uniform and hat away now — bundle it under a bush. God will forgive us for littering just this once, I think," replied Harry.

Maisie jumped down and went over to inspect Purnah.

She sniffed and mewed her approval.

"Right," said Harry. "We must press onward. The farther we can get from where you jumped out of the train, the better our chance of confusing your pursuers."

"We walkings to Shott-land? Grurk!" said Purnah. "Is farlings, then?"

"It's probably three hundred miles, which is much farther than you should think about walking," replied Harry. "Let's see if we can travel in style."

He turned and pointed toward a cart coming along behind them, stacked with bales of hay. "Smile and touch your hat, Princess — but keep your long hair tucked up under it. Maisie will do her little turn here."

As the cart slowed down, Maisie stood in the roadway and did a little pirouette on two legs. The driver grinned broadly.

"Where are you headed for, then?" he asked. "Wherever you are going, my friend," replied Harry.

Purnah thought that was a good reply, much better than asking a farmer to drive her all the way to Scotland, which would have been her first answer.

Samuel Soap was cursing his bad luck once again. He had escaped from a savage hound by the skin of his ... skin. He'd hurled himself over a wall, trousers ripping, dog chomping, housewife yelling. Now he was hiding amid a clump of bare bushes. They weren't the only things that were bare. The dog had taken the whole seat out of his breeches — underwear, too — and he had toothmarks in places that he'd never be able to mention to anyone.

He'd have to hide all day until nightfall. Even then, it would be difficult —

No, wait! There was something under that bush over there! It was a pair of trousers!

Oh. It was a maid's uniform, with a silly little white cap.

It was that girl's uniform. That was why she was stealing from the clothesline.

Glumly, Soap pulled on the maid's costume. He was a small man, and it fitted, more or less. Even so, he had never enjoyed donning a new disguise less than he did today. Normally it was a point of pride for him to turn into some-one else by means of a change of clothes. Now it was sim- ply humiliating.

Perhaps it was his mustache. No self-respecting lady's maid had a mustache. No self-respecting lady had a maid with a mustache.

He headed back the way he had come.

Angus paced tirelessly uphill, his metal feet springing against the rocky slope of the mountainside. Emmaline bounced and jolted as the automaton carried her. She peered back along the trail; Titch and Hercules had given up the chase and were dragging Professor Bellbuckle down to a carriage halted by the tiny village green.

"We must save the professor," declared Emmaline.

"It is not possible," replied Angus. "We are unable to defeat the large human. He will subdue us and take us captive also, hoots mon. Besides, it is you that he wishes to seize, not the professor." The mechanical man kept striding onward, onto a broad open steep of bare hillside. Then, turning, he scanned the distance. "They are unable to pursue us here. The slope is too steep for a horse-drawn vehicle, and they are less nimble on foot than am I." He put Emmaline down.

They watched as the horse-drawn carriage started along the road at the edge of the sea-loch. "We could fol- low them and free the professor," said Emmaline. "Or, at least, see where they are going." Her words were based on hope rather than good sense.

"We cannot catch them, and if we did, I refer you to my previous comments about the very large man, who is a most formidable opponent. As you will have observed, I was unable to make any impression on him, despite my boxing skills. I have been programmed to defeat opponents in the middleweight categories and below. My creator, Mr. McVasilieff, was most definite on that point. And yet, although I laid several scientific punches upon my adversary's person, he appeared completely undaunted and undamaged. I can make no physical impression on the man. I doubt that you could, despite your admirable technique with that boat hook." Then, remembering that he was sup- posed to say something Scottish as part of his disguise, Angus added a mumbled, "Och aye, the noo."

Emmaline thought for a moment. "What did you say about those men wanting to seize me?"

"I heard them clearly. The tiny person told the big one known as Titch that he should grab you and 'Stop messing abaht wiv the old bloke.' I can replay the conversation if you like — my hearing receptors save recorded sounds on a brass disc."

He flicked a switch under his arm, and the whirring disk played back a tinny replay of those precise words.

"That makes no sense," protested Emmaline. "Professor Bellbuckle is a famous scientist. Well, perhaps not really famous, but he's been doing it a long time. I'm just a girl."

"You are a girl who invents flying machines," answered Angus. "The professor invents things that explode accidentally. It may be that the Collector is more interested in yourself than Professor Bellbuckle."

Emmaline shook her head in confusion. That couldn't be right. "But they captured him."

"I think it is more accurate to say that he flung himself on the large one and would not let go. The professor's concept of personal defence is a strange one. Although he was trying to avoid capture, his behavior made it almost unavoidable."

Emmaline nodded miserably. "Well, then. We must go on to find our friends. Later we can plan to rescue the professor. I assume we should not go down and catch the next train?"

The automaton shook his head in a whirring, springy fashion. "They will simply await us at Nochtermuckity railway station."

"Right then, we won't go there," said Emmaline. She pulled out her train timetable, which featured a small map. It had nothing except railway lines and stations, but Emmaline could at least work out the shape of the landscape, with its jagged coastline indented with deep sea-lochs. It was possible to get to Nochtermuckity overland. There was just an inch or two of blankness in the way.

She looked up at the mountain ridge above her. That was what the blankness must be.

———◦◦◦———

Dr. Smoot had laid out the pieces for his Transatlantic Passenger Catapult. Rubberbones could tell that the inventor had been stung by the jeers of his colleagues. The lad wasn't sure if he should have said that a parachute and an adjustable throwing device would improve the catapult's chances of success. Rab was certain that they would increase the probability of not hurling the unlucky passenger straight into a rock; he just wasn't sure how much better that particular improvement would make the poor beggar's chances of survival.

Rab understood the laws of aeronautics better than Dr. Smoot. He did not believe that the future of manned flight lay in flinging people across oceans. He wasn't certain how far it was across the Atlantic, but he knew it was a long way. Enough to eat a cheese sandwich, at least. Probably two.

The cottage door opened. "Hello," said Dr. Grockle. The monkey chattered its own greeting.

"Afternoon, Grockle," replied Dr. Smoot sharply. Rubberbones could tell that he was not happy to see his visitor.

"Erm, I wanted to apologize to you. My friends were very sarcastic at lunch. I'm sorry if I seemed to laugh along with them." Dr. Grockle's voice was low and apologetic. "The fact is, your invention has great potential. It needs development, of course. Testing. But I believe that this is the ideal place to do that."

"Indeed," replied Dr. Smoot. "That is why I remain here when the fair-weather inventors go back to their warm homes for the winter."

"I admire your dedication," Dr. Grockle continued.

"Indeed, if you had someone to help you — a brave, youngish sort of chap with a sense of adventure — you might really make great strides forward with the catapult."

"Like yourself, perhaps?" replied Dr. Smoot.

"Ah, no. I have a bad knee and a fear of heights. And glaucoma. Diptheria. The Brazilian Ankle-Wobble. I'm not suited for actual field tests at all. No, I was thinking of the young chap you have with you now." He looked straight at Rubberbones.

"But," Dr. Grockle went on (before Rab could say a word), "I am more than willing to help in any way.

For instance, I could arrange for a large net to be set up to catch the young man. And I could donate a proper set of protective clothing. And that parachute thing the  young fella mentioned. I could buy the very best available. Have one sent up from the best silk merchant in London."

"That would be marvelous!" said Dr. Smoot.

Rab could see that the mad scientist was enthralled by this sudden show of support.

Dr. Smoot had probably always been the butt of his colleagues' jokes. He was, after all, a very mad scientist indeed.

And, if Rubberbones could help, well, he would.

⊰ CHAPTER 23 ⊱

The Transatlantic Passenger Catapult

The farm cart trundled its way to a village some miles to the north. It was the right direction and, if slow, it did the thing most important for Purnah's continuing freedom; it took her beyond the area where Inspector Pike was marshaling every policeman he could gather to look for the princess. At least, that was what she had picked up from the cart driver.

"Any news, farmer?" Harry Hawkes had asked. The driver was probably not actually a farmer himself, but simply worked for a farmer. Purnah thought this was flattery and filed it away in her memory. Harry, like the smooth butler, Strand, understood that cleverishness was often better than stabbings.

"Oi just come from town. Grandchester. There's a roight hows-yer-do there. Lots of coppers about lookin' fer a lost princess. Fell out of a train, they say. Very careless of her." "Indeed," replied Harry. "You'd think that royalty would be better supervised."

Purnah chuckled at this, but quickly turned her laugh into a cough. She pulled the hat further over her eyes and tried to look as much like a vagrant boy as she could.

Samuel Soap's cabbie was still waiting for him. He'd seemed startled by Soap's bizarrely unconvincing disguise as a female house servant, but the expression on the mustachioed maid's face told him to say nothing. When they arrived at the hotel in Grandchester, Soap gave the driver a handful of silver and ran inside through a back entrance.

Ten minutes later, Soap appeared again, properly dressed in formal black suit and bowler hat. He was off to the police station to make inquiries about Mrs. Lucy Butterworth, who had been taken in for questioning the night before.

———

Emmaline was sweating, despite the icy blast, as she forced herself to walk upward, step after step. Great raw rocks jutted through the thin soil every few paces. The mountain, windswept and treeless, seemed to go on forever.

"Do you wish me to carry you, Miss Emmaline?" asked Angus. The mechanical man showed no sign of tiring. If he had slowed his springy pace at all, it was simply to allow the girl to keep step with him.

"No, I'll be fine," wheezed Emmaline. "Really, I will. All we need to do is find a —"

What did she need to find? A short-cut to Nochtermuckity? A tea shop? A place where she could exchange some of the money borrowed from Angus for a hot meal, a warm sweater and some dry socks?

She might as well wish for a complete flying machine, all equipped for two, and a fair wind for the Island of Mad Scientists.

She kept on going because what other choice did she have?

Rubberbones was surprised to find that Dr. Smoot's catapult was a fine piece of carpentry. He'd expected that, like the stilt shoes, it would prove likely to fall apart in a stiff breeze. Instead, it was a nicely made wooden machine that was assembled by means of tabs and slots into a light yet sturdy apparatus for flinging brave aeronauts through the air. A couple of people could carry it without much difficulty. Three people easily.

Stanley thought it smelled interesting.

"Did you make this, Dr. Smoot?" Rab asked.

"Oh no, I had it made by — um, I don't remember. But it's a jolly nice catapult, isn't it?"

Rubberbones thought that Dr. Smoot was very eccentric indeed, even compared to Professor Bellbuckle. Rab hero-worshipped the professor, but at the same time he knew that you shouldn't really expect him to behave like a grown-up all the time. Any of the time, really. Dr. Smoot was the same.

They dragged the catapult onto the plateau above the scientist's cottage, with the help of the sheeplike servant boy. Rubberbones realized that he had not actually talked to the lad so far. That was very rude of him. So he introduced himself.

"My name's Rab. What's yours?"

The boy looked at him warily, as if nobody had ever spoken to him like that before. "Will," he whispered. That was all.

"Er, glad to meet you, Will. You work 'ere, then?" Rubberbones stated the obvious, but that was all right. The lad was clearly shy.

"Yes."

Rab waited for him to say more. He didn't.

They set up the catapult and aimed it along the open flatness of the upper island. "What are we going to, ah, throw?" asked Rab.

Dr. Smoot looked surprised. "I thought we were planning on throwing you!"

Rubberbones grinned. "We are, but not to begin with. We need to see if it works properly."

"Hmm. I hadn't thought of that. What, then?" Dr. Smoot looked around him. Rubberbones couldn't believe that he, himself, was the careful, responsible person here. That had never happened before. "What did you throw before?"

"Oh," replied the scientist. "Sacks of something. Dirt and rocks, I think." He brightened. "I still have the sacks. I didn't keep the dirt, though."

Within an hour they had fetched the sacks, found a shovel and prepared for a test run. Rab tried to guess how much soil and stones equated with his own weight, since a bag that flew a hundred feet must weigh the same as a boy who hopes to fly the same distance. Dr. Smoot didn't seem to worry about details like that. Will said nothing, but dug dirt and filled sacks. Stanley ran about and occasionally gnawed at a sack.

"Right," said Dr. Smoot as they stood ready to fling the first sack. The catapult arm was ratcheted back, and the sack hoisted into the cup. "All ready?"

Rubberbones stepped closer to see how it worked. Will stepped back nervously. Dr. Smoot pulled a lever, and the bag hurtled away into the sky as the arm slammed forward. Rab peered as the sack arced over the island and landed at least four hundred yards away. It was a tremendous throw, elegantly curling through the air.

Stanley rushed after the sack, but it had a massive head start, and the dog never had a chance of catching up with it.

Of course, the sack dissolved into a cloudburst of dust as it struck the ground.

"That was jolly good!" declared Dr. Smoot. "It were champion!" agreed Rubberbones.

Stanley stood, evidently shocked that the thing he was chasing had exploded. He was probably glad that he hadn't caught up with it. Will looked scared. Rab realized that the boy had thought the whole thing through a little more than its inventor had. "It's all right," said the Yorkshire aeronaut. "I'll 'ave a parachute."

Well, he would. They'd have to make one, of course. But Rubberbones had spotted a silk flag at Dr. Smoot's cottage. He wasn't sure what country it represented, but he had no doubt that the proud banner of Bolivia or Montenegro or wherever it was would make a fine parachute. He hoped nobody from those countries would be offended, but it was all in the cause of scientific experiment.

They shot off six more sacks of soil and rocks, each with the same beautiful result. If the Smoot Transatlantic Passenger Catapult was not yet ready to deliver paying travelers across the Atlantic, it did a fine job of dropping dead weights of dirt over a quarter-mile distance. That was step one.

Foglamp decoded the message with his usual efficiency. He liked what it said:

Confirmed identity of Robert Burns. Can deliver him to you shortly. Can you set up large net on shore facing island? Tomorrow, if weather permits, or ASAP. Boy will come to you as parcel. G

The secretary smiled. He would deliver the news to the Collector in a moment. But first he had to write a brief reply to the note. He could, indeed, arrange for a large net to be set up on the narrow beach opposite the frowning cliffs of

Urgghh. And some men to watch in case anything should land in it. Probably not a fish, he thought to himself.

Foglamp folded the note and passed it to the monkey.

The Island of Mad Scientists

⚔ CHAPTER 24 ⚖

Victoria Regina

Princess Purnah, currently in disguise as a junior tramp, was enjoying herself immensely. Maisie had taken to riding on Purnah's shoulders, wrapped around the back of the royal neck. The farm cart had dropped them off outside a village. Harry took out a compass to check directions and pointed toward the north. "We should go that way," he said. "Assuming there's a road that heads in that direction. Otherwise, we'll tramp across country."

"To Scottishlands?" asked Purnah.

"To a railway station. There's one at Pilkington-under-Hill, which isn't far from here. It's just not possible to walk to Scotland except by taking weeks to do it. It's too late in the year to be sleeping in hedges, my dear. We will find our way to somewhere where you can catch a train. You do know how to catch a train, don't you?" asked Harry.

That was a good question. Purnah knew how to sit inside a train. She probably could ride on the roof or hang on to the sides. She certainly knew how to jump out of a moving carriage. What she had never done was the boring but important aspect of train travel in which you buy a ticket and, using a timetable, take a succession of trains to your destination, changing along the way at different stations. That had been Auntilucy's job. Purnah did not know how to read a timetable or the strange maps that showed lines leading to dots with names.

"Prrk! Can you comes with mees? You and dear little Maisie?" She flashed a smile, intended to be charming (but actually appearing a bit deranged).

"My dear, Maisie and I have to be at home for the start of Advent. To do that we would have to travel to, where was it, Urgghh, and then back again by train. As you'll note, we wander the roads with very little money. I simply cannot afford a ticket to Scotland and back again."

"I paylings for yous. How much is cat ticket?" asked the princess.

"Cats travel free. But I don't, alas, and I can't expect you to pay my way," replied Harry Hawkes.

"Is notly your way. Is my way! You go helplings my Royal Majesty! Is settled!"

Harry protested as they climbed a stile and began to hike across a ploughed field. Purnah would have threatened him with much beheadings, but she liked him, and Maisie would disapprove.

———

Samuel Soap's first act was to walk to the police station to ask about "his aunt, Mrs. Wrigglesby," who he'd heard had been arrested in some frightful mix-up. The desk sergeant looked at him as if he were mad. "No, mate," replied the policeman. "We 'ad an old lady in, but not by that name. Some fake spiritualist. She's been released."

Soap went through a display of relief that he had been misinformed about his (imaginary) aunt, and strode down the street to the post office, considering what he should do.

The post office personnel weren't just going to agree if he said, "I think an old lady may have sent a telegram from here after the police let her go. Can I have a look through those you've sent today, please?"

"I say," he began. The postal clerk peered at him through the grille. "My aunt was in here earlier. Older lady, short and plump. Mrs. Butterworth." This time it was important to use her real name. The clerk gave him a quizzical look. "Oh, yes?"

"Well, she sent me down here because she thinks she made an error on a telegram she sent," said Soap, trying to look as sincere as he could.

"Very unfortunate for her," replied the clerk. "But I can't let you look at the copy. Only the original sender can do that." "My aunt is old and has a rumbling spleen. She's resting, on doctor's orders."

"I'm sure the copy will still be here when she's well enough to walk again. The message has already gone, of course." The clerk was very curt in his manner.

"I don't want to read the message. I just have to make sure my aunt got the address correct. She's not sure she sent an important telegram to the right place. Did I say that she's old and in poor health?"

The clerk relented. "All right, then. She sent two telegrams. Which is it, the one for London or the one for Scotland?"

Soap made a guess. "Scotland." The clerk showed him a form, and he copied down the following: *Lal Singh, C/O The Royal Society of Experimental Science and Invention, Urgghh, near Nochtermuckity, Scotland.*

Emmaline had crested the ridge of the mountain and looked out over a fine panorama. If she had had a camera or a paintbrush and palette, the view would have been exactly what she wanted to see — a landscape of somber moorland hillside dropping into a steep valley, with a matching ridgeline rising on the opposite side. The afternoon sun cast shadows on the bare heathery mountainside. Patches of trees clung to the lower slopes. It was all very grand. It was what people came to Scotland to see. Only she had to climb down the mountain and up the other side. And the sun would be going down behind that mountain much too early. Traveling in the dark would be difficult.

She was cursing her luck as Angus looked on without emotion (being an automaton and all) when something new appeared at the edge of her vision, moving along a rough track no more than a hundred yards ahead of her. She turned her head and saw a figure on horseback. No, there were more figures, emerging from behind a rocky ... um, a big rock thing that had hidden them from her view. Angus assessed the new arrivals in his usual manner.

"Four riders — professional manner — one closed carriage

— one other vehicle — treat with caution."

Emmaline had come to respect Angus's assessment of danger, so she dropped to her knees while Angus dropped flat behind a slab of granite. They were a fraction too late, as one of the horsemen whistled; he and a second rider trotted toward the place where Emmaline and Angus had taken cover.

Dash it all, thought Emmaline. I've staggered all the way up a mountain for the Collector to nab me when I'm completely winded. But there was something about the men on horseback that was far different from the little thug and the silent giant. The riders were, as Angus had put it, "professional"; they wore civilian garb, but they rode like soldiers — like men without fear. The first one pulled up within thirty feet of her position. She rose to her feet.

"It's a fine afternoon to be out on the mountain," the man called out. "Who are you?"

Emmaline decided that she'd keep her name to herself for now. "Just out for a walk, sir. On our way to Nochtermuckity."

The rider shook his head. "You'll not be there before dark. It's at least eight miles, perhaps ten. Why is your friend hiding from me?"

Angus rose sheepishly from behind his flat stone. Emmaline realized that she had to explain his strange appearance. This man's interest was not simply mild curiosity, she could tell. The local landowner? His steward? "My friend is in fancy dress. It's all a bit of a lark. We hadn't planned on walking so far in costume." It sounded unlikely, even as she said it. Still, it was better than "My friend is a mechanical creature, assembled by a lunatic Russian and my deranged tutor."

"I'll tell you what, miss," said the rider. "I'll stay here with your chum while you go and talk to my superior." He gestured at the other horseman, who had halted while the carriages came along the track. Emmaline walked toward the man, feeling several pairs of eyes sizing her up. As she walked forward, the first vehicle halted. The man turned and walked alongside her toward the light, one-horse closed carriage. A window slid down, and an elderly woman looked out. She didn't smile. With her sat a man in Indian dress, and for a brief moment Emmaline thought that Lal Singh had somehow managed to get a coach to bring her to the island. But it was not Lal Singh.

"You don't look like an assassin," snapped the old lady. "Erm, no, ma'am," Emmaline replied. She'd never wondered whether anyone would mistake her for an assassin. It was a very odd thing to say. "I'm just, er, walking to Nochtermuckity with my friend. Am I going in the right direction, do you know?"

"I believe you are, young lady, although the captain of my escort can tell you precisely. You won't get there today. You'll need food and blankets if you are to spend a night out on the moors. Speak to my attendants in the wagon behind, with those instructions. And say 'Your Majesty' when you address me, child."

Your Majesty, thought Emmaline. Like an elderly Purnah, issuing orders to everyone, but without the threats of stabbing and strangulation.

Oh.

Emmaline curtsied. The old woman chuckled. "I think we can manage a hamper and some warm bedding for a young lady wandering about the highlands. Your friend looks very strange, doesn't he?"

"Oh, yes, Your Majesty. He's in fancy dress. He's costumed as an automaton."

"Oh, yes, I see. Very convenient for hiking across Scotland in the wintertime." Queen Victoria guffawed. Her Indian companion laughed as well.

"Oh, my dear, thank you for entertaining an old lady. I am very amused."

The Collector was not amused with his employees. Hercules and Titch were hearing exactly how disappointed he was in their efforts today.

"Let me see. I sent you to bring in Miss Emmaline Cayley, a young girl of fourteen years. Instead, you have brought me Professor Ozymandias Bellbuckle, a well-known imbecile whose incompetence and irresponsibility have been bywords in the scientific community for thirty years. How did you confuse the two?"

"Ah, well, see —" began Hercules. "It were like this —"

"I don't care how it was!" screamed the Collector, pushing his sharp white face toward Hercules. "I care that I ordered one adolescent female aeronaut. I was very specific about that. Instead, you bring me

Bellbuckle! What am I to do with a Bellbuckle?"

"Er, file him under 'B,' sir," suggested Hercules.

Titch was glad he hadn't said anything. Even though he was almost seven feet tall, he was terrified of the Collector. So Titch was relieved that it was his friend Hercules who was picked up and thrown out of the room. You wouldn't have thought anyone so old and spidery could be so strong.

⇜ CHAPTER 25 ⇝

Purnah in Search of Chocolate

Rubberbones was amazed at what Lal Singh had brought back after his day away from the island. New furniture had replaced the battered chairs and table. There were piles of blankets, and rugs covered the floor. The shelves were laden with supplies of all sorts.

"I knew you were busy, young Rab, so I did not disturb you from your efforts," explained Lal Singh. "Mrs. McGinnis assisted me. She feels that this cottage, in its previous condition, was not suited for a lady and her household. And the lady in question will be here tomorrow."

"Aunt Lucy?" asked Rab, full of excitement. "And Purnah?"

"That is the problem," replied Lal Singh. "I have here two telegrams, which you must read." He offered the papers to Rubberbones.

The first telegram was from Aunt Lucy, sent from somewhere called Grandchester. As always, Aunt Lucy had no concept that telegrams were charged by the word; this one had probably cost a week's worth of groceries.

> *My dear Lal Singh! Lots of excitement — but worries, too! After all sorts of adventures involving my pretending to be a spiritualist and Purnah my protégée, we were accosted by the police, most rudely I thought, on our voyage by train toward London. I was able to fend them off while Purnah made a bolt for it. The good news is that I was able to take an umbrella to the scoundrels for long enough for Purnah to escape. The bad news is that she did so, and nobody has the faintest idea where she has got to. Fortunately, I was able to give her money beforehand. The police haven't charged me with anything (I think they are embarrassed by how easily I overcame so many of them in combat) and have let me go. I admitted that I was a fraudulent medium called Hepzibah Foozleberry, knowing that no complaints will be lodged against that fictional personage.*
>
> *I will catch the next train to Scotland, and expect to see you tomorrow.*
>
> *I have sent word to Mr. Holmes about these events. I do hope that Purnah is all right and has not stabbed anyone. I worry so about her. Lucy Butterworth.*

Rab's brow furrowed in concern. Purnah should not to be let loose in the English countryside alone. It wasn't fair to the English countryside.

The second telegram was shorter, and much more to the point:

> *My dear Lal Singh; have received word from Mrs. Butterworth as to recent events. Most concerned re missing girl P. Meanwhile, brother Mycroft seeking to change policy of India Office toward P's status regarding That School. More news in due course. Holmes.*

Rubberbones thought through the cryptic words. The part about "brother Mycroft" confused the boy. He asked Lal Singh about it.

"Mr. Sherlock Holmes has an older brother of that name, young Rab. Although most unknown to the general public, Mr. Mycroft Holmes has a position of considerable importance in the British government. I assume that Mr. Mycroft Holmes will be persuading those in charge of the India Office that Princess Purnah ought not be returned to St. Grimelda's. He will perhaps mention the pterodactyls kept by that appalling school, and point out that almost no effort was made to teach the princess to speak the most rudimentary English in her four years there. I believe that he will suggest that Princess Purnah's best interests are being served by placement at Professor Bellbuckle's Academy for Gifted Asiatic Royalty."

"That's us, right?" asked Rab. "Indeed it is," confirmed Lal Singh.

"That'd be champion," said the boy. And, of course it would, if only it weren't for Purnah being lost somewhere in England. Rubberbones knew she would not ask for directions or even head in the right general direction. He thought there was a very good chance that Purnah would do something horribly ill-advised.

Purnah was about to do something horribly ill-advised. She did not realize this at the moment. She just thought she was doing something nice for her new friends. The day had begun with her awakening from a night spent shivering in a ditch by a railway line. Things had improved since then, and she could look forward to a cozy night in a barn full of hay, with a supper of bread and sardines from the knapsack of Harry Hawkes.

Most royal personages would not have considered that plan to be particularly regal, but a Chiligriti princess knew how to make do. Besides, it was much nicer than being at St. Grimelda's or — she privately admitted — the palace she had grown up in.

The barn was about a half-mile outside the little town of Pilkington-under-Hill. As they'd passed along the high street, Purnah had noticed a shop selling sweets. Now, as Harry settled down to sleep, with Maisie curled up around his head, the princess wondered if the shop was still open. She decided to buy presents for everyone. Chocolate, mostly. She pulled Harry's hat low on her head and snuck as silently as a Himalayan mountain goat out of the barn.

The shop was indeed open. It sold newspapers and groceries and the sorts of things you might need at any time. Purnah had been practicing her impersonation of an ordinary English voice, although it was mostly her idea of how Rubberbones spoke, and some odd sayings she'd picked up at St. Grimelda's.

"Oi say," she began, "Oi'll 'ave a jug o' cream fer me catlings, a jar o' fish paste and muchly choklitings! Trikk! Champion! Jolly hockeysticks!"

It was bizarre, but not at all bad by Purnah's standards. The shopkeeper, a fellow with a long-established frown, grunted. "You can pay for this, can you?"

"Of coursely I payish! Champion!" replied Purnah. "Let's see the money, then." The shopkeeper evidently did not trust an adolescent tramp to pay for his groceries.

Purnah pulled out her wad of banknotes. "Get me shoppings!" she snapped. The man eyed her with even more suspicion, but began to fill a bag with slabs of chocolate, a bottle of cream, chocolate biscuits, a jar of fish paste, chocolate cakes and every item in the shop that might conceivably contain chocolate. "Right," he announced. "That'll be seven shillings and fourpence." This was a great deal of money for anyone to spend on chocolate. It was almost a week's wages for the lady's maid that Purnah had begun the day by impersonating.

Purnah confidently offered a ten pound note. This was half a year's wages for that same lady's maid. The shopkeeper was torn between greed and his normal suspicious nature. The latter won out.

"Here, where did you get that?" he shouted, grabbing Purnah by the wrist and jerking her forward so hard that Harry's hat fell off.

Purnah responded in her traditional way. "Lemme go, big bullyish! Glekk! Porok!" she screamed, loud enough to deafen her assailant. But the shopkeeper tightened his grip and stared at her from close up. "You're that foreign princess they're looking for, ain't yer? There's a reward for turning you in." He nodded toward a bulletin board, where a "wanted" poster was tacked up among offers of bicycles for sale and requests for light housekeeping. It featured an artist's impression of a thin-faced girl with long dark hair who looked uncannily like Purnah.

"Just hold still and I'll call the constable," hissed the shopkeeper. "Don't think you are going anywhere, missy." Princess Purnah was afraid that she wasn't going anywhere, except to a police station. But, as a Chiligriti princess accustomed to regular threats of assassination, she was not about to accept her fate. Her left hand dug into the pocket of her coat, and she withdrew the knife made by the master blade-maker Sharposwishi the Toothless. Brandishing the dagger dramatically, she yelled once more, "Lemme go or I slits you gizzards like sacrificial monkey!" (Actually, monkeys are not sacrificed in Chiligrit. Purnah said that for effect. Sensitive readers should understand that, and not be upset. I'm sorry I mentioned it at all.)

The shopkeeper's mouth opened in stunned surprise, and he let go of Purnah's wrist. "Don't hurt me!" he whimpered. "Hah!" she replied. "Hah! Vishti Parukh nonnu hripp!" Then, pulling his necktie out from under his apron, Her Royal Majesty jerked the man's head toward the counter, and pinned the tie to the wooden surface with a firm jab of the dagger. "Forgettings you ever seed me!"

It was a good dagger, and she hated to lose it. Still, a man who is pinned to his own counter by a six-inch blade through his necktie is hardly likely to run for the police right away. Purnah decided that such a fine knife was payment enough for the bag of provisions, so she took back the ten pound note, grabbed the bag and sauntered out of the shop, humming a traditional love ballad that translated as "I Shall Bring Fine Yaks to Your Father to Prove My Love to You."

All the same, as soon as the shop door closed behind her, Purnah ran like the wind.

———

Samuel Soap had no idea where Princess Purnah was. But he thought it likely that she would go to Scotland, to the place called Urgghh. He'd found it on a map. That must also, surely, be where the Burns and Cayley youngsters could be found. If he could catch the girl and deliver her to the Collector, then he'd go to Urgghh himself and pose as "a friend" who could help find the missing princess. With a bit of luck, he could then snatch the other two kids and hand them over to the Collector. That'd be three rewards for one job. Very nice work, if he said so himself.

———

Emmaline couldn't believe that she'd been so stupid as not to recognize Queen Victoria. Who else would be traipsing around the Scottish highlands like that? Everyone knew that the queen loved the mountain landscapes and spent much of the year at her palace at Balmoral. The Indian man in her carriage was not, of course, Lal Singh, but a royal secretary known as the Munshi. The riders, with their military air and strict questions, were with the secret service.

Still, the really good thing was that the queen had ordered her attendants to provide a picnic hamper and a pile of blankets. Angus carried these easily as he strode across the moors, often far outpacing the girl. "Slow down!" called Emmaline. "We won't get there tonight, so there's no point in racing."

Angus was clearly prepared to walk all night. But he swiveled his brass head all the way round to address Emmaline. "As you wish, miss. There is a cottage ahead." The whirring noise that indicated he was analyzing his surroundings began. "Cottage — abandoned. Roof — fallen in. No human inhabitants. Sheep present in considerable numbers."

Ah, thought Emmaline. A ruined building inhabited by sheep. It was the perfect place to spend the night.

The Collector was forced to admit that, despite his best-laid plans to collect only the most promising scientists, he had somehow caught a Bellbuckle. This was not at all what he had planned. He considered what other collectors — enthusiasts for stamps, for instance — did when they found a specimen they had no use for. He understood that they swapped them with like-minded hobbyists, or sold them for what they could get. He shook his head. He could not imagine there was a market for an excess Professor Bellbuckle.

He'd also had a very pushy letter from that Wackett woman — the headmistress. She wanted to know why he hadn't delivered her lost princess yet. She suggested that his hirelings might not be trying very hard. He didn't like the woman, and he hated to admit that she might be right about his employees.

Foglamp brought the professor to the Collector's study. The American scientist looked dejected. He also looked as if he'd been fighting with a much larger, younger man, but that was misleading; he always looked that way.

"Good evening, Professor Bellbuckle," began the Collector. "Nothing good about it," the professor snapped back.

"Your dad-blamed owlhoots dry-gulched me and hogtied me and flung me in your hoosegow!"

The Collector looked blank. "I have no idea what you just said."

"I mean to say, that pair o' rascals ambushed me, tied me up and threw me in your jail."

"Oh, yes, of course. That was simply a misunderstanding," said the Collector.

"A misunderstandin'?" The professor was dumbstruck for a moment.

"Yes, indeed. I had instructed my employees to capture Miss Emmaline Cayley. I had not intended that they make you their prisoner," continued the Collector.

"You don't want me — an eminent pioneer in my field — for your goshdurn collection?" Professor Bellbuckle was now irate.

"No. I'll keep you for the moment, then arrange to have you released into the wild."

The professor stuck his chin out. "I won't have it, no sirree! When you have collected a Bellbuckle, a Bellbuckle you shall have! I insist upon my rights!"

The Collector was getting a headache. He gestured to Foglamp to return the prisoner to the dungeon, then summoned Titch and Hercules. He ordered them to set up a net at the edge of the loch before sunrise, or there would be trouble.

Titch and Hercules didn't want any more trouble from their spidery employer.

⊰ CHAPTER 26 ⊱

Flinging Dirt

Rubberbones was woken by the smell of breakfast. Lal Singh was up and dressed. Rab could not possibly imagine the Sikh butler in a nightgown and cap.

"I must go to Strathcarrot to greet Mrs. Butterworth as she arrives by the train. Alas, she was not clear as to the time of her arrival, so I must be prepared for her to take the 7:45, 12:27 or 15:04 from Glasgow. I marvel at the regularity of trains to this most underpopulated region of Great Britain. Truly we live in an era of high civilization!"

Rab wasn't sure he agreed with Lal Singh's assessment that regular train service was the highest point of human achievement, but he did recognize the man's ability with bacon, eggs and curried potatoes. Lal Singh went on. "You must remain here in case word comes from Her Royal Majesty, or Miss Emmaline and the professor."

Rubberbones was happy that Miss Aunt Lucy would arrive shortly. He'd help Dr. Smoot this morning, then he and Stanley would be ready for Aunt Lucy to get there. He might wash his face and everything. But for now, he was going to see what catapult tests were planned for today. The thing showed promise.

Rab was surprised when he reached Dr. Smoot's cottage to find a note on the door. "Meet us at the cliffs at the far end of the island," it said. That wasn't far for a lad with a good pair of legs for running and a dog who liked to chase. Fifteen minutes later Rubberbones, bounding over the rocks in pursuit of Stanley, reached the farthest tip of Urgghh. The catapult was set up. Doctors Smoot and Grockle stood beside it, along with Will, the sheeplike boy. They were looking out over the water toward the gray stone bulk of Invermisery House.

Dr. Grockle turned to greet Rab. "Glad you are here, my boy! Exciting news! I persuaded the people at Invermisery to set up a net. We can try the catapult safely today. I brought a padded costume for you, and that parachute- thingy made from this very nice flag of — where was it, Smoot? Paraguay? — anyway, it's all ready for you!"

Rubberbones was not expecting this at all. "Er, we've only tried a few shots with the catapult so far, wi' bags of dirt."

"Yes!! Fantastic results!" added Dr. Smoot.

"Right, yes," admitted Rab. "But we've not tried it out with a person at all. Not even to see if they — I — fit into the cradle."

Dr. Grockle brushed that aside. "We'll do that right now. No time like the present, is there?" The monkey, astride his master's shoulder, flicked a banana in agreement.

"But don't we need to know if the catapult can hit the net?"

"Ah, we've tried it with the sacks of dirt that young Will here has been kind enough to dig for us. Works jolly well, I'd say. Three out of five hits so far," said Dr. Grockle breezily.

Dr. Smoot nodded in agreement. "We'll try it again, so you can see!"

Dr. Grockle continued, "You know, it would be such an achievement for Smoot here. And we'd all love to get one over on Sneed and the secretary with their know-it-all ways, wouldn't we?"

Rubberbones thought about it. After all, he was the indestructible flying boy. And he really did want to score a point for Dr. Smoot over the sneering scientists. There remained a nagging doubt in his mind, but he ignored it.

"All right, then. But let's see the bags fly first. There's a boat ready if I land in the sea, in't there?"

"Of course there is, my boy," said Dr. Grockle, putting his arm around the lad. "What could possibly go wrong?"

The monkey made a noise that sounded like a hoot of derision.

Morning light streamed into the barn, and Purnah (who had spent the night burrowed deeply into the hay, to keep out cold and policemen) had woken to find Maisie rustling around in search of the jug of cream she could smell. Harry Hawkes was making tea. He listened to her account of the suspicious shopkeeper in silence before he spoke.

"You aren't going to like this," said Harry. "It might be against your dignity and traditions."

"What izz?" replied Purnah suspiciously.

"We'll have to disguise you properly. That means buying some new boys' clothes, and getting a boy's haircut. Do you mind getting your hair cut off?"

Purnah's dignity and traditions would be much more offended by being caught by the police than by getting her long hair shorn. "Is orlrightings," she muttered.

"And you can't wear ballet shoes."

"Glekk!" said Purnah. That bothered her more than a haircut.

They ate chocolate and fish paste for breakfast (although not together — Maisie ate the fish paste), then Harry pulled out his own knife and cut Purnah's hair to above the ears.

"It's a rough job," he said, "but you can't be seen out with your long hair. I know a barber and a tailor in this town; I've changed out of my tramp get-up here before."

They walked into town. Purnah wanted to duck between buildings and lurk in shadows, but Harry told her to act normally. Purnah had no idea what that meant. Maisie walked ahead in the apparent knowledge that nobody would look at a small boy with a bad haircut when there was a fine tortoiseshell cat to admire.

"Right! Here's the barber," said Harry when they came to a red-and-white striped pole outside a shop door. The good thing is that old Sam is half-blind, so there's no chance he'll recognize you as the missing princess. The bad thing is that Sam is half-blind, so he won't give you a very good haircut. But he's not cut anyone's ear off yet. At least, not that I've heard."

<hr />

Samuel Soap had studied his maps and realized two things. The first was that he could wait at Strathcarrot for the girl. It was a small station, and there was little chance of missing her in the crowd. The drawback was that the authorities might grow suspicious of a man hanging around. Perhaps he'd use a selection of disguises and swap them every couple of hours. That'd be an interesting challenge in itself. The second thing was that Urgghh was remarkably close to his employer's address at Invermisery House. Soap did not believe in coincidence. He wasn't sure what it all meant, but his fear was that, somehow, the Collector would lay hands on all three youngsters without Sam Soap getting the credit for their capture. By which, of course, he meant getting the reward.

Emmaline spent about as restful a night as anyone could expect in an abandoned cottage with most of its roof collapsed and a goodly number of sheep coming to see what she was up to. Even with the royal donation of blankets it was freezing cold. Still, Angus was the perfect companion in this situation. He prepared breakfast from the hamper — tea, sausages, fried and poached eggs, kedgeree, grilled tomatoes, bread rolls and a selection of fine jams and marmalades. It was clear that the queen did not go short while traveling. Her servants had included cups, plates, cutlery and a frying pan, as well as other necessities that a lady might need on a moor. Of course, the hamper weighed seventy pounds, and Emmaline could not pick it up herself.

The lavatorial facilities were nonexistent, of course, but Angus (ever the mechanical gentleman) had brought Emmaline a basin of hot water, a toothbrush and a bar of soap with the royal crest, "VR," embossed on it. He also steered the curious sheep away from the tumbledown wall where Emmaline went for privacy. That was nice of him.

And then they were off, striding across the hillside. Nochtermuckity was a few short miles away. They'd be at the island by afternoon at the latest. Everything would be fine. It wasn't even raining.

Titch and Hercules set up a very large net on the patch of sand facing the cliffs of Urgghh. Titch set it up, of course, while Hercules complained about the ingratitude of their employer (although not too loudly, of course). They'd gone to a lot of trouble to bring the Bellbuckle bloke in, and there was "nuffink" they could have done about the Cayley girl with her boat hook. She was a dangerous savage, that was what she was. Titch listened to this tirade in his usual silence.

Still, assuming that the Burns lad really did fly into the net, they'd have him captured good and proper. There was a rowboat available in case he landed in the sea; they'd fish him out if he did.

The first bags of dirt came flying over the water. Hercules ducked for cover, but Titch watched impassively as three of five landed safely in the net. One landed in the water, and the last one smashed against the rocks with a burst of dust and stones.

Well, thought Titch, good enough. All except that last effort.

⚔ CHAPTER 27 ⚔

Under the Flag of Paraguay

The costume fitted Rubberbones surprisingly well. Dr. Grockle had taken old clothes of his own, cut short the arms and legs and stuffed padding into the linings. There was a helmet that Rab suspected had once been a lady's corset, now filled out with socks. The effect was like an unconvincing fatman suit in a cheap theatrical production, but the boy could tell that it offered good protection. He might be a rubber boy, but he wasn't a complete idiot.

The parachute was indeed the flag of Paraguay. Rab didn't know much about parachutes, although he'd read that an American had used one to jump safely from a balloon over San Francisco a few years before. This one was attached to the suit by strong twine and was tucked into the collar of his jacket; he'd have to tug it out by hand at the right moment. That might be fiddly.

Stanley barked at him with enthusiasm for the costume. Doctors Smoot and Grockle applauded as well. Will looked at him shyly, and the monkey gibbered coarsely. It was time to try it out.

Rubberbones climbed into the cradle — "I call it the Flingerator," said Dr. Smoot — of the catapult. This was the spoonlike seat where the passenger began his flight across the Atlantic, or at least across the quarter-mile from the top of the cliff to the net. The steel cables that held the throwing arm back were tight. All that Dr. Smoot had to do was turn the catch that operated the clockwork release mechanism.

Which he did now.

"Good luck, Richard," he said. "Bon voyage!" boomed Dr. Grockle. "Woof!" added Stanley.

The monkey cackled, as if it was all hilarious fun.

Then the arm whipped forward and Rab was hurtling through the air, arms wrapped around his knees like a human ball.

The wind rushed against his face. Without goggles, he found it hard to see properly. He was traveling upward in a steep arc; then he leveled out and felt himself dropping. There! He saw the net, and two figures close by.

Rubberbones reached behind his head and tugged at the parachute. It unfurled behind him with a jerk as the strings tightened. He leaned forward and tried to judge his flight path. Was he too high to land in the net? He tugged at the parachute. Rab needed to change course fast, or he'd fly over the net and crash into the roof of Invermisery House. Rab pulled on the strings and stretched his legs out. He willed himself to turn downward. Slowly he mastered the parachute, aiming his feet toward the net. It was harder work than maneuvering the kites he was accustomed to.

Indeed, it was difficult enough that the boy didn't take any notice of the two men running to assist him.

Rubberbones landed softly, the parachute covering him. "That were champion!" he announced.

"Yeah, champion," agreed a voice.

Rab peered out from under the banner of Paraguay to see a tiny man and a giant. They were laughing, and not in a friendly way.

He'd met them before.

Purnah sat in the barber's chair while a very elderly man nearsightedly attacked her head with scissors. As Sam the barber snipped at her, Purnah felt that all the assassins in the royal palace of Chiligrit were no more dangerous than small children compared to this mad scissors wielder. Then he whipped out a comb and some smelly liquid, and suddenly

Purnah was staring at a neatly coiffed boy with his hair parted severely down the middle and plastered to his skull. The boy stared back.

"Eeky!" muttered Purnah. It was indeed a transformation. In the chair beside her, Harry Hawkes was becoming the Reverend H.D.F. Hawkes, vicar of St. Bogwell's-in-the-Marsh. His face was clean, his hair was trimmed and brushed and his beard was pruned, like an overgrown bush attacked by a determined gardener.

Maisie snoozed on a chair, because she was already perfect. "Right," said Harry. "Time for some decent clothes. There's a tailor I know who'll dress us both in the manner that will suit us best. "

An hour later the Reverend Hawkes, a fine, respectable example of a clergyman, sat in the waiting room at Pilkington-under-Hill railway station, tickets for Scotland in his hand. He was accompanied by a cat in a wicker basket and his nephew Algernon, a boy of perhaps ten or eleven, a casual observer might guess, in a pale blue sailor suit with a white collar and matching cap. The same observer might think that young Algy seemed a touch discontented, but that was probably because small boys get bored easily, and tend to fidget. Actually it was because Princess Purnah knew that, in her disguise as the Reverend's nephew, she looked more ridiculous than she had in her whole life.

Emmaline walked into Nochtermuckity at a quarter past one in the afternoon, Angus pacing away tirelessly alongside her under his load of blankets and a giant wicker hamper. She went into the first shop she came to.

"Please," she began, "can you tell me how to get to Urgghh?"

"Aye," replied the shopkeeper, sizing her up. "Ye'll have to take a boat doon at the wharf. Ye might look for old McGinnis. It's his boat. And it's his island."

Emmaline thanked him. He sniffed, evidently feeling that she ought to buy something to repay him for his assistance. Emmaline, however, did not feel like buying a pound of liver (it was a butcher's shop), and left to rejoin the mechanical man outside.

"To the wharf," she told him as she headed toward the loch. "To find someone called McGinnis."

The first person Emmaline met when she reached the jetty was a motherly woman who projected kindness and efficiency. "Excuse me," said Emmaline. "I am looking for a Mr. McGinnis. I need to get over to the island to meet my aunt."

"Ach, so," replied the woman in a surprising German accent. "I am Frau McGinnis. The vife of the McGinnis. And you must be — not zer princess, no." She clapped her hands. "You must be Emmaline!" She seemed unsurprised at the automaton's presence.

Emmaline stared at her. How did this stranger know who she was? Surely she wasn't another agent for the Collector? Fear welled up in the girl.

"It is Lal Singh who tells me you are coming. You and your aunt and this princess and a scientific gent from the United States. He asks me to vatch for you while he conducts his business elsewhere. But — look at you! You need a bath and a hot meal. Come vith me to the hotel and all vill be in order right away!"

"I really want to get over to the island. My friend Robert — Rab — must be there," persisted Emmaline.

"In correct order, my dear. As you vill note, there is no boat at present, for the McGinnis is off doing errands in it. He will return at 2:45 sharp, so I have instructed him. Meanwhile, you and your metal friend need a proper luncheon."

"Just some oil," said Angus.

"Ach, so."

The Collector watched from the window, almost beside himself with joy as he peered through the telescope. The Burns boy was coming right to him, actually flying in like a bluebottle toward a web. And, aside from the thrill of the capture, the Collector could enjoy the sight of young Master Burns as he maneuvered the parachute, with elegance and grace, into the net.

The Collector rubbed his hands in anticipation of his new addition's arrival. His black eyes glinted.

CHAPTER 28

The New Specimen

Rubberbones couldn't believe what was happening. The two unpleasant characters he'd encountered at Strathcarrot station were pulling him out of the net. They weren't gentle about it, either. The little one chortled while his massive colleague hoisted Rab up and out of the netting and flung him over his huge shoulder.

"Straight to the boss," said the smaller man. "Wants to see his new specimen right away."

Rubberbones found himself unable to escape the giant's grip as they passed through a narrow door cut into the gray wall of Invermisery House, along a succession of hallways and up several flights of stairs. They were met by a fussy- looking man who ushered them into a study. The big man flipped Rab upright, keeping an iron grip upon his shoulder. He faced a strange old fellow who somehow gave the impression of an oversized spider. It was something to do with his long arms and legs. The man was uncannily frightening for someone so obviously ancient.

The man twined and untwined his hands as he peered at Rab. Then he spoke.

"Young Master Burns, I presume? I thank you for joining us here. I expect that you will be an asset to my Collection. You are a remarkable young man."

"You what?" replied Rubberbones. What was the man talking about?

The Collector explained all about his hobby. Rab didn't like the sound of it at all. And he had no idea why this strange man considered him to be some sort of scientist. He was just a lad who could fly a bit.

"You can share a cage with Professor Bellbuckle." Rubberbones didn't want to share a cage with anyone, and the news that his friend Bellbuckle had been captured was no comfort, either.

"I have one question. Now that I have added you to my Collection, I would like very much to pair you with your female friend, Miss Cayley. When can I expect her to come my way, do you know?"

Rab knew that in his "penny dreadful" stories, the gallant hero would grit his teeth and say something about not giving away a lady. Or he'd laugh in the villain's face. But the boy wasn't very good at off-the-cuff witty retorts, and his attempts at lying were always disastrous failures, leaving him red-faced and stuttering. So he simply told the truth.

"I don't know."

———

Purnah sat with her back to the engine as the train steamed northward. She was still scowling about Harry's choice of clothing for her.

"Why is picking this sailor-man suitings?" demanded the princess. "Why not bigling-boy robes?"

"Clothes, not robes, Purnah."

"Whichlingever. I lookish like tiny childlings. Hripp!" She was not at all happy. The boy's haircut was understandable.

She accepted the loss of her ballet shoes. But the shop had had racks of boys' clothes cut like adults' that would fit her. Anything was better than a sailor suit in pale blue.

"I regret the necessity, my dear," said Harry. "But the object is to make you look as different as possible from the princess on the posters. So, instead of a long-haired girl of, what, thirteen, I think you told me, we have a short-haired boy who looks about ten."

Purnah thought about it. She was slender and not especially tall. In these clothes she did look younger. Harry was right all along. Maisie climbed into her lap and began to purr, as if to agree.

She decided it was fine to be in all these disguisings, looking like an imbecile. Purnah was so pleased that she almost started singing a favorite ditty, "I Can Hit Your Grandmother with a Rock from Here." But then she remembered that small English boys in sailor suits do not sing popular Chiligriti folk songs.

Harry — the Reverend Hawkes — grinned at her. Purnah decided that when she regained her throne she would ask Harry to become her Minister of Sneakiness.

At precisely 2:45, a short, stout figure appeared at the Nochtermuckity Station Hotel. "Good afternoon, my dear," he said to Mrs. McGinnis. "I'm done wi' all the little tasks ye set me."

Emmaline understood that this must be the McGinnis himself.

"Hello, Vilhelm. Ve are about to escort young Miss Cayley here to the island. She is the girl that nice Lal Singh spoke of. Her aunt is due to arrive later this day."

The McGinnis grunted but in what Emmaline took as a friendly way. He looked at Angus but — being accustomed to mad science on a daily basis — did not comment.

The boat ride across the loch from Nochtermuckity took a few minutes. At the single stone dock that served as Urgghh's harbor stood a small animal. He was keening in a voice of deep doggy sorrow and loss. "That's Stanley!" exclaimed Emmaline, trying to shout over the clatter of the boat's engine. "Where's Rab?"

As the McGinnis cut the motor and drifted up to the pier, Emmaline scrambled out of the boat. "Stanley! Where is he?"
"The boy is probably with Dr. Smoot," said Mrs. McGinnis.

"He has been assisting him with a project of some sort."
"Dr. Smoot?" said Emmaline. The name, of course, meant nothing to her.

"One of our scientific gentlemen. His cottage is just over there."

Dr. Smoot was at home. Mrs. McGinnis rapped once and pushed open the door. Emmaline, following her into the little house, saw a man poring over a jumble of blueprints. His home looked exactly like Professor Bellbuckle's former residence, although without the arsenal of explosives.

"Dr. Smoot," said Mrs. McGinnis. "This young lady is looking for young Robert. Is he vith you today?"

The inventor looked about him in clear confusion. He walked over to a pile of wooden planking and peered beneath it. "No, it seems he isn't."

"Have you seen him today?" asked Emmaline.

The scientist appeared baffled. "Today? No, I don't think so."

Stanley sat at Emmaline's feet and howled.

"There, my dear," said Mrs. McGinnis. "He's probably at your own cottage."

They checked. He wasn't. The cottage was empty. Stanley was yipping and barking like a mad thing. "What are you saying, boy?" asked Emmaline.

The dog gazed at her intently and ran off across the island.

Emmaline followed as fast as she could, with Angus alongside her and Mr. and Mrs. McGinnis trundling along behind them. Stanley periodically turned and looked meaningfully back at them, urging them to follow swiftly.

He trotted to the edge of a cliff.

"What's he doing?" asked Emmaline. "Be careful, you silly dog!" The last thing she wanted was for Stanley to plunge a hundred feet into the loch.

But Stanley had no such thing in mind. He stood and pawed at the ground, whimpering softly.

At first, Emmaline could not understand. Then she spotted two sets of marks gouged into the damp soil. Two straight lines indented in the ground, like the runners on an over- sized sled. But these were not sled marks, because there was no sign of movement. Something had sat in this place, making these marks. But what was it?

.⚒ CHAPTER 29 ⚒.

The Dungeon of Invention

"Robert, my boy!" exclaimed Professor Bellbuckle. "I'm so glad to see you here!" Then he corrected himself. "Not actually here here, you understand."

The giant had flung Rab into the dungeon with more force than was absolutely necessary, the little man encouraging him with a shout of, "Go on, Titch! Toss the blighter in!" The boy bounced down the stone steps, landing among a heap of assorted scientific equipment. "Er, hello, Professor," he replied. "I've gone and got myself captured, too."

Several scientists looked up from their research and — seeing nothing but a new arrival — continued with their studies. Professor Bellbuckle, however, ran and pulled Rubberbones to his feet. The boy wasn't hurt, of course.

"Let me show you around," said the professor. "It's quite impressive. For a prison, I mean."

The dungeon had been hewn out of stone; Rab could tell that it was very old. There was a succession of caverns, roughly shaped into large chambers. Green mold spread across the ancient rock. The steps were worn and uneven. The great chambers were divided by wooden screens. Some of the

rooms were studies or storerooms, one a library. The bigger chambers were large laboratories, clanking with machinery or reeking of chemicals. The worst-smelling cavern, however, was the refectory.

"That's where we all eat," said the professor. "The food is terrible. I don't think these fellas notice, though. You'd be surprised how these science boys get distracted from what's going on."

Rab thought that anyone Professor Bellbuckle thought distracted must really be disconnected from reality.

Most of the dungeon was lit by a system of electrical bulbs, according to Mr. Thomas Edison's method. The chemistry lab, however, had a skylight. Night had fallen, so there was no circle of sunlight playing on the floor. Rubberbones walked over and stood underneath it. Looking up, he saw a chimney slicing through the rock, the opening broader than his outstretched arms. There was a window frame of tiny panes at the top of the shaft, silhouetted by the faint moonlight. The boy pointed this out to Professor Bellbuckle.

"Probably there to keep the rain out," said the professor. "Stops stray livestock falling down as well, I guess."

Rab looked at the chimney carefully. How far up was it? Could he climb it?

———

It was past dark when the train reached Glasgow. Purnah, with Maisie curled up on her lap, had enjoyed the journey. Harry had asked her many questions about life in Chiligrit, and especially about the traditional beliefs of Chiligriti religion. Purnah told him tales of the many gods and goddesses and how they played tricks on one another. Eejit, the God of Stupidity, for instance, had spent many thou- sands of eons (or, at least, all weekend) with a heavy stone inscribed "Thou may'st kick me" attached to his back. Many practical jokes involving powerful glue were employed by the deities of her homeland. They appreciated the humor inherent in flatulence as well.

It was too late to proceed on to Nochtermuckity. "The early train to Strathcarrot is after breakfast tomorrow," said Harry Hawkes. "But no barns full of hay for us tonight! We are dressed as respectable people, so we must stay at a hotel."

While Harry made arrangements, Purnah sat with Maisie on a bench next to the ticket office. She was beginning to nod off when she heard a voice she recognized. No, two voices.

"Look, Mr. Botts. If you hadn't taken so long to get here, we'd have been at Urgghh already." It sounded like that horrible detective, Inspector Pike.

Purnah pulled Maisie up closer to her face, so that she might seem to be rubbing noses with the cat. She peered around Maisie's ears. It was Pike, the angry policeman with the shiny bald skull. With him was Mr. Botts, the foolish man from the India Office. They must not see her!

"I've arranged a private train as far as Strathcarrot, Inspector," replied the bureaucrat in his fussy little voice. "And accommodation there. We shall have to take the first train to Nochtermuckity in the morning. Of course, the princess might not be there."

The inspector grunted in disgust. "The Butterworth woman sent a telegram there. We had to get a magistrate's order before the post-office fella would show it us. No, my detective's nose tells me that's where we'll find the foreign girl. I'd bet a sovereign on it."

Purnah peeked again — Maisie didn't wriggle or complain — and watched the two men walk away.

———

Emmaline had stared at the marks in the soil for a long time. They meant nothing to her. Angus had no ideas, while the McGinnis and his wife argued as to whether the traces matched an old picnic table that Mrs. McGinnis remembered one of the scientific gents had once owned. Darkness had fallen as they discussed.

They walked disconsolately back toward the quay. Mrs. McGinnis was extremely concerned and suggested they talk to the secretary at the clubhouse. "I shall ask him vat he knows," she announced. Her eyes narrowed, and Emmaline thought that she looked formidable, like Queen Victoria herself. "I shall hold him responsible if anything has happened to the boy."

When they reached the society's building, Emmaline asked Angus to stay outside; she knew that the arrival of the metal man would excite the scientists enormously, and there was no time for that. It was a time when straight answers about Rab were needed. They found the secretary playing cribbage with his friends Sneed and Grockle. Mrs. McGinnis wasted no time on small talk. "The boy known as Robert is missing. Has anyone seen him today?"

"No, dear lady," replied Mr. Secretary. "Not at all."

Sneed shook his head. "Busy with research all day!" This was only true if playing cards counted as a valuable mathematical exercise.

Dr. Grockle was more helpful. "Not seen him myself. He was helping Smoot all day yesterday." The monkey nodded in agreement and checked under his arm for a tasty flea.

"We've spoken to Dr. Smoot," Emmaline chimed in. "He says he hasn't seen Rab recently."

"Well, then," said Dr. Sneed. "The boy's probably wandered off onto the Cuillin somewhere. He'll be back. Probably he didn't notice the time. And it's slow walking in the dark. After all, he doesn't want to fall off a cliff."

"Fall off a cliff!" exclaimed Emmaline.

"I'm sure he's done nothing of the sort!" said Mrs. McGinnis.

"Naebody's fallen to their death in almost a year," muttered Mr. McGinnis. "And he who fell was drunk. Yon Rab's no' a drinker, is he?"

At that moment the door opened, and Lal Singh ushered Aunt Lucy inside. "I'm sorry I'm late, Emmaline!" she said. "I've impersonated a medium, been questioned by the police and lost the princess. But aside from that —"

She noticed the grim mood in the room. "What's happened?"

The Collector was happy. The Burns boy had fallen nicely into his trap. Never before had he been able to get a subject of his interest to actually fly into the web. He thought about his reply to that annoying Wackett woman at her appalling school. He looked forward to telling her that he couldn't help her with her missing princess after all.

CHAPTER 30

"No Escapes Are Permitted!"

Rubberbones was happy to discover that he didn't really have to sleep in a cage. It was a cell with bunks, a rail for clothes and a nightstand. Professor Bellbuckle was his roommate, since they were neighbors alphabetically. Rab could usually sleep well through any tribulation — he'd once slept in a coffin on top of a coach — and did so now. Kidnapping was no reason to miss a good night's kip.

He was ready for breakfast as well. There was no point in starving just because he'd been imprisoned. Professor Bellbuckle accompanied him to the refectory, where a surly woman served him a bowl of lumpy porridge, followed by burnt sausages and runny eggs swimming in grease. Rubberbones cleaned his plate and returned for seconds.

The other scientists noticed this, at least. None of them had ever asked for more. The oldest, as senior among them, made the introductions. He seemed pompous.

"I am Aronnax," he said. "I was with Captain Nemo in the Nautilus. You may 'ave 'eard of me." Rab recognized the name of the French scientist who had journeyed around the world under the sea. "This is mon ami, Lidenbrock, who traversed the caverns under the earth." He gestured to another elderly man. "And here is Mr. Summerlee, Professor of Comparative Anatomy, and also the famous Tesla. Mr. Tesla is an electrical inventor, as is well known, but we do not permit him to do anything dangerous. That is why he appears so sad, for all that he ever does is dangerous. We do not approve of 'is wild tricks with lightning bolts." Aronnax almost spat.

Rubberbones could tell that Tesla, whom he'd read about, was miserable. A dark, thin man with an intense face, Nikola Tesla was wasting away in the dungeon.

"How long 'as Mr. Tesla been 'ere?" asked Rubberbones. "Zey 'ave kidnapped 'im after the World's Fair in Chicago," said Aronnax.

Summerlee added, "Apparently his friends don't know he's missing. They think he's just preoccupied with a project and keep leaving sandwiches outside his laboratory door in case he gets hungry."

Tesla slumped in his chair.

Aronnax continued, "A cette table, là, sont the deranged astronomer Mizzarbeau and his friend Monsieur Synthesis — quite insane, you know, the both, tsk tsk. Over there is the brain expert, Freud, who will no doubt ask you about your dear mama; we do not know why. That man there is the occult science man, Van Helsing." Aronnax sniffed in disapproval. "There is old Wadley of the Zoological Institute, and Cavor, who 'as joined us most recently. The fellow sitting there does not give 'is name. He says 'ee 'as a time machine." Rab could tell from the way that Professor Aronnax said it that he wasn't convinced. The man without a name waved coolly.

"My name is Robert Burns," said Rubberbones. He said it carefully, and without his mouth full. "I can fly a bit."

"Pah! What is zis 'fly a beet'? You are not a proper scientist. You are a boy 'oo make outrageous claims!" Aronnax stuck his nose in the air. "I will 'ave none of eet."

Rab thought the old scientist was quite rude, but he had other things on his mind than whether he could fly or not. "I want to escape," he said flatly.

There was a good deal of laughing at that.

"We all said that for the first week or so," said Mr. Summerlee. "But it can't be done. We've all come to accept it. Our captors provide very good research facilities, and — let's face it — most of us spent all our time in the outside world inside our laboratories."

"I want to escape," squeaked Professor Cavor. "I very much want to go home."

"Yes," replied Summerlee. "But you've only been here a week. You'll get used to it."

"We will not tolerate zis 'escape' idea!" snapped Aronnax. "We 'ave it vairy comfort-able ici. No escapes are permitted! Any attempts at the runnings away may bring punishments upon us all. Non, you will not be permitted to endanger our quite civilized captivity with any stupid escapes!"

Purnah slept nervously, with Maisie on her pillow. She had hoped that she had seen the last of Inspector Pike and Mr. Botts, but now they had suddenly reappeared on her trail. In fact, they were now ahead of her. She could not fathom how this had happened. Was it magic?

Harry Hawkes told her it wasn't. "I don't know how they know where you are going, but at least we've spotted them, and they haven't seen us. So we must decide what to do next. If you want to go on to Urgghh to meet your people, we'll do that. If you want to go somewhere else, we can do that instead. You could pretend to be my nephew and stay with

Maisie and me at St. Bogwell's vicarage if you like, although you'd have to dress like that every day."

Purnah thought about that. At thirteen she was thin and small and could pass as a young boy. It seemed unlikely that she could get away with that at sixteen or seventeen. Besides, she missed her friends, and the costume was humiliating. "No, we goings onwardish! Rukh!"

"I think that's the best choice, my dear. Tackle the trouble head on!" said Harry. He began to sing a hymn about facing life's travails, but Purnah wasn't in the mood to join in. She was silent throughout the journey to Strathcarrot. Two hours later they were waiting for their connecting train to Nochtermuckity. Harry was certain that (unless Inspector Pike and Mr. Botts had overslept horribly) they would have gone on ahead already. He assured Purnah that her disguise was good enough to fool anyone, but she was unsure. The princess was well aware how easily she could give herself away. She needed to be more cunningish. Her temper led her into trouble.

She sat on a bench, Maisie purring on her lap. Yet Purnah was as alert as the golden gazelle of the Hooty Hoot Hills. She watched. She listened. She noticed a man dressed in the uniform of a railway worker and pushing a broom. An hour later, she saw a man she'd have sworn was the same person, but older and with one leg missing, lurking beside the departures board. She scowled at him, and he stepped behind a pile of luggage.

The two were probably related, thought Purnah. But neither one of them looked like policemen with the big tackety boots she knew well.

The train arrived, and the clergyman, his nephew and his cat all got on.

Samuel Soap had spent the night at Strathcarrot's only hotel, planning to be at the station to meet the first train of the day. However, as he sat down for breakfast at 6:30 sharp, he was shocked to see his old enemy, Pike, across the dining room. The policeman was facing away from him, sharing a table with a tall, weedy-looking man who did not look like a detective. Soap finished his breakfast swiftly, a newspaper held up like a shield between himself and Inspector Pike. He crept out and slipped from the building. He hadn't been spotted. Still, seeing his adver- sary startled him badly. He watched from across the street until Pike and the other man left the hotel, each with a suitcase, and headed for the station.

Soap knew they must be after Princess Purnah. He followed the two men at a distance and observed them taking the early train to Nochtermuckity. He considered sneaking onto the rear carriage himself, but instead decided to keep to his original plan. He'd look out for trains coming in and people transferring to the Nochtermuckity line. So he spent the morning lurking around the station, changing his disguise, and watching for the girl to arrive. But the only people to catch the Nochtermuckity train were two old ladies who chatted in Gaelic, a country doctor and his dog, and a clergyman with a small boy and a cat. The small boy stared at him once before getting aboard.

Then it hit him. Samuel Soap, the master of disguise, had been spotted by the small boy. Except that it wasn't a small boy at all. In fury he tried to kick a wastepaper bin, but put his foot through it and had to call the porter to free his leg from the remains of the broken receptacle. "Very careless of you, sir. That will be seven shillings and ninepence to replace it, thank you very much. No; we don't accept checks."

It was another four hours before the next train to Nochtermuckity.

It had been an unhappy night at the cottage. There was no sign of Rubberbones. Aunt Lucy wept, Stanley howled and Emmaline could barely keep her fears from overwhelming her. Even Lal Singh appeared glum as he served breakfast. Angus jerked along mechanically behind him, rattling the tea tray. Surely, thought Emmaline, her friend had not fallen from a cliff? Or was he lost on a rocky hillside? Unthinkable! And yet, he wasn't here, and there was nowhere else he could be.

Emmaline broke the news about Professor Bellbuckle to Aunt Lucy. She took it well. "Dear Ozymandias! I'm sure he'll be all right. He's had a lot of experience being imprisoned, you know." She looked up at Angus as he poured tea in and around her cup. "Nice young man you've brought along. Very helpful." Emmaline considered saying something about Angus being an automaton, but if her aunt hadn't noticed yet, no doubt she would later.

They gathered early to decide on a plan. Mr. and Mrs. McGinnis appeared, bearing food to feed a hundred. "Ve vill search the whole island," declared Mrs. McGinnis. "And ask everyone here."

"We've done that, my dear," said the McGinnis. "Ve'll do it again," snapped his wife. He shut up.

By eight o'clock the entire population of Urgghh had gathered, as ordered by the formidable German hausfrau. By eleven they had scoured the island, twice. Rab was not on it. The scientists were no use whatsoever since (now that they had been introduced to Angus) all they could do was jabber about the possibilities of metal servants. It was all Angus could do to stop them dismantling him on the spot. "We should interview everyone," said Emmaline. "And compare what they say." She thought this was what Mr.

Sherlock Holmes would do.

"We've done that," replied Aunt Lucy.

"Not one at a time," said the girl. "That's the important part."

The secretary was happy to let them use the society clubhouse for interrogation. He volunteered to go first. He knew nothing useful.

Mrs. McGinnis ushered the suspects (as Aunt Lucy insisted on calling them, which Emmaline thought was a bit rude) into a back room and stood guard to ensure that none of those waiting in the main room had a chance to put their ear to the wall.

Emmaline asked questions, such as "When did you last see Rab?" and "Do you have any idea where he might have gone?"

Aunt Lucy alternately glared at the interviewees and asked questions designed to trip them up, like, "Where exactly were you at the moment when Rab vanished?"

Lal Singh stood silently. Stanley whimpered disconsolately. Angus used his analytic skills to process each interviewee, but it seemed that McVasilieff's programming was better suited to identifying people who were about to attack with cudgels rather than those who told subtle lies.

Dr. Sneed thought he'd seen the lad with Dr. Smoot. Two days ago.

Dr. Grockle maintained his theory that Rubberbones had fallen off a cliff. "Poor kid!" His monkey chattered in agreement.

Dr. Smoot was extremely vague about everything, including where he was and why people were asking him questions.

"That's all, then?" asked Aunt Lucy.

Lal Singh thought for a moment. "No. There is a boy who performs simple tasks. He is a quiet youth, and I suspect that his presence here is disregarded by most."

The McGinnis knew where the boy could be found and went to fetch him.

Will was clearly scared to be brought before an interrogation. Emmaline looked at the boy. There was something odd about him. Still, his memory was as good as anyone's — certainly better than Dr. Smoot's.

Aunt Lucy could tell that the boy was shy, and did not try to trick him into a confession. Instead, she offered him some cake. Gradually, he seemed to open up.

"Do you remember another boy who was here on the island?" asked Aunt Lucy.

He nodded that he did.

"Do you know what happened to him?" Again, he nodded.

"Please tell us what happened." Aunt Lucy's voice was soft and grandmotherly. Emmaline hoped that the boy would talk. Indeed, could talk. And he could.

"He flew in Dr. Smoot's catapult. He went over the cliff."

"Get Dr. Smoot in here!" snapped Aunt Lucy.

Mrs. McGinnis stomped out of the building and returned in a minute, almost dragging the hapless inventor. "You vill tell vot you know!" she hissed.

The man appeared shaken by her force. "What?" he pleaded. "What do you want from me?"

Emmaline pointed at Will, who sat terrified. "This lad says that Rab went flying from your catapult."

Dr. Smoot had the glazed expression of a stuffed buffalo. "What? The catapult? My catapult? Well, that was ages ago. It was, ah, what day is it? Erm. Yesterday."

"Let me get this right," said Mrs. McGinnis in a voice that could have cracked granite. "You sent this boy flying off a cliff yesterday?"

"That's right!" replied Dr. Smoot, as if he had suddenly remembered a vivid dream. "Right off the cliff into the net outside Invermisery House. Just as Grockle arranged! Excellent piece of work!" Then he paused thoughtfully. "Yesterday. Hmm. Seems like much longer. No, I haven't seen the boy since then."

Mrs. McGinnis shouted through the wall, "Vilhelm! Don't let Dr. Grockle go anywhere!"

Her husband stuck his head through the doorway. "I'm sorry, my dear. He gang oot a few minutes ago. He was in a right hurry. He left his monkey here!"

The monkey perched on a chair, chattering to himself.

⊲ CHAPTER 31 ⊳

Dr. Grockle Runs Away

Rubberbones looked up at the skylight. It was, as he'd thought, a natural fissure in the rock that brought a shaft of daylight into the cavern. The chimney was perhaps forty feet up. For the first twenty it was wider than the boy was tall, and the sides were worn smooth; probably water had sluiced through the opening for eons before anyone closed off the upper opening with the window.

"You'll never get up there," said Professor Cavor from behind him. "I've been looking at it for the last week. The rock is too smooth to climb."

Rab turned around to look at the speaker. The squeaker, actually. Professor Cavor had the smallest, highest voice he'd ever heard from a grown man.

"We could make a ladder," suggested the lad.

Professor Cavor shook his head. "I've looked for material. I could rip apart the furniture and save the nails to assemble it all in a rickety sort of staircase, but nobody wants to help, and the people upstairs — the midget and the ogre — come down to make sure we don't misbehave."

Professor Bellbuckle came to look. "Why, we could pack the chimney with gunpowder and blow the whole thing in. It'd be spectacular."

Professor Cavor looked at him as if he was a lunatic; Rab had seen that expression before. "You'll bury us under a hundred tons of rubble!" he squeaked.

The American inventor nodded, as if this was an unfortunate side effect that might be overcome with a little thought. "We could put saucepans on our heads," he replied. "And hide under the lab tables."

Even Rubberbones knew that this was a scheme too mad to consider. He let his mind range around things they could make in the laboratory. The professor could, of course, make something dangerous and explosive out of almost anything. Trying it out in a way that didn't involve crippling injury to the user was the hard part.

"What is it that you do, Professor Cavor?" he asked.

"I have invented an alloy that counters the effect of gravity," answered Cavor. "But it's difficult to make in any but the smallest quantities. I had planned to build a ship to travel to the moon, but that would demand far more than I could make."

"But they've provided you with materials to make some?" asked Rubberbones.

"A little. Enough to perhaps make a chair float in the air." Professor Cavor gestured dismissively.

"Enough to make me float in the air?"

Cavor heard a noise behind him and raised his finger for silence. Professors Aronnax and Lidenbrock walked by, the former glaring at the new arrivals as if to forbid them to escape.

"Why are they so dead set on stopping us from escaping?" asked Rubberbones.

"As far as I can tell," replied Cavor, "it's because of

that fellow who talks about a time-travel device. Titch and Hercules brought his machine down here so the chap could develop it further, but the time-traveler decided to go back twenty years to tackle the Collector when he — the Collector, not the time-traveler, you understand — first bought the house."

"That's brilliant!" declared Rab. "So the old man would never build these dungeons!"

"Yes, but the scheme failed when the time machine arrived a year too early and the traveler was trapped in the caverns before anyone had built the steps down from the house. He almost starved before he was able to return to our time. The Collector's men noticed his absence and ordered everyone's experiments to be confiscated for a month. And no ginger biscuits, either! So Aronnax and Lidenbrock forbade any more escape attempts."

"We'll have to make sure they don't find out what we're doing, then!" whispered Professor Bellbuckle. It was lucky that he kept his voice down, because Dr. Wadley walked by, chatting with Van Helsing about the habits of vampires. Rab shook his head, because he wouldn't have collected any of these lunatics.

————◦◦◦————

Purnah and Harry had devised two plans as they approached Nochtermuckity. If Inspector Pike and Mr. Botts had come and gone home again (as might be hoped), they'd go straight to the island. If the policeman and the bureaucrat were still pursuing their inquiries, they'd act like winter tourists, staying at a hotel until the coast was clear.

Purnah assumed that Pike would be sneaky and cunningish himself (she dismissed Botts as an "idiotical bakrishnashtik"). She would not make any mistakes. She remembered an old Chiligriti proverb, "Do not follow the snow tiger into his cave just to stick your tongue out at him." That would not do. She had not come so far, in such a stupid outfit, to be captured by Inspector Pike.

They got off the train and were almost knocked down by a wild-haired man in a lab coat running to catch it as it steamed back toward Strathcarrot.

"Rude man!" said Harry Hawkes.

"Mad scientist!" replied the man who took the tickets. "Dr. Grockle. Loonies, the lot of them." As if that explained it.

Purnah's stomach was filled with butterflies as she stepped out of the railway station. She liked that British expression; in her country it was termites instead.

"Straighten up, Algy!" commanded Harry in his best clergyman-uncle manner. "Let us stroll toward the loch and take the air." Purnah scowled, but remembered her role and followed meekly.

As they approached the wharf, she spotted her two enemies arguing by a rowboat. She'd hoped that, with their head start, they'd have gone to the island and returned empty-handed by now. It was clearly Botts's fault. She could hear them quarreling.

"Look, if we wait for this McGinnis to fetch us in his steam launch we'll be here all day. It's been hours and there's no sign of him. Let's just borrow this boat. It's police business, after all." Inspector Pike was not a patient man.

"But it isn't our boat, Inspector. If we take it we are no better than those scallywags who stole my cousin's motor car. Besides, I might get splashed."

Purnah smiled to herself as she watched the detective manhandle Mr. Botts into the rowboat and clamber into it himself, splashing water over both of them.

"We waitlings here!" she declared.

"Yes, let's go and find a nice cup of tea," replied Harry.

"And cream cakes!"

Maisie mewed in agreement. They'd let Pike and Botts go and search for Purnah on the island, while the vicar, his cat and his nephew took afternoon tea.

———————

"I shall throttle that Grockle!" announced Mrs. McGinnis as they all ran down to the wharf.

Luckily for Grockle, he was nowhere to be seen. Emmaline looked down toward the jetty where a man wearing a postman's cap was tying up a rowboat.

"Afternoon!" he called out. "Telegram for a Lal Singh or Mrs. Butterworth!"

"Postman!" announced Angus, using his amazing powers. "Did ye see yon Dr. Grockle go this way?" demanded the McGinnis. "Ye know the fellow — one o' thae science gents."

"Oh, aye. He was in a boot an' rowing like a maniac!" replied the postman.

"Which way?" asked Emmaline.

"Toward Nochtermuckity. There's a train due aboot noo." "So he hasnae made for Invermisery House," said the McGinnis.

"What's Invermisery?" asked Emmaline.

"It is a house on the far side of the sea-loch," said Mrs. McGinnis. "It faces the island. The owner is — vot is the vord? — 'reclusive.' He has nothing to do with anyone. I do not even know his name."

"So according to Dr. Smoot," Emmaline mused, "Rab flew off the cliff and landed in a net at Invermisery House. And Dr. Grockle arranged it, somehow. Does this make any sort of sense?"

"Well," said Aunt Lucy. "We'll just have to go and ask for him back."

Emmaline instinctively knew that there was more to it than that. Rab was being held prisoner. Just as Professor Bellbuckle was a captive. Someone wanted to kidnap her. These things must fit together. Somebody wanted to possess all three of them. No, that was wrong. Professor Bellbuckle was not the intended victim. He'd just got himself captured accidentally, in his own deranged fashion. Someone wanted to seize Emmaline herself, and Rubberbones.

Her thoughts were interrupted by a voice from the water. "You! Someone! Help us with this boat!" She looked over to see two men trying to maneuver a boat up to the jetty.

The one who spoke was a fierce-looking man with a bald head. His companion was — oh no! It was Winthrop Botts of the India Office, last seen being thumped with an umbrella at Aunt Lucy's house.

The Collector was musing on his good fortune. He had sent a telegram to the Wackett woman expressing, in curt language, that he had no further interest in finding the eastern princess. He enjoyed these little acts of cruelty. He imagined how she would react and wished he could see it. Then he spent a few minutes deciding whether he could reasonably billet Miss Cayley — when he caught her — with the Burns lad or with Professor Cavor. Probably decency demanded that he give her the lone single room at the end of the corridor, but he disliked anything that changed the alphabetical symmetry of his collection.

≈ CHAPTER 32 ≈

The Amazing Cavorite

The three conspirators were huddled in a corner, discussing a way to experiment with the Cavorite. Rubberbones came up with the idea that if he had enough to lift his body weight, it might be possible to float up the chimney, open the skylight and escape.

Professor Cavor looked at the boy as if he was a genius. Or a complete lunatic. Rubberbones couldn't tell which. "Right," said Cavor. "I have the Cavorite in my room. My captors were kind enough to break into my laboratory the day of my abduction."

"That was thoughtful," agreed Professor Bellbuckle. "After all, it's not as if you'd be carrying any in your pockets."

No, thought Rab, otherwise Professor Cavor would have been floating at the level of the rooftops.

Professor Cavor led them to his cell and a lead-lined chest. "Watch out! Catch it if you can!" As he released the catch and slid back the lid, two bars of a shiny metal rose from the box. Quick as a flash, Rab grasped one, and Professor Bellbuckle, fumbling as he had the day he taught the youngsters to play baseball, managed to clutch the other to his chest.

"Well done," said Professor Cavor. "Now, shall we see what we can do?"

Rubberbones took both bars and stuffed them beneath his arms like crutches without legs. Slowly he began to rise, until his head hit the ceiling.

"That's champion, that is!" announced the boy. "I can get up the chimney wi' these!" Then a thought struck him. "Only I don't know how to get down."

"Don't let go!" squeaked Professor Cavor. The two scientists grabbed Rab by the feet and hauled him to the ground. With some difficulty, they shut both bars of the amazing alloy back into the box.

Angus scanned the visitors with intense concentration. "Fierce mustache! Unreasonable!" He seemed unable to find the right words to describe Mr. Botts of the India Office. After a few moments of clicking and whirring, the words "Complete bumbling idiot!" came out of his little brass trumpet.

The bald man with the mustache had an air of dignity, despite his wet trousers. "I am Inspector Pike of Scotland Yard," he announced. "And you!" — he pointed at Aunt Lucy — "are most definitely Mrs. Butterworth, wanted in connection with the abduction of Princess Purnah of Chiligrit! You are not Lady Flagstone, as you told me. It's a very serious offence, lying to a police officer, it is!"

"So put the handcuffs on me, Constable!" retorted Aunt Lucy, showing how little she cared.

Pike didn't seem to notice. "Where is this kidnapped princess, then?" he demanded.

"Yes, where?" queried Mr. Botts. "I have to get her back to St. Grimelda's!"

That statement was enough to get Emmaline's blood boiling, but Aunt Lucy remained calm. "She's not here. I have no idea where she is. But she's not going back to that school."

"I shall search the place for her," said Pike.

Mrs. McGinnis stepped forward. "Do you have the proper varrant to do that? This whole island belongs to my husband," she said, poking the McGinnis to make sure he knew to agree with her. "And there vill be none of the searching vithout his permission — vich he von't give, vill you, dear? — unless you present a varrant, properly signed and certified in the correct manner."

Emmaline could tell from Inspector Pike's face that of course he had no warrant signed by a judge. Probably he could get one, but not today. She was amazed that a man's face could turn so red so quickly.

Aunt Lucy was enjoying this immensely, but she tried to

cover her urge to laugh by opening the telegram she'd been holding for the past ten minutes. Then, as she scanned the paper, she broke out in a very unladylike whoop.

"Oh, Inspector Pike and Mr. Botts. It seems you've had a wasted journey! Mr. Sherlock Holmes writes to me regarding the princess. It says this:

M. had tea with Lord S. today. Explained position re P. Completely understands inadvisability of return to St.G's. Princess to remain with you. India Office will be instructed — Holmes."

Aunt Lucy flourished the telegram at the inspector. He deflated like a football pierced by a six-inch nail.

Emmaline listened to Mr. Holmes's terse prose. The man hated to spend money on extra words. But it meant that his brother Mycroft had taken tea with "Lord S." — that must be Lord Salisbury, the prime minister! — and that the whole stupid scheme to send Purnah back to the strictest school in the world had been quashed. Cancelled.

"Well, in that case, gentlemen," said Mrs. McGinnis, all kindness again, "you must come and have something to eat. And ve can find some dry clothes for you."

———————

The cream cakes were excellent. Purnah thought all cream cakes were excellent. (Maisie had the same attitude, although she simply knocked the pastry onto the floor and licked the cream.) Still, Purnah found it hard to wait for Botts and Pike to return from the island.

"We coulds going overly by boatings!" she suggested to Harry.

"We could, but that would draw attention to ourselves," he replied. "I don't imagine that the inspector would simply assume that a clergyman, a small boy and a very fine cat have chosen to spend a cold afternoon visiting Urgghh for reasons of tourist interest."

"We could lurkings in the rockses. Pilkh!" In Chiligrit there was a lot of lurking among rocks. It was a popular pastime for young and old, armed and unarmed.

"We could indeed. Although lurking in this dining room seems more comfortable and less likely to draw unwanted attention," replied Harry.

Purnah knew this was true, but it was very hard for her to remain quiet and still when she was so close to her friends, Errand Boy and Emmaline Cay-lee, Auntilucy, Lal Singh and the perfessur. Ptish!

"No licking the plate," whispered Harry. "It's considered rude." Although Maisie was permitted to do so.

Samuel Soap needed only sixpence to help the station porter remember an elderly clergyman, a boy and a cat. Another sixpence reminded the porter that two men (one bald and fierce, one tall and thin) had arrived on the early train and had not returned.

Where had Purnah and the old man gone? The porter didn't know, but a quick look around the village told Soap that there weren't many places they could have gone. If they'd taken a boat to Urgghh he'd have to follow them, and encounter all the problems that went with kidnapping people from islands. It would be a lot easier if they were still in Nochtermuckity. Perhaps at the only hotel. That would be the first place to look. Now dressed as an English visitor to Scotland (with a horrible tartan tie that no Scot would dream of wearing), Samuel Soap sauntered into the hotel. A glance into the dining room revealed a small boy, his face smothered in cream, sharing a table with a cat. The cat was licking the plate, and the boy clearly wanted to. Soap chortled with glee to find his prey so easily. Now, all he had to do was catch her.

———————————

"What if I can't open the skylight?"

The two older scientists looked at one another. Rubberbones had a good point. They hadn't considered that a skylight at the top of a forty-foot shaft, placed there at an unknown time in the past, might not simply open at the merest touch.

"We could find a hammer around here somewhere," said Professor Cavor. "And a chisel."

"Explosives!" offered Professor Bellbuckle with enthusiasm. "Or a screwdriver," said Cavor. "I know there are screw-

drivers in the laboratory."

"There must be ingredients for explosives in a science lab," continued Bellbuckle.

"Er, let's think about it a bit more!" said Rubberbones. He was the sensible one here. That was an unfamiliar feeling. "If I'm 'olding the Cavorite bars under me arms, I can't be 'ammering at the skylight. Besides, the glass will fall in my face."

Professor Cavor's expression turned glum. "Ha!" exclaimed Bellbuckle in triumph.

"And I can't set off an explosion while I'm floating right next to the skylight, can I? That would be even more dangerous!"

Professor Bellbuckle's face fell, while Cavor chortled at his discomfiture.

Then the American's spirits lifted as he had a "Eureka!" moment. It was, of course, the same "Eureka!" moment that came to Professor Bellbuckle again and again.

"A rocket!" he exclaimed.

Rubberbones didn't like this idea at all. "Professor, I'm

not riding on a rocket. They get really 'ot. And they don't always, er, go straight." Being an indestructible rubber boy had its limits. Catching on fire and slamming into a rock wall were beyond those limits. You had to be reasonable about these things. Again Bellbuckle's face fell. Again his resourceful attitude toward rockets (and why they were the solution to any daily problem) came to the rescue.

"No. I shoot the rocket up the chimney, smash the window and then — after all the broken glass, wooden debris and so on has fallen down — you float up using the Cavorite. You can float all the way out!"

"Try not to lose the Cavorite!" said Professor Cavor.

Rubberbones thought that losing the Cavorite would be the least of his problems. It would probably just float away. But it seemed unhelpful to mention that, so he didn't. He had enough to worry about.

They all suddenly shut up as Lidenbrock walked past. It was hard to keep a secret, especially if explosives were to be involved. Rab was relieved that the professor understood that. Professor Bellbuckle loved to chat about things that might blow up.

"How did Grockle arrange it?" asked Emmaline. She was in Dr. Grockle's room at the clubhouse.

She and Lal Singh were going through the scientist's belongings, searching for clues or anything else that would help them rescue Rubberbones. Angus whirred through books, papers and a selection of rude postcards from Paris, seeking information. Stanley had been locked outside, since his concept of helping consisted of ripping things up.

"I believe that he had a way of communicating with someone at Invermisery House," said Lal Singh. "For reasons I am not comprehending, Dr. Grockle arranged for young Robert to be shot from the catapult into a net. Thence he was seized, for reasons that also are unclear."

Emmaline realized that it must be the same adversary who had sent the two thugs to seize her and who had taken Professor Bellbuckle. It just had to be. He collected scientists, and Rab — although just a lad — was a pioneer of aviation. As was she, of course.

Angus suddenly stopped his rapid scanning of papers and handed one to Emmaline. It was a coded message. "What does it say?" she said.

"I am not programmed to decode," replied Angus. "But I can dust and tidy with amazing efficiency. And box, as well."

The McGinnis surprised her, poking his head in. "Aye, it's a simple substitution code. The alphabet has been shifted, so that, say, 'P' means 'A' and 'Q' equals 'B,' and so on. Get some paper and we'll sort it oot in a couple of hoors, nae problem!"

Between them, they did. Even Inspector Pike and Mr. Botts joined in, the detective apparently feeling that, if he couldn't arrest anyone in the foreign princess case, he might as well solve some clues in the matter of a flying lad gone astray. The secretary and Dr. Sneed, embarrassed by their friend Grockle's betrayal, did their part as well. Aunt Lucy, who wasn't good at that sort of thing, made tea. They didn't ask Dr. Smoot to help, for reasons too obvious to mention. "This is a note from Grockle to arrange for Rab to be captured. And a reply from someone doing the capturing!"

said Emmaline, shocked.

"But how did the note get to Invermisery and back again?" asked Aunt Lucy.

Angus held up a small, waxed-cotton pouch, with a tiny belt attached.

"That vould not fit a child!" declared Mrs. McGinnis. Lal Singh smiled, without humor. Emmaline understood.

"The *monkey*!"

⊰ CHAPTER 33 ⊱

A Terrible Plan All Round

Professor Bellbuckle could make a rocket out of almost anything. It was his one genuine ability. Rubberbones admired this talent.

It was long past suppertime. The three conspirators gathered secretly, Rab standing guard while Cavor helped Professor Bellbuckle. Locked up with a full chemistry lab at his disposal, the American inventor made a very large rocket. It was amazing to watch him. The hardest part was finding a bottle big enough to fit the stick (broken off from a mop) into the rocket's head.

Rubberbones understood it wasn't a good idea to let the other scientists find out what the professor was up to. They had opposed any efforts to escape and certainly weren't going to like a scheme that involved setting off an explosion in the dungeon. He thought they were a useless bunch, really, with no spirit of adventure.

Fortunately, most of the scientists had gone to bed early, so Professor Bellbuckle could work undetected. The only one to come poking around was the man who claimed to travel through time. Rab tried to look casual as he barred the lab doorway.

"What's your friend working on?" the man asked Rubberbones.

"Oh, he's 'ad an idea," replied the boy. "Something 'armless. A clockwork teapot, I think." It was a bad lie. Rab was a bad liar.

The scientist smiled. "Good work, lad. I wish you'd been with me when I traveled into the future."

Obviously he was as deranged as any of them, thought Rubberbones.

"Just don't let old Aronnax and Lidenbrock find out. They'll snitch on you in a heartbeat."

The plan was Emmaline's idea, and all the adults (except Lal Singh, who smiled gravely) had tried to dissuade her. It was too dangerous. It was mad. It depended on Dr. Smoot, who couldn't remember what day it was. It involved bribing the monkey with out-of-season fruit. But she had to deliver herself into the clutches of the Collector. She could think of no other way to rescue her friends.

Once the code was broken, it was easy to write a new message to send to Invermisery House.

Have convinced Miss Cayley to try Smoot's catapult. Same arrangements as with boy. Have net in place tomorrow morning. Grockle.

That should tempt him, thought Emmaline. He'd agree, of course. Then she'd be shot from a catapult across a wild stretch of freezing water to land in a net where brutish men would seize her. But Aunt Lucy and Lal Singh and the McGinnises and the rude police officer and the useless Mr. Botts would step in to catch them in the act. There would be arrests, and Rubberbones and Professor Bellbuckle would be released from captivity.

It all sounded horribly dangerous. And tremendously unlikely to work out properly. In fact, it was a terrible plan all around. Completely hopeless.

So they put the note in the little pouch and brought the monkey in. Lal Singh handed the monkey a banana. The creature accepted the bribe with a grave expression, ate it in three bites, then deftly strapped the belt around his middle and popped out of the window, dropping the banana skin behind him. Emmaline watched in astonishment as the animal darted through the rocks to the shore. It tugged a tiny canoe out from a hiding place, pulled it down to the loch and began paddling in the direction of Invermisery House. The sun had gone down. She watched as the monkey disappeared into the darkness.

Mr. McGinnis was about to complain about the terrible cost of bananas, but his wife shut him up.

Samuel Soap had decided on a risky plan. Cunningly distracting the hotel clerk (by stealing the desk bell and ringing it incessantly after taping it to his knees), he had checked the hotel register. The Reverend Hawkes was in Room 3, his nephew in Room 4. It was a stroke of luck that they had separate rooms. Soap took a moment to memorize where each room was. He would simply put a ladder up to the window and abduct the boy … er, the girl. He wouldn't normally dream of such a dangerous scheme, but it was likely his last chance, and the reward was enough for a winter in the South of France at a much nicer hotel than this one.

Things looked good. Room 4 overlooked an alley behind the Station Hotel. There was a ladder leaning against a fence, and a wheelbarrow. Whether he could push a wheelbarrow full of irate princess three miles to Invermisery House in the middle of the night was another matter. Still, he hadn't got to be a jewel thief, a swindler and a fake private detective by being too cautious. He'd give it a try.

Purnah slept soundly. She always did. So it was lucky that Maisie woke her up by leaping onto her chest and mewing urgently.

Someone was breaking in through the window. Purnah's experience with hotels was limited, but as far as she could tell this was a normal event. When she'd shared a room with Emmaline in London, the place had been overrun with masked men in leather trying to abduct her. It had been annoying. At present, Purnah had no sharp objects of her own, but under the bed was a chamber pot (unused). It was heavy and had a good handle for swinging. (Chiligriti princesses always make sure that suitable weaponry is on hand at all times.) So she crept over to the window. An intruder was attempting to pry it open. Hah! Let him try!

Maisie jumped up onto the window ledge. The burglar, surprised, stopped to stare at the cat. Purnah flung open the window and swung the chamber pot. It collided with the burglar's face with a satisfying smack. He began to topple, so she helped him do that by seizing the top rung of the ladder and pushing with all her might.

The intruder fell with a loud shriek, and Purnah was happy to drop the chamber pot on top of him. It made an excellent noise as it smashed, and the burglar shrieked again. Lights appeared in windows, and someone shouted, "Who the b^%&*y h*%# is making that racket?!"

Purnah thought the man's face was familiar, but then again, most British people looked alike to her. He strongly resembled the skulking one-legged man from the railway station at Strathcarrot. Although, when she thought about it, one-legged men must make hopeless burglars.

She slammed the window shut and went back to bed.

Foglamp opened his window when he heard a familiar tap at the glass. The monkey climbed in and held up the pouch. The secretary gave him a handful of nuts from a jar and took the message up to his master's study. Ten minutes later he returned with a reply, which he wrote carefully in code on the back of the message. The monkey finished his nuts, chirped a businesslike farewell and went out through the window. Foglamp smiled to himself. His employer was in an excellent mood tonight.

The time-traveler knocked on the bedroom door at dawn. Rab let him in.

"Look, the other chaps here don't know what you have planned. Of course, I don't either, but I think you need to make sure that old Aronnax and Lidenbrock don't actually prevent you from accomplishing your scheme. It's a rocket, right?"

Rubberbones nodded.

"Up through the chimney?" The boy nodded again.

"And then you climb up the rock face and escape?"

"Something like that," agreed Rab. He didn't mention the Cavorite.

"Probably complete lunacy, but I wish you luck! Make sure that you fire off the rocket during breakfast. I'll cover for you in the dining hall. Clear away the glass before the others finish their bacon and eggs. Then wait 'til the morning tea break to make your escape attempt." The time-traveler had thought it all out.

Rubberbones instructed Professor Bellbuckle what to do. The older man skipped breakfast and instead took the rocket to the chimney, hidden under his coat. Rab and Professor Cavor went to the dining hall. Professors Summerlee and Van Helsing had drawn a diagram on a tablecloth, while Mr. Tesla was doing something complex and scientific to the coffee machine, which was engulfed in shimmering waves of electricity. Rab thought he seemed a little happier than before, but Lidenbrock pulled out the plug, scowling at Tesla for apparently having fun. Dr. Freud had made old Wadley lie down on a couch in the corner and was asking him questions while they both munched on toast. Mizzarbeau and Synthesis argued about ways of knocking the earth off its orbit, as if this would be a good thing.

"Where is Bellbuckle this morning?" demanded Professor Aronnax.

"Er, not feeling too well," replied Rubberbones, head down.

He hated to lie.

"Yes, he was up late working on a clockwork teapot," said the time-traveler. "Still in bed."

There was a muffled boom from outside the room. The time-traveler instantly dropped his tray. Crockery shattered. Professor Cavor squeaked in surprise. "Oh, sorry!" boomed the time-traveler. "Clumsy me!"

"What was zat noise?" asked Aronnax.

"This chap dropped his tray!" shouted Professor Lidenbrock.

"Oh! It sounded louder than usual!"

"I'll adjust your ear trumpet!" replied Lidenbrock.

Rubberbones smiled at this cunning trick. He winked at the time-traveler as he finished his (fairly horrible) breakfast and didn't even ask for seconds. He wanted to see what the professor had accomplished, so he hurried to the foot of the chimney.

Professor Bellbuckle had done well. He was just emptying the last charred bits of wood and broken glass into a dustbin. "Come and see," he said. "My best work, I feel."

Rab had to agree. The skylight was smashed to smithereens. Only a piece of the frame remained in place.

If you wanted something blown up, Professor Bellbuckle was the man to do it.

The Collector watched as several figures set up the catapult on the cliffs. Through his telescope he identified Dr. Smoot, the society's secretary and that odd boy left behind by Dr. Moreau. He'd have liked to capture Moreau, but the famous physician had left for the tropics before it could be arranged. The figure swathed in thick clothing must be the Cayley girl. No sign of Grockle.

There was a knock, and Foglamp entered. "Sorry to disturb you, sir. I heard a strange noise in the dungeon. I will investigate it, of course."

The Collector waved him off. It wasn't important. The efficient Foglamp could handle it.

———◦◦◦———

Purnah didn't mention the incident with the burglar to Harry. She thought he might have insisted she pay for the chamber pot, and she wondered if it was a priceless antique. After all, she only had so many of those colored sheets of paper that people here used to barter with. Harry had slept like a log after singing a few rousing hymns in bed to help him slumber better. He was probably the only person in the hotel who hadn't been woken up by crashing and screaming after dark.

"We goes much islanding today!" announced Purnah over breakfast. "Bad men leavings in disgrace 'cos not findings of myselfish anywhere aboutly. Oh hooty-hoot! I here all timely, in stupid costumes eating cake!"

She was, in fact, eating cake for breakfast.

"I very much hope so, my dear," replied Harry. "I'll buy my ticket back to St. Bogwell's today, and see how much of your money is left. I am afraid that if we have to wait too much longer we shall have to revert to trampdom and sleep in a haystack. It's expensive staying in hotels like respectable people!"

Right, thought Purnah. No more lurking about. She disliked haystacks.

They walked to the ticket office. While Harry was paying his fare, Purnah (who had no patience for waiting) stepped outside, holding Maisie. It was a bright day, and she could see the little harbor with boats on the water. There was almost nobody about. She began singing a cheery Chiligriti tune about endless feuds that wiped out whole families. Then she heard a noise behind her. She turned. It was that man. The man from Strathcarrot station. The man who had tried to break into her room.

He had a bandage around his head and a broken nose today. She ran.

There was a penny farthing bicycle leaning against the station wall. It had a giant front wheel as high as she was tall, and a tiny, rear wheel. She'd seen them but had never actually ridden one. Grabbing it, she pushed it forward, leapt, like a mountain goat in frolic, onto the footrest and vaulted into the saddle. Maisie jumped into the basket at the front. Purnah stamped on the pedals and gripped the handlebars, and the bicycle turned into the high street. Suddenly she was moving quickly, her feet revolving in an unfamiliar way. Maisie hunkered down, ears flat, as the wind rushed by. Behind them, the man stole a second bike and followed in hot pursuit.

Harry stepped out from the station building and waved helplessly in the distance.

Everything was in place. Emmaline would be fired from the catapult at eleven o'clock. She would land in the net at 11:01. Meanwhile, Mr. and Mrs. McGinnis would round up every able-bodied man, woman and child in Nochtermuckity and its surroundings, gather them at their home, Hard Knox House, and — this part seemed even more unlikely than the catapult flight — have them ready, on land and in boats, to rush Invermisery House and overwhelm the inhabitants.

Emmaline thought that this was more likely to resemble the scenes in gothic novels where mobs of enraged peasants stormed the mad doctor's castle than any sort of police arrest. The little town didn't have a policeman of its own but shared one with the next village. A boy had been sent to fetch him. Meanwhile, Inspector Pike would be lording it over the locals, impressing them with his power and experi- ence as a representative of Scotland Yard. Lal Singh was with the crowd, so at least there was someone reliable to storm the castle. Emmaline was certain that storming fortresses had been a key part of Lal Singh's previous career. Angus and Dr. Smoot set up the catapult at the exact spot where the gouged earth showed it had stood before. Will had come out to help with the apparatus. The secretary was present, apparently feeling that it was his job to supervise, or at least remind Dr. Smoot where he was supposed to be aiming. Emmaline could tell that he was embarrassed that Dr. Grockle had let the whole Royal Society of Experimental Science and Invention down very badly. Smoot was a forgetful lunatic, but that was what the society was all about; Grockle was a traitor to all it stood for.

Emmaline was dressed in about seven layers of clothing, gleaned from rummaging through the cottages. She wore a balaclava helmet, thick mittens, heavy winter boots and a parachute made from a flag not of Paraguay but of mighty Ecuador. She had no idea where Dr. Smoot had acquired his surprising collection of South American flags, but they were of excellent quality. He had more, if she'd like to go again, he said.

"Just please get it right the first time!" she exclaimed. "I'm not like Rubberbones. If you aren't on target, I will hit those rocks!" She pointed at the rocks in question. Dr. Smoot looked at her vaguely.

"I'll do it," piped up Will. "I'll see you there safely."

◄ CHAPTER 34 ►

Like the Mad Dervishes of Ikhty-poo!

It was time for the eleven o'clock break, and most of the captive scientists left their desks and workbenches in favor of a cup of dreadful brown liquid and a stale currant bun. The others were so occupied with their experiments that they didn't notice three of their number engaged in a desperate escape attempt. They probably wouldn't have spotted elephants in ball gowns dancing through the laboratory.

"Hush!" squeaked Professor Cavor. "I have the Cavorite here." He opened the lead-lined chest hidden under his worktable. They caught the alloy rods at the first attempt. Rubberbones tucked them under his armpits, and — with both professors holding onto his arms to prevent him from floating upward — they made their way to the chimney. The time-traveler stood in the dining hall doorway to prevent any of the others from seeing what was happening. He winked at Rab.

Rab looked up the chimney shaft. It would be easy enough. He'd use his feet to guide him up the wall. When he reached the top, he just had to scramble through the broken skylight. Then it was a matter of skirting the house, keeping out of sight and making a bolt for the village. He'd find Lal Singh and Mr. and Mrs. McGinnis. They'd know what to do.

"Good luck, son," whispered Professor Bellbuckle. Professor Cavor nodded and squeaked. They let go of his shoulders, and Rubberbones began to rise.

It was simple. With the buoyant metal rods supporting him, Rab simply floated up through the chimney. His feet kept him from hitting the rock walls. As he reached the smashed skylight, the lad straightened up and passed easily through the gap. Dead easy. Champion!

His feet cleared the broken glass and burnt wood, and he kept rising. Ey-oop!! thought Rubberbones as he suddenly realized that the Cavorite rods would lift him high into the sky. Whoops! He hadn't considered what would happen after he rose through the chimney. Rab let go and jumped. The rods drifted upward as Rubberbones flung himself for- ward onto the grass. "Sorry about that, Professor Cavor," he muttered.

Rab lay in a patch of meadow, a stone's throw from the gray mass of Invermisery House. The dungeon extended into the rock beyond the layout of the building itself. Ahead of him the ground appeared to drop away. He crawled forward to the edge. He could see the cliffs of Urgghh not far across the sea-loch. He looked toward the place where he had catapulted into trouble.

And there, on that same cliff, the catapult was set up again. Someone was getting ready to make the same mistake he had made.

A voice came from below him. "She'll be 'ere in a moment, Titch! Any time now!"

Rubberbones peered down. Twenty feet or so below him, the two thugs were standing by the same net they had caught him in.

The lad wasn't certain who was about to be catapulted this way, but he was going to help her, whoever she was.

Purnah pedaled like the mad dervishes of Ikhty-poo, known to all Chiligriti children from the old tales their grandmothers tell them. Maisie crouched in the basket, ears slung back. The penny farthing rattled along the high street of Nochtermuckity, then along the coast road northward. The machine moved very fast, as Purnah's legs pumped like pistons. Every time she hit a bump on the ground, the bicycle bounced and rattled. She could hardly keep her seat on the saddle, but she leaned forward and gripped the handlebars tight. She looked over her shoulder to see Samuel Soap (although she didn't know his name) keeping pace with her, a stone's throw behind.

She wished that she had a stone. A nice, big, round one. Alas, she didn't, so she kept pedaling, head down and elbows out. She struggled up a hill, legs straining and muscles burning, then came to the crest and raced downhill.

Ahead of her a large white house appeared, with a big knot of people gathered outside. Among them she spotted Auntilucy and Lal Singh, and wonderful unclean doggy beast Stanley! But next to them was the villainous Inspector Pike — had he arrested them all? Surely not, for Lal Singh would not permit it. The Botts man was there as well. Glekk!

She barely had time to wave at her friends and poke her tongue out at her foes as the speed of the penny farthing took her hurtling past them. For the first time, Princess Purnah wondered whether the contraption had brakes. If it did, she had no idea where they were.

Emmaline sat in the spoon of the catapult, waiting for the moment when she would be hurled upward toward the net awaiting her across the expanse of the sea-loch. This would be the third time she had left the ground in an absurdly dangerous manner.

The first time, she'd flown in her rickety homemade kite to escape from St. Grimelda's School for Young Ladies; she'd been attacked by pterodactyls, narrowly missed by Professor Bellbuckle's rocket and fished out of the North Sea. The second time, she'd taken charge of a device belonging to the Belgian Birdman, who had broken down from an attack of nerves in front of a cheering crowd on London Bridge. That flight had ended with a crash into the River Thames, with Rubberbones and Purnah forming a human chain that swung from her feet.

This attempt seemed the craziest yet. This time she didn't even have a grossly unsafe, completely untested flying machine. She just had herself, a lot of padding and the flag of Ecuador tied to her sweater by strings.

And she still hadn't got over her fear of flying. In fact, it was no longer an irrational phobia. It made complete sense to be afraid of flying.

Dr. Smoot was counting to three. "Ah, one! Ah, two! Ah, oh, let me see —"

Will reached for the latch. If Dr. Smoot could remember how to count to three, he'd catapult Emmaline into the sky.

"Was that Purnah?" Aunt Lucy asked Lal Singh. "The clothing was all wrong, but there was something Purnah-ish about the cyclist."

"Yes, I am most certain that the small boy in a sailor suit, accompanied by a cat, was indeed Her Royal Highness. Unfortunately, I was unable to converse with her since she was passing by at thirty-five miles per hour," replied the Sikh. Inspector Pike scowled. He'd seen that boy and cat before. His keen eyes didn't miss a thing. He had simply failed to make the proper identification.

A second figure on a penny farthing flew by. This time Inspector Pike trained his highly developed policeman's brain on the rider. He knew that man — but without a mustache. And dressed differently.

"Hey! Stop that man! He's Emerald Ernie, the notorious jewel thief!"

The crowd had gathered to hear why the McGinnis and his formidable wife had summoned them. But the effect of a deep, authoritative voice telling them to stop a jewel thief was powerful. All together, like one man (also woman, automaton and dog), the population of Nochtermuckity swarmed down the road after the two cyclists. The McGinnis had been about to stand on a box to address them all, but the moment was lost.

"Ach, ye get them to tell 'em the one thing and they go harin' off after another!" he complained.

"Get in the carriage," replied his wife. "As long as they are headed toward Invermisery, the exact reason does not matter!" She pulled her husband into an open carriage, and they sped after the mob.

Aunt Lucy could not keep up with the crowd. "Go on ahead, Lal Singh. Take Stanley and Emmaline's mechanical friend and get to the front. You'll know what to do when the time comes."

Purnah looked behind her. Glekk! Porok! Not only was the "nastee" man after her, but a whole mob of people — some on foot, some in carts or on horses, although she could see no yaks or camels — was pursuing her. She hammered down on the pedals. She was going very fast indeed. Even Maisie — ears flattened against her head — seemed concerned about what would happen next.

The road curved around a headland. Out on the loch there were boats, all rowing in the same direction that she was going. Hripp! The mob had a navy! The road curved again, and a big gray house with a tower loomed up.

Perhaps she could hide in there! The people might be nice, and protect her from the rioting mass that surged along after her —

The penny farthing hit a bump. Hard. Purnah lost her grip on the handlebars and went sailing through the air. Maisie flew out of her basket. Both of them somersaulted across the road toward the loch, dropping down to a sandy beach —

Into a net.

A voice rang out. "We've got the Cayley girl, Titch! I never saw the catapult go off!" Then a face appeared, looking down at Purnah in puzzlement. "Only it's a nipper in a sailor suit. How'd that 'appen?"

———

Rubberbones looked down with astonishment. In an instant, from out of nowhere, a small figure in a sailor suit and a furry animal of some sort had appeared — airborne. They'd landed in the net. But — and this part made no sense at all — they hadn't been thrown from the catapult. He peered out across the water; that was still in the "loaded" position. The number of people waiting to land on this beach today was apparently inexhaustible.

He heard the child yelling as the little thug reached to pull it out of the net.

"Lemmee alone! Villainish Prrkk! Wretchling! Porok! Tring!"

Purnah!

The Island of Mad Scientists

The tiny man fell backward as the furry animal launched itself at his face. Purnah leapt out of the net and stood, fists clenched, as the massive bruiser known as Titch approached her. He moved slowly, saying nothing. Rab could see a sly smile on his face as he advanced, huge hands ready to grip her by the throat.

Rubberbones took three steps backward ... and launched himself off the rocks.

Emmaline was flying for the third time. The sensation was strange. She had no flying machine, no fabric-and-wood craft around her. It was just her and the sky.

The sky didn't worry her. The ground did.

Still, it was a marvelous feeling as the wind rushed past and she arced upward, then leveled and began to dip. Now she could see the beach properly. The net was just as she'd observed it from the cliffs, but something was going on. There was an argument on the little strip of sand. An alter- cation. A fistfight.

It was Hercules and Titch, bullying someone. A small boy. And — wait — Hercules was under attack by — by a cat! The cat was winning.

But the giant Titch was facing the little lad, threatening him with violence. He was reaching out to seize the boy —

And then another figure dropped into the picture. Rubberbones! She'd know him anywhere! He landed at Titch's feet and launched himself at the huge thug. The lit- tle boy screamed — a war cry, not a shriek of fear — and hurled himself at the giant. They could have no chance against him. They were brave, but they were tiny.

They were getting bigger by the second, as Emmaline hurtled toward them. She reached behind her to tug the parachute. She should have done this as soon as she began to descend; the scene on the beach had ruined her concen- tration. She yanked at the flap that would release the Ecuadorean flag. Nothing happened.

She was coming down like one of the professor's rockets. The parachute unraveled behind her, too late to slow her down. She tensed, balling up to protect her head and hoping to land feet first.

Emmaline was going to die. Or, at least, have a very hard landing indeed. She closed her eyes.

⚔ CHAPTER 35 ⚔

The Really Exciting Part You've Been Waiting For!

Purnah knew that she was going to die. It was a rare thing among the royalty of Chiligrit to pass away, old and in bed, surrounded by grandchildren and great-grandchildren. She'd been raised to expect bad things from cousins with daggers and aunts with poisons. Even so, she hadn't expected to be crushed by an enraged bully on the shores of a Scottish loch. Still, she was kicking and punching and — yes, she got in a savage bite to the fleshy bit at the back of his leg! She'd happily bite his nose if only he'd bend down a little more. Her friend Errand Boy had appeared from out of the sky and was landing solid blows of his own. It was really unfortunate that the enemy was so very, very big. And she was without any knives whatsoever, which showed poor planning on her part. She was going to die. Turok!

The princess began singing the traditional Chiligriti death song, "O Mine Ancestors, Save Me Some Goat Soup and Not Just the Gristly Bits," when a miracle happened. Emmaline Cay-lee also appeared out of the sky, slamming into the giant's ear with her stout winter boots. The huge man lurched forward, almost crushing Purnah underfoot. His eyes rolled back in his ugly giant head, and he silently collapsed. Emmaline bounced off the falling monster, flipped once and landed in the net. Purnah changed in mid-shriek (Chiligriti tunes are loud and not to most people's taste) from the death song to the anthem of victory, which began "I Have Cut Out Your Bowels with a Hairbrush," and continued singing.

Rab got up from the patch of sand where Titch had flung him. He was dazed. Even a rubber boy cannot emerge from a brawl with giants completely unscathed. Emmaline lay in the net, seeing stars.

"Get off me, you brute!" shouted Hercules. They'd forgotten about him. The little man had been struggling with a nine-pound tortoiseshell cat attached to his face by her claws. Even a fighter as puny as Hercules could eventually overcome a cat. He knocked Maisie to the ground and was about to kick her.

"No you kicklings friendling-cat! Parrp!" screamed Purnah and launched her own flying kick to her undersized enemy's stomach. Hercules collapsed like a sack of spuds. Rab pulled her off him before she trampled him into a quivering pulp. She would have, too. The tiny criminal leapt to his feet and ran. He scarpered across the sand, turning to see whether the enraged princess would strike him again.

That was why he didn't see the second penny farthing bicycle before it ran him over.

There was a crunch, followed by two shrieks, and a thin, ratty man with a mustache piled into the squealing Hercules. The bike lay on its side, big wheel still revolving. And then there were other people, the fastest among the mob that had pursued Purnah from Hard Knox House. Harry Hawkes, riding a borrowed donkey, had caught up at last. He rushed to the princess, now cradling a purring Maisie. "All right, my dear?" She nodded assent. Lal Singh examined Titch to ensure he wasn't about to wake up, then gently lifted Emmaline out of the net.

"Miss Emmaline? Are you joining us?" he crooned.

Emmaline opened her eyes. "What happened?" she asked. "I am uncertain, although I am sure we will find out shortly. Meanwhile, can you stand up?" She could, gingerly, with one arm on Lal Singh's shoulder.

Inspector Pike had seized Samuel Soap. "Emerald Ernie — or whatever your real name is — I arrest you for the Chimpleigh Manor burglary, for the theft at Beebleborough Jewelers, for the ..." He continued in this vein for a while and concluded, "Also, causing a public affray and assaulting this midget wot you have run over today!"

Out on the water a rowboat pulled onto the shore, the Jolly Roger flying from an improvised flagpole. "Arr!" announced Mr. Blackbeard. "We come to 'elp 'ee landlubbers!" He held up a prisoner, trussed up with rope. "We captured 'is ship!" It was the monkey, looking wet and unhappy, the parrot keeping watch over him. The tiny canoe was tied alongside the boat. "We always looks out fer our old shipmates!" shouted Blackbeard. "Got any rum?"

The Collector watched, astonished and enraged, as his scheme fell apart before his beady black eyes. Why had this happened? Had Grockle betrayed him? What was that explosion he'd heard earlier? Was it Bellbuckle? Of course it had been Bellbuckle! But there was no time to lose. He reached into a drawer and pulled out an ancient pistol, then ran on spidery legs down the stairs to the dungeon.

It was chaos. Even Foglamp's famous efficiency was unable to quell the joy among the scientists. In fact, they'd tied him up to a piece of heavy brass apparatus. He was arguing with Professor Aronnax while Dr. Freud tried to measure the secretary's skull with a tape measure. Van Helsing and Wadley poured glasses of celebratory brandy (made using lab equipment) to toast the escape. Now that Rubberbones had succeeded, everybody was suddenly in favor of his escape bid. Yes, they'd encouraged the whole enterprise. It had been a group effort all along. The mad astronomer Mizzarbeau was singing in French, and Summerlee was grinning at Tesla, who had set up his own celebratory display of flashing lights on top of a sad- looking cake. The time-traveler wore a small smile.

"Quiet! Shut up!" shrieked the Collector. "All of you! When he brandished the pistol, they did shut up. There's nothing like pointing a loaded weapon at a person to take the giggling out of his day. "Where is Bellbuckle?" he demanded.

Professor Bellbuckle was still standing at the foot of the chimney, pointing out the excellence of his rocket's effect. The Collector took two spidery paces toward him and pointed the pistol at his head. The professor continued to explain the precise mix of saltpeter he had used in his gunpowder mix to Professor Cavor until his listener cleared his throat. Then Bellbuckle noticed the gun aimed at his temple.

"Now, there's no need to get unpleasant," he told the Collector. "If you wanted to interrupt me, you could have just coughed or something."

"Bellbuckle!" screamed the Collector. "You have ruined everything for me!"

The professor took a careful step backward. He'd seen crazy people with guns before. He was from Georgia. "Hold your horses, there, friend! Things ain't gonna improve for you if you start shootin' folks."

That was good advice, but the Collector could see his whole world collapsing around him. There was an angry mob at the front door. His pair of bullies had somehow been overcome by three children and a pet cat. His secretary was tied to an expensive bit of equipment that he'd paid for out of his own pocket. And his Collection, the ungrateful curs, were in outright mutiny. One of them had done the unthinkable and escaped his clutches.

It was all Bellbuckle's fault. Furiously, the Collector cocked the pistol, still pointing it at the professor. "You have ruined all my plans!" he screamed, fangs dripping with saliva. His mad black eyes gleamed with hatred.

A metal bar dropped from high above. Two of them, actually. The first one knocked the gun out of the Collector's hand. It fired, harmlessly, against the ground. The second struck him on the top of his skull.

He whimpered. And fell.

Professor Cavor squeaked in relief. Professor Bellbuckle grinned.

"My Cavorite!" exclaimed Cavor. "There must be some limit to its anti-gravitational property."

"About seven minutes," answered Bellbuckle. "Give or take a few seconds."

"Most disappointing," said Cavor.

"You don't see me complaining," replied Bellbuckle. Then the dungeon was swarming with people. Mrs. McGinnis was organizing everyone, and her husband was guessing how much everything had cost. Angus was surrounded by scientists admiring his fine engineering features. Purnah clasped Maisie, and Lal Singh still supported the groggy Emmaline. Rubberbones brought Aunt Lucy to where Professor Bellbuckle was once again discussing rocketry with Professor Cavor, who had some interesting ideas about moon travel.

"Oh, Ozymandias! My hero!" Aunt Lucy flung her arms about Professor Bellbuckle and kissed him on the cheek.

"Lucy, my dear," he began. "It wasn't really my fault —"

"Of course not," she replied. "It was his!"

Pulling out a brand new umbrella, she started beating the groaning Collector with it, until it was completely broken into bits. Nobody tried to stop her. The Collector whimpered a little, flapping his spidery legs. Stanley ran over and peed on his trousers.

In the headmistress's study at St. Grimelda's School for Young Ladies, Mrs. Malvolia Wackett read the note from the spidery old man she'd met with. He regretted to inform her that he would not be able to help her in the matter of the runaway princess. Mrs. Wackett knew that the old man had taken the information she'd given him and simply dis- carded their bargain as soon as it suited him to do so. It was not so much the content of the note that bothered her as it was his choice of words; there was something insolent about him. She did not take insolence from anyone! Her face reddened as she ripped the paper into shreds, her huge hands tearing the note and hurling the tatters into the fire. She'd get that girl back, whatever it took. "Matron!" she bellowed. "Once term is finished, we have some unfinished business to resolve. Is the pterodactyl ready to fly?"

"So, ye'll not be wanting to stay on the island over the winter?" asked the McGinnis. "Ye've paid for it, ye ken. The rent is non-refundable."

Mrs. McGinnis slapped him. "Do not be foolish. It is absurdly cold and vindy here in the vinter. I do not blame them for leaving. Give the lady her money back, Vilhelm!"

"I think we should go home," replied Aunt Lucy.

There was no reason to stay. Mr. Botts had received a telegram confirming that Purnah could remain with Aunt Lucy. Inspector Pike was so happy that he'd finally caught the long-sought Emerald Ernie that he'd forgotten the embarrassing failure of his wild-goose chase in pursuit of the missing princess. Indeed, he took command of every policeman for fifty miles around to handle the arrests of the Collector and his underlings. Dr. Grockle had been caught changing trains at Strathcarrot. Pike was in his element. At one point he was even observed smiling, briefly.

The captured scientists all took the train from Nochtermuckity to return to their former lives, which Rubberbones thought was actually a bad thing in the case of the more dangerously mad ones. Professor Mizzarbeau loudly described a future scheme involving destroying most of the earth with a giant ray from space, while Monsieur Synthesis argued with him over the details. They all shook

Rubberbones's hand. The time-traveler winked and gave him a rock he said was "from the future"; Rab thought it was just a rock. Tesla offered the boy a job if he ever needed one in America. Van Helsing gave him a pamphlet entitled "What to Expect When You Are Undead" as a parting gift. Dr. Freud told him to look after his mother, but never to listen to anything she said.

"Strange bloke!" muttered Rab.

The Reverend Harry Hawkes and his very fine cat had taken leave of Princess Purnah; they had to be back at St. Bogwell's-in-the-Marsh in time for the First Sunday of Advent.

Purnah had absolutely no idea what that meant, but she understood that Harry did not want to offend his god. Offending various gods had led a lot of her royal relatives into trouble over the years.

"Come and visit!" said Harry. "We'll have cream cakes." Maisie allowed Purnah to pick her up and rub her tummy. "That means she thinks you're very special," said Harry. "Oh, is beee-oootifulish catlings!" cooed Purnah. "You writes me from homings, yesly?" Harry said that he would. Emmaline, overhearing, was fairly certain that

Purnah expected Maisie to write her own postcards.

The train pulled away from the station. "Good-bye-eeh!" Purnah cried out, waving madly until the last carriage disappeared from sight.

The secretary of the Royal Society of Experimental Science and Invention was staying, of course, as was Dr. Smoot. They had promised Mrs. McGinnis that they would treat young Will with much greater care than before.

"You know, he's not a normal person," said Emmaline. "You what?" replied Rubberbones.

"Dr. Moreau created him. He's famous for his terrible experiments. It's wicked. I think Will may have been born a sheep. Well, born a lamb, I mean."

"That's just wrong," said Rab flatly. "I'm not sure I like mad scientists as much as I used to."

"Exceptings our Perfessur Bellbuckings!" interjected Princess Purnah.

"Except for Professor Bellbuckle," replied Emmaline. "Well, we should all go back to Lower Owlthwaite," said Aunt Lucy. "Rab's grandmother will want to see him. And Princess Purnah can finally stay with us without anyone interfering. I don't expect any trouble from now on!"

"Hip, hip, hooray for a quiet life!" shouted Professor Bellbuckle. (Emmaline thought this was partly because he disliked having a gun pointed at him.) Stanley yipped in agreement. Purnah was trying to poke Rubberbones with a brass wire device that Mr. Tesla had left behind, laughing as he grumbled, "Stop that, Yer Majesty. I'm warning you —" Lal Singh grinned behind his beard, then changed his expression quickly when the princess noticed. "Ha! Trikk! All funnee now!" she declared, and jabbed the end of the wire apparatus in Rubberbones's left ear.

Emmaline hoped for quiet as well. She would be able to work on her flying machine at last.

Angus coughed politely. "I intend to accompany you. Professor Bellbuckle owes me sixty-four million and forty dollars, American currency only, minus the cost of a piece of walnut cake — that was my treat. I do not intend to let a man who owes me so much money out of my sight again." The professor began to protest, but Aunt Lucy pushed a sardine-and-plum-jam sandwich into his mouth. "Into the boat, everyone!" she shouted. "We are going home!"

A NOTE ABOUT PEOPLE AND PLACES

Readers will no doubt have guessed that while cities like Glasgow, Leeds and Liverpool actually exist, such places as Urgghh, Podgemout Parva and Nochtermuckity cannot be found on any real map of Great Britain. Most of the characters appearing in this story are the products of my deranged imagination, but Queen Victoria and her Indian secretary clearly existed, as did Dr. Freud and the genius Nikola Tesla. Several of the scientists are taken from period literature: Professor Cavor and his gravity-defying "Cavorite" is the invention of the great pioneer of science fiction H.G. Wells (as are the nameless time traveller and the terrible Dr. Moreau) while Professors Aronnax and Lidenbrock are taken from the books of Jules Verne. Mr. Summerlee is from Sir Arthur Conan Doyle's The Lost World, Van Helsing from Bram Stoker's Dracula and some of the other scientists come from lesser-known fiction of this period. The whole Podgemout Castle section is my tribute to P.G. Wodehouse, possibly the funniest writer ever, who specialized in sheer nonsense at country houses with everyone impersonating someone else and only the butler showing any sense at all. Harry Hawkes is loosely based on a genuinely eccentric clergyman, the Reverend Frank Tatchell, Vicar of Midhurst in Sussex; his hard-to-find book The Happy Traveller (1923) is a joy to read.

There was very little piracy in Victorian Britain, and not much in the way of mechanical men serving haggis.

From Winged Hussar Publishing

Steps to Deliverance

Drowned Secrets

Markov's Prize

America in Flames

Read on about a mighty warrior from the froze
north, who wears chain-mail underwear and a
helmet with really big horns.

Unfortunately, he's also very stupid. Mistaking-
the-family-cow-for-a-monster kind of stupid.

BOGBRUSH
the Barbarian

Howard Whitehouse
Illustrated by Bill Slavin

PROLOGUE

(The bit that comes first.)

The July snow was blowing sideways across the frozen plain toward the village. The brief summer of the Northlands was still days away. Yet inside the log-walled settlement there was rejoicing. A new baby was to be named!

Villagers gathered in front of the ceremonial fire, wearing their best bear-furs, shining armor and weapons, and their finest helmets with horns. That was just the womenfolk. The men were dressed up as well. Someone had polished the skulls above the gateway that welcomed visitors. Everyone was drinking ale from huge flagons, although the children weren't allowed more than five cups of the thick, sticky brew. Whole oxen were roasted as snacks. You could eat as many turnips as you liked.

The naming ceremony took place in the temple, which still smelled of the cows who lived inside. For this special occasion, most of them had been moved outside. The old priest, an ancient figure draped in the pelt of a great wolf, with the teeth of a sabre-toothed cat around his neck, cackled to the assembled village. He was too old to talk and could only cackle.

"Grock brig giss wrooorrrkk figgle naaammigg hiierrkk? Hwurkgh!"

This meant something like "Who brings this child to be named?" Or possibly "I have swallowed the knucklebone of a goat and may choke if nobody helps me."

The villagers assumed it was the first of these sayings. A young yokel and his wife stepped forward. You could tell they were yokelfolk because they had straw in their hair, very few teeth and no armor at all.

WORD OF THE DAY: yokel — *an insulting term for someone who lives in the country, which suggests that he or she is uneducated and probably stupid.*

See how many of your schoolmates you can call a yokel before one of them smacks you in the head.

An old man, who had a massive bronze helmet with horns on either side and many swords, spears and axes — so many that he paid a boy to carry most of them — stepped forward as well. "I am the grandfather," he announced. "I shall name the wee lad."

He wasn't really a "wee lad" at all. His mother was straining under the weight of the babe, who was twice the size of every infant ever seen in the village. The older ladies had passed him to one another, each comparing him to prize-winning pigs they had owned. Nobody had ever hoisted a baby of such size.

The grandfather looked around, challenging all to argue with his right to name the boy. The baby's parents obviously weren't about to quarrel with a heavily armed grandpa.

"He shall be named Bogbrush, and he will become a mighty barbarian warrior. Like myself, of course."

"Bogbrush," whispered one of the old ladies at the back. "That's a nice name."

A MOMENT FOR EDUCATION:
Bogbrush *is British slang for a brush used to clean a bog.*

ANOTHER MOMENT FOR EDUCATION:
Bog *is British slang for a toilet.*
See also loo *(page 398).*

The most muscle-bound of the village grandmothers hoisted the infant, who burped loudly,
and tossed him at the old priest; the holy man
staggered as the baby flopped into his arms, and he
began to cackle wildly yet again. The baby, now known
as Bogbrush, threw up all over him.

"A mighty warrior shall he be," intoned the grandfather.

CHAPTER 1
(I'm holding up a finger.)

It was a perfect evening for monster slaying. Bogbrush, the mighty barbarian hero, was ready. He was hunched behind the barnyard wall, a gigantic sword gleaming in his huge fist. The night was dark, but not so dark that the warrior couldn't see his own feet; he recognized them both at the end of his legs. It was cool, so he wouldn't be sweaty, even with all the hacking and slashing he'd have to do. It was dry, which was good because nobody likes to be out in the rain, horrible man-eating creatures included. And tomorrow was laundry day, so his mother could get the monster blood out of his trousers.

He had only one pair, and his mother washed clothes just twice a year.

The young barbarian thought about all these things, one by one. He was a slow thinker. Big, blond, rippling with muscles, but not quick between the ears.

His grandfather, Bumrash, had been a great slayer of foul beasts, vile things from the marshes and the smaller, less athletic sorts of demon. The people of the village spoke of the old man, now dead, as a great swordsman, a mighty hero. He'd been killed by a snake when he was ninety-four; he didn't cook it properly and got food poisoning.

Bogbrush had heard the men talking about his grandfather.

"That Bumrash. He was an idiot as a boy. Later on, he grew into a lunatic," said old Bedsock.

"I remember him as a raving maniac," recalled Lardgut the Elder.

The young man didn't know exactly what it meant to be an idiot or a raving maniac, but he thought these were high compliments. His grandfather must have been greatly admired. And now he, Bogbrush, a boy of at least fifteen and maybe even eighteen summers (none of his family were good at counting), held the mighty sword once carried by Bumrash. The sword was called Headlopper because it was made for lopping. Heads, mostly, although Bogbrush was only allowed to practice on turnips. Still, the lad was ready for heads. Monster heads. Big monster heads. The kind with horns.

Suddenly a sound pierced the air. A terrible scream of evil. It went "Moooohh! Moooh!"

Bogbrush shivered with a jolt of fear but — being a mighty barbarian hero — he jumped up onto the wall. Headlopper was in his hand, the massive blade shining in the moonlight. He stared into the field and saw the bright (and clearly evil) eyes staring back. The monster had big savage horns with which to stab and gore and . . . stab and gore. There were probably other words for it, but Bogbrush couldn't think of them. The vast beast paced fiercely, its wicked, poisonous breath making fog in the cold air. The moon disappeared behind a cloud. He had to strike now!

"I must cleave this foul thing in twain!" said Bogbrush to himself, but quite loudly. "I shall smite it ere it knoweth I am here!" Luckily, the monster showed no signs of understanding any of this. Almost nobody understood Bogbrush, exactly. He always spoke as his grandfather had taught him —like a barbarian hero. He used complicated sentences full of important-sounding words, sometimes with strange *eths* on the end of them. It was hard for him to remember how to talk like this, and often he even confused himself.

The rest of his family (who, as you'll remember, were yokels) didn't even try to understand what Bogbrush meant when he said things like "I hadst closeth the pigsty ere bedtime, yet forsooth I hast forgeteth to shuteth yon gate!" They just followed the squeals of the pigs he had let loose in the flower beds.

Bogbrush leaped forward, sword in hand. The huge blade swung through the night, slashing into the monster's hide before the savage beast could strike against the hero. The fiendish creature toppled with a grunt.

WORD OF THE DAY: twain *means "in two pieces." Use it in conversation with your brother or sister, as in "I shall cleave this mushroom and sausage pizza in twain, and thou shalt choose which bit to take."*